SUBSTANTIAL THREAT

SUBSTANTIAL THREAT

Nick Oldham

Severn House Large Print
London & New York

This first large print editi
SEVERN HOUSE LARG]
9-15 High Street, Sutton, Surrey, SM1 1DF.
First world regular print edition published 2005 by
Severn House Publishers, London and New York.
This first large print edition published in the USA 2007 by
SEVERN HOUSE PUBLISHERS INC., of
595 Madison Avenue, New York, NY 10022.

British Library Cataloguing in Publication Data

Oldham, Nick, 1956-
  Substantial threat. - Large print ed.
  1. Christie, Henry (Fictitious character) - Fiction
  2. Police - England - Blackpool - Fiction 3. Organized
  crime - Fiction 4. Detective and mystery stories 5. Large
  type books
  I. Title
  823.9'14[F]

ISBN-13: 9780727875747

Printed and bound in Great Britain by
MPG Books Ltd, Bodmin, Cornwall.

One

There was a particular combination of words that gave Henry Christie a very special thrill and sent a shimmer of unadulterated pleasure all the way down his spine. They were words Henry had been privileged to read out loud to about forty people in the course of his career as a police officer. Henry did not care what sort of person it was who had to listen to what he said, they could be the hardest, toughest, meanest bastards in the world – and some of the recipients of his words had been pretty near to that description. No, Henry did not care who they were because he was certain that the words would, inwardly at least, make anybody brick themselves.

Henry ran the words through his head once more. They were clear and recent in his memory. He had only spoken them two hours before.

'You are charged that between the sixteenth and seventeenth of March this year you did murder Jennifer Walkden, contrary to common law.'

The murder charge.

Yes! Henry thumped his steering wheel with glee. He did not care a damn who the person was because no matter who the hell they were or

5

what they purported to be, those words meant they were going to prison for a life sentence ... all things being equal. That is if Henry did his job right, if the prosecution brokered no deals, if the jury believed the evidence ... yeah, okay, all those things, but even that uncertainty did not detract from the feeling of utter triumph he felt when slowly reading out the charge.

Henry yawned and shook his head as he drove his car into the Lancashire police headquarters at Hutton, just to the south of Preston.

It had been a long day, but one which had been deeply satisfying. It was 9 p.m. by the time he parked in the car park near his office, fourteen hours after first coming on duty. It did not matter that he was physically and mentally exhausted, that the day had stretched his skills, abilities and personal resolve to their ultimate. None of that was important. What was crucial was that the suspect had been charged with the gravest offence, bail had been refused and he would be appearing at court in the morning.

Temporary Detective Chief Inspector Henry Christie had nailed the bastard and the feeling of elation that fact gave him over-rode anything else.

It had been touch and go. It could so easily have gone the other way and the suspect, by the name of Sherridan, could have walked. Henry knew the evidence against him was paper thin, but as he was totally convinced in his own mind that the guy was guilty of sticking a ten-inch kitchen knife into his girlfriend's heart and skewering her to a kitchen table, Henry had been

6

grimly determined to take it to the wire.

The whole thing had hinged on the interview: on clear, persistent, incisive and clever questioning. The suspect had to be made to admit the job because there was nothing else to tie him to the murder: no witnesses, no forensic, no weapon. Maybe a little circumstantial evidence and a pretty creaky alibi ... and, of course, Henry Christie's cold-blooded gut-wrenching belief that Sherridan was a killer. The man needed to be pushed and pushed to the limit, but not intimidated or frightened; there was a fine and dangerous line between the two. A line Henry was very good at treading.

Henry had been up at three that morning, planning his interview strategy. He went on duty at 7 a.m. and talked the whole thing through with the local detective sergeant who was to be 'second-jockey' in the interview. At nine he put the plan into effect, talking to Sherridan, who had been in custody since the previous evening.

Eight hours later, after many furious, fractious and heated verbal exchanges (but with plenty of rest and refreshment breaks to keep suspect and solicitor happy), Henry truly thought he was on the verge of losing it. The clock on the wall behind Sherridan seemed to be ticking double time. Twenty-four hours was almost up, only sixty minutes to go, and Henry already knew that he would have major problems convincing the very cynical and pedantic on-call superintendent to grant an extension to the period of custody. Sherridan would either have to be charged or set free. And at that point – 5 p.m. –

7

charging him was not even a remote option.

Then it came.

The chink of light. The opening. The lie that Sherridan had forgotten he had told ... or maybe not forgotten, so much as forgotten in which context he had told it.

Excitement surged through Henry as his adrenaline sluices opened. Moments like these made life worth living. Henry even felt the detective sergeant next to him tense because he, too, had spotted the opening. The trick was not to let on to the suspect because he could have wriggled free, even at that point. He had to be manoeuvred into an ambush. It was all Henry could do to refrain from smiling, to prevent himself from fidgeting, to stop himself clenching the cheeks of his bottom and rising ever so slightly in his seat. It took every last ounce of restraint not to let on that he was in and that the whole fabricated story that had been spun was about to be shredded word by word, lie by lie.

Henry felt like a chess grand master who had just seen the last six moves to certain victory. He was cold, ruthless and precise. His voice, however, remained calm and polite.

At first Sherridan did not see it coming. He prattled on blithely, smugly, digging his hole, well aware of the time passing in his favour, believing he would soon be walking free. Then, like a spectre, it materialized in front of him. Suddenly he clammed up tight and locked eyes with Henry for one chilling instant, the colour draining from his face.

His solicitor sat bolt upright and emitted a tiny

gasp of despair.

Checkmate, you murdering bastard! Henry blinked innocently, face impassive.

'Shit,' mouthed Sherridan and dropped his head into his hands.

And from that moment on it was plain sailing. Despite his desperate back-pedalling and frenzied denials, he was like a fish caught on a hook. Henry revelled as he reeled the slippery son of a bitch in. After a fifteen-minute spirited, but ultimately useless fight, Sherridan cracked and caved in. Tears welled up as he finally unburdened himself and admitted committing murder.

Henry charged him with the offence five minutes before the twenty-four-hour deadline, milking each syllable of every word.

After this Henry and the local DS congratulated each other with a flurry of high fives and a few slightly hysterical, 'Hey, yo de mans' and an Irish jig around the CID office. After the brief celebration they quickly cobbled together the court file for the morning, then Henry left it with the local man to do the admin side of things – fingerprints, descriptives and a DNA swab of the prisoner.

Henry walked out of Blackburn police station feeling emotionally elated yet mentally drained from having concentrated so hard and so long. His temples were throbbing like pistons.

Before setting off back to his office at HQ, he gave his ex-wife Kate a call on the mobile. He let her know where he was and when he was likely to be home. They were taking things on a day by day footing, trying to get back together

9

again, and regular communication had been part of the deal Kate had thrashed out with him. Henry told her he needed to get back to his office and clear up a few things before heading home.

Henry Christie was now a member of the Senior Investigating Officer team based at Lancashire police HQ. His temporary rank of Detective Chief Inspector and the move to what was in essence the murder squad had been the parting gift to him of an ACC who had gone to pastures new. The SIO team was based in offices in a building that had once been a residential block for students attending the training centre at HQ. It had been gutted and refurbished for the sole purpose of housing the team. Henry's office was on the middle floor of the three-storey block and had a view through the trees to the rugby pitch in front of the main HQ building beyond. A nice, fairly peaceful location at the dream factory – as headquarters was often referred to by cynical front-line coppers.

The corridor outside his office was quiet. A light shone out from an office at the far end, otherwise there was no sign of habitation. This did not mean that no work was going on. At present, including the murder Henry had been dealing with at Blackburn, the SIO team was involved in six ongoing murders and assisting at least a dozen enquiries into other serious crimes.

Henry's pounding headache had subsided. The drive from Blackburn to HQ with the car windows open had relaxed him, given him time to

10

chill with David Gray on the CD. He could have done with a strong drink, but the days of having alcohol on police premises were long gone. He settled for a cup of water from the cooler, which he took back to his office.

After completing his housekeeping chores by about 9.45 p.m. he decided to call it quits for the day without feeling too guilty about it. The thought of the king-size bed and his warm ex-wife was very appealing. As he stood up, stretched and creaked, ready to head off, he heard steps approaching slowly down the corridor. Henry peered round his office door and smiled when he saw Detective Chief Superintendent Bernie Fleming, the head honcho of the SIO team. Henry admired him greatly, both professionally and personally. Although he was a career detective, Fleming was not narrow-minded and had a good head for strategy on his shoulders. He had supervised some extremely complex murder investigations in his time and been successful on every one. He was holding a thick box file and a video-cassette tape.

'Henry, I thought it was you. Result?'

'Coughed it ... court tomorrow.'

'Well done,' Fleming said with genuine feeling. 'Off home now?'

'Yep.'

'Can I just give you these before you go?' He held out his hands. 'Bit of a pressie for the new kid on the block,' he added slyly. 'A cold case I'd like you to review.'

Henry took the file and video eagerly. 'Thanks, Bernie.'

11

'Fancy a swift one at the Anchor before you hit the road?' Fleming asked hopefully.

Henry declined with a sad shake of the head. 'Love to.' He shrugged. 'But y'know...?'

'Yeah, no probs,' Fleming said with a trace of disappointment. Henry knew that the Chief Super did not have anyone to go home to and felt slightly mean at refusing the offer of a drink. Now that he did have someone to go home to, he was not going to jeopardize the relationship.

Fleming trudged back down the corridor towards his office and Henry watched him go. Then he glanced down at the thick package and video in his hands. Cold-case review was one of the functions of the SIO team, it involved looking again at unsolved murders and other serious crimes which came under their remit. This was the second one Henry had been given since joining the team two months before. The prospect of it excited him. He was very tempted to open the file there and then, sit down and start work on it. But that would have been as bad as going for a drink with the boss. That was another condition of the package with Kate: come home when you can.

He called her from the office phone and announced his imminent departure.

Twenty-five minutes later he was sitting next to her in the lounge of their house on the outskirts of Blackpool, sipping Blossom Hill red, discussing each other's day. They hit the sack at just gone eleven, both bushed. They cuddled and kissed for a while but did not make love and fell asleep quickly.

About 4 a.m. Henry woke up groggily, dying to pee. After relieving himself, sleep would not return. He tossed, fidgeted, began to sweat and could tell he was affecting Kate, though she did not wake up. Eventually frustration got the better of him: there was no point staying in bed. He slid out, wrapped his dressing gown tightly around himself and stepped quietly on to the landing.

He checked on his daughters, Jennifer and Leanne, soundly asleep in their rooms. Good kids, good to be back with them ... almost back with them. He experienced that overwhelming sense of love he always felt when he was with them, then sneaked downstairs, knowing exactly why he could not sleep.

He had brought home the cold-case review.

It had been a frenzied attack. The girl had been mercilessly beaten, battered to death by an assailant who had lost total control. Blood had splashed everywhere around the dingy basement flat – floors, walls, ceiling – indicating she had been pursued relentlessly through the premises, desperately trying to defend herself from the onslaught.

Her life had come to an end in the tiny, grubby bathroom. Here, it seemed, she had been cornered by her killer. Trapped. Her head had been repeatedly smashed on the rim of the toilet bowl until she died from massive internal bleeding in her brain. Her face was a gory, unrecognizable pulp. The killer had probably continued to pound her head against the toilet long after she

13

had died.

She had been found on her knees, slumped over the toilet, her head hanging into the bowl as though she might have been vomiting. It was estimated she had been there for forty-eight hours. And if that was not bad enough, rats had gnawed her buttocks, legs and feet.

Henry sighed. His nostrils dilated. He rubbed his gritty eyes. He paused the crime-scene video, holding it on a framed shot of the dead female's bare back – she was completely naked – which was latticed by a network of wheals, abrasions and cuts. She was thin almost to the point of emaciation, resembling an inmate of a concentration camp. Not that her gauntness had prevented her from being a prostitute. Semen from four different men had been found inside her during post-mortem.

Henry pressed the stop button on the remote control and the TV screen went blank. He had seen enough for the time being. He took his mug, stood and walked quietly through the silent household into the chilly conservatory. The house backed on to agricultural land and a pale dawn was approaching. He gazed across the field and jumped with pleasure when he saw a big dog fox bouncing through the grass. Then it was gone. Elated by the sight, he sat on one of the cane chairs, shivering a little and holding his hot mug of tea between the palms of his hands, drawing heat from it into his body.

He placed the mug down on the glass-topped coffee table, reached out and flicked on the fan heater, gazing unseeingly into the garden. He sighed again, interlocked his fingers behind his head, but did not allow his mind to go blank. His inner concentration was absolute as he tried to imagine himself as a fly on the wall at the scene of the particularly brutal and senseless murder he had been asked to review.

This thought process was a vital part of the job of the murder detective: making assumptions, constructing hypotheses to be tested, retested and most probably discarded en route to the truth. Then maybe one or two lines of enquiry eventually turning up information, facts, evidence, and then, hopefully, a suspect.

There was not much to go on here. The flat the girl had died in was located in a poor area of Blackpool's North Shore. It could easily be accessed directly from the street down a set of steps from the pavement. This, unfortunately, meant that visitors or customers, or the killer, could come and go without having to enter the main building above, which was a large terraced house converted into a warren of tiny flats. The main point about this, and what made it particularly frustrating from a police point of view, was that people could enter her flat unobserved and very quickly. All they had to do was slip in from the pavement.

At the foot of the steps the front door was almost hidden from view from anyone who happened to be passing. It opened into a tiny vestibule and from there into a bed-sitting room. This was meagrely furnished with a three-quarter-width camp bed, adequate in size for the business of prostitution, some cheap chipboard units and an old, but comfortable-looking settee. There was a portable TV in one corner of the room which looked quite new. The room was lit by a single bulb swinging on a bare wire from the damp ceiling and a lamp on a unit next to the bed. Curtains, worn and frayed, were drawn across dirt-streaked windows, giving the room, at best, a very grainy-grey light.

Also on the bedside unit were an empty wrap of heroin, a blunt, blood-filled needle and a packet of condoms.

The kitchen, reached through this room though an archway, was fitted with a two-ring electric hob and nothing else. No fridge, no kettle, no toaster. Just a brown-stained, germ-filled sink. A cupboard on the wall housed food supplies. Pot Noodles and a selection of instant soups, a bottle of curdled milk, little else. The boiling water required to make these delicacies had to be heated in a pan on the hob.

The cupboard under the sink was the route by which the rats had been able to infiltrate from the foundations. They had obviously been trying to break through for some time, having gnawed their way through the laminated chipboard from which the cupboard was made. Had the girl been alive, the rats would have come through anyway. As it was, they had found her dead and feasted on her.

Henry shivered involuntarily at the thought. It was ghastly enough to have been murdered so horrifically, but then to have been lunched on did not bear thinking about. In his time as a cop, he had been to several deaths, usually from

16

natural causes, where the deceased had lain undiscovered for some time and their pets, driven crazy by hunger, had started to nibble them away.

Cats were the worst.

Henry's mind, distracted momentarily by these thoughts, flicked back to the crime scene.

Whether she had actually had four customers on the day of her death was difficult to determine for sure. It seemed to be a likely scenario, according to the scientists, and very likely that her last customer had been her killer.

She had had sexual intercourse with a man who had then pummelled and battered her until she died.

The assault had started in the bed-sitting room. She had been beaten while still on or near the bed. Blood splashes were all over the bed clothes, together with semen stains from another three men. Her assailant had smashed her head against the wall next to the bed, strands of blood-matted hair and indentations in the plasterboard confirmed this.

The grim fight had continued around the room.

She had either banged her head, or had it banged for her, against the sharp corner of one of the home-assembled units. The pathologist and forensic scientists had matched up the triangular point with the indent on the back of her skull.

At some point during the struggle, killer and victim crashed through to the kitchen and boiling water from a pan on the hob had been tipped up. A scald mark was found on the dead woman's back: more excruciating pain to add to

17

the suffering she was already enduring at the hands of the person destined to take her life. From there the crime-scene analyst reckoned she had managed to escape, but only as far as the bathroom. She had locked the door, which had been booted down off its fragile hinges.

Henry's thought processes paused at that point. His mind's eye saw the moment when the door had been whacked down, splintering. He wondered if the woman had thought she had found some sort of sanctuary in the bathroom, a place of safety. But all she had found was that she had backed herself into a corner from which there was no escape.

Was she screaming as her assailant threw himself against the door? Or was she cowering, huddled down on the floor, whimpering, terrified as the door burst open? What was she thinking as the killer, breathless, red-faced and raging, stood in the bathroom doorway?

He had probably launched himself across at her in a flash of violence. Maybe she had already been on her knees by the toilet bowl, begging for mercy, and all he had done was grab her and started pound-pound-pounding her face against the porcelain.

Or had she fought him at that point? Did he have to wrestle her down, overpower her again, drag her to her knees and then murder her?

Henry finished his tea and walked back to the lounge. The sky was much brighter now, the sun not far away, spring in the air. He went to the TV and switched the video on again. He sat on the settee, hunched forwards, and watched intently as the tape continued from where he had left it. The camera drew back from the woman's spine then circled within the confined space of the bathroom, picking out the blood splashes on the wall, in the washbasin, in the bath, and the mass of coagulation in the toilet. The screen faded to black, then faded in a few seconds later. Now the body of the woman was laid out on a mortuary slab just prior to post-mortem taking place.

Henry's face was emotionless as the camera inspected the wounds on her head and face and the scald mark on her stomach. A commentary from the Home Office pathologist, Professor Baines, accompanied this footage. His latex-gloved hands came into shot, pointing out the various injuries, his voice describing and commenting on them with relish.

Henry stuck with it up to the point where the PM was about to take place, then switched off. He felt no need to watch her being hacked to pieces.

A sigh escaped from his lips. His toes tapped agitatedly in his slippers as he pondered and summarized in his mind what he had learned in the last hour about a crime that had been committed over eleven months before.

There were no particularly good witnesses. No one had been seen entering or leaving the flat, despite the investigation team having interviewed dozens of people in the area. Nor were there any fingerprints which matched anyone on record, and no forensic evidence other than the DNA profiles on the semen. Low copy DNA – DNA left by a person merely touching objects –

had been tested too, but this very expensive process had been inconclusive.

The DNA profiles from the semen were crucial, of course. But only when they could be matched to a particular individual. As with the fingerprints, no match could be made to anything currently held on record. That did not mean that the men who had left their semen did not have criminal records. It might just be that they had not been arrested recently enough to have provided a DNA sample for the database.

Henry knew that new DNA samples were continually being checked against the database of outstanding crimes, but it was a slow process which might or might not bear fruit. He felt he could not sit back and wait and hope that something of that sort happened.

Still cogitating, Henry mused that he was looking for a man who was quite powerful and very handy with his fists, which, together with the rim of the toilet bowl, had done a lot of damage to the prostitute's face. It could be someone who had convictions for assaulting women, particularly hookers. It was an avenue that had been pursued in the original investigation. A lot of likely suspects had been pulled in and questioned without success. That was a line Henry intended to re-open and maybe fling the net more widely across the whole north-west region.

He bent down to the VCR and ejected the cassette. He would not have liked Kate or his daughters to see it by accident.

Perhaps the biggest hurdle faced by the murder squad had been that they had been unable to identify the victim. She was faceless and name-less. Either no one knew who she was, or they were not telling. No identification papers had been found in the flat and the landlord knew her only as Miss Smith. A media campaign, including an item on *Crimewatch UK*, produced no leads whatever. Her DNA, dental records and fingerprints were also dead ends. No one on the national missing persons register fitted her description.

Which was bloody amazing, Henry thought, because her age had been estimated at just four-teen.

No one had missed a fourteen-year-old girl. Fourteen. A prostitute. Now murdered. And nobody knew who the hell she was?

But Henry was not surprised. He had long since stopped being surprised at anything. He knew how ruthless and uncaring the world was.

'Thanks very much, Mr Fleming,' Henry said to himself under his breath, 'for giving me a no-hoper of a case.'

It was 5.45 a.m and Henry had to be at Black-burn Magistrates Court at ten to see how his murderer fared during the remand hearing. He stifled a wide yawn and crept upstairs, knowing the household did not stir until seven thirty. He checked his daughters again to see if they were sleeping soundly, his fiercely protective parental instinct roused by the thought of a fourteen-year-old girl missing and murdered. If either of his two went, he knew he would never rest until he found them. The thought made him judder.

He slid back in bed, ensuring he did not rouse

Kate. She murmured something and turned over, taking the duvet with her.

With a wry smile, Henry closed his eyes, then thought about his cold case. If only for the sake of some parent out there, he would give this one his best shot in the time he had available ... then within seconds he fell into the sleep that had been eluding him for the last couple of hours.

Two

Ray Cragg surfaced from sleep with a storming headache, but did not have any time to brood about it. He had some serious work to do, a busy day ahead. He groaned as he rolled out of the same bed he'd been sleeping in since the age of ten: single, narrow, with a deep indentation down the centre of the mattress into which his thin, wiry body fitted perfectly. It was the only bed he could ever sleep comfortably in.

Once on his feet he staggered a little to keep his balance until the blood made it up to his brain. He kicked some discarded clothing out of the way and lurched out on to the landing dressed only in the ragged, loose underpants he slept in. On the way to the main bathroom he passed his mother's bedroom. The door was slightly ajar.

Cragg paused outside, listening. Then, unable to resist, he peeped in.

Deep asleep, his mother lay splayed on the king-sized bed, naked, the duvet only half-covering her. There were numerous roach ends in the ashtray on the bedside cabinet and the sickly-sweet smell of stale cannabis hung in the air. Cragg shut his eyes momentarily as the sight of his mother's pubes made him shudder. Next to her was the bulk of some sleeping guy, breathing deeply but not quite snoring. On his bedside cabinet were two used condoms half-wrapped in tissue. Cragg had no idea who the man was. Didn't particularly want to know. Didn't actually care either, because he loved his mum. So far as he was concerned she could do anything, or shag anyone, so long as it made her happy.

The only thing Cragg would not tolerate was any bastard who dared slap her round. Two guys had suffered for doing that in the past. One had even thought he could do the same to Ray Cragg.

A knife plunged into the guy's left buttock had made him squeal and think differently.

Cragg closed the bedroom door quietly. He padded barefoot along to the bathroom, had a piss, a power shower, then shaved, although there wasn't very much to shave off, even at the age of thirty. His almost pure-white blond hair, cropped right back to his skull, frustrated the life out of him. Sometimes he thought he would never get any facial hair other than odd tufts here and there which reminded him of Shaggy in *Scooby Doo*.

He left the bathroom annoyed by this thought and also because he had razored the head clean

23

off a big yellow pimple on his chin which refused to stop bleeding. Holding a tiny triangle of pink toilet tissue to his face he stomped angrily back to his bedroom to get dressed.

Transformation time. He tossed his less than clean underpants across the bed and opened the wardrobe. Inside was an array of designer everything. His pulled on a pair of boxer shorts, CK T-shirt, jeans, trainers, and set them off against an Omega wristwatch, a line of single diamond studs in his pierced ears and a state of the art mobile phone (pay as you go, so therefore no records of calls made) slotted on his black leather Gucci belt.

'I am the fucking biz,' Ray Cragg said to his reflection in the mirror while hunching his shoulders in a threatening way. 'The effin' biz,' he said again. 'I think I might just shoot some bastard today.'

He was ready to operate.

His half-brother Marty was in the kitchen waiting for him. He had let himself into the house earlier, was munching toast and listening to Oasis on a portable hi-fi placed on top of the fridge, while perusing the racing pages of the *Sun*. He was dressed similarly to Ray but was more sturdily built.

Ray turned the music off immediately. 'Stuff that for a game of soldiers,' he said, complaining at the noise. 'Got a shaggin' headache.'

'I was listenin' to that,' Marty whined half-heartedly, turning to appraise his half-brother for the first time.

Ray batted his eyelids blandly, daring Marty to challenge him. Though Marty was bigger and physically more powerful than Ray, no aggression from the younger man, he knew his place in the hierarchy.

Marty sneered secretly and looked back down at his racing tips for the day, hiding a smirk at the little pink dab of toilet tissue with the red dot of blood in its centre stuck on Ray's chin. Marty took a huge, rude-sounding slurp of tea from his mug.

Ray rubbed his head, feeling slightly faint again. He dropped a couple of Nurofen Meltlets into his mouth and washed them down with ice-cold orange juice from a carton in the fridge.

'Heavy night?'

Ray shrugged. 'So-so.'

'You wanna keep off that Pils. Fuckin' kills you.'

'Thanks for the crap advice.' Ray slotted a couple of slices of thick white bread into the toaster and re-boiled the kettle. He trimmed the crust off the toast and spread it thickly with butter and seedless raspberry jam (he hated food with bits in it and bread with the crust on, had done since childhood). He sat next to Marty and snatched the *Sun* away from him. Marty let it go without a murmur of protest. Ray ate in silence while leafing through the tabloid.

'What time's Crazy coming?' Ray asked. He turned to the back page. Now that he had some sustenance inside him he was coming to life.

'Should be here by now,' muttered Marty, checking his watch.

25

'Tosser's always late,' Ray commented. His thin-lipped mouth twisted distastefully. With a 'tut' of annoyance he unhitched his mobile from his belt and punched in a number. With the phone to his ear he crossed to the sink, dropping his cup and plate into the washing-up bowl, already brimful of dirty crockery, water, scum and food particles.

'Crazy?' Ray demanded. 'It's me, yeah, now where the fuck are you? ... Yeah, right,' he said, sneering at whatever the response was. 'Not fuckin' good enough ... we've got things to do, a bloody busy day ahead, so put your foot down, will you?' Ray folded the mouthpiece of his mobile back into place and shook his head.

'If that twat's on his way like he says, I'm a fuckin' Dutchman,' Marty said. 'Marty van-fuckin'-Cragg's my name. I'll swing for the unreliable tosspot.'

'He'll be here,' Ray said.

'Still up t'maker's name in that slag of his,' Marty surmised.

'He'll be here.'

They migrated into the living room and watched the best bits of a slasher-type movie while waiting impatiently for Crazy's arrival. He was the driver for the day, Ray's number-two man after Marty. Hopefully he would turn up in a fairly nondescript, clean and reliable motor which would not draw any undue attention to them.

Half an hour later he pulled up outside, honking his horn as though he was the one who had been kept waiting.

'Fuckin'-hoo-ray,' Ray said, jumping up. He pulled a baseball cap on, peak twisted backwards, a denim jacket, and fitted a pair of Full Metal Jacket sunglasses on. He was ready to roll. 'C'mon.' He brushed past Marty who, also clad in sunglasses, was at the front door, opening it for his brother. They trotted down the driveway, past the Mercedes and the BMW, and jumped into the waiting Astra GTE. Ray went in the front passenger seat next to Crazy. Marty hunched in the back.

Ray twisted side-on to Crazy, made the shape of a gun with his first finger and stuck it against Crazy's temple. 'Bein' late pisses me off.'

'Hey, hey,' Crazy's voice creaked nervously. 'I been working, sorting stuff out for you.'

'Yeah? More like screwing that bint of yours,' Marty interjected, his mouth curling.

Ray removed the pretend gun from Crazy's head and sat properly on his seat, allowing Crazy to look disdainfully over his shoulder at Marty. 'No – actually, no.' He turned back to Ray. 'Sorting out today for you, that's what I've been doing, and checking this area real careful, like, for cop surveillance, just in case.'

'And?'

'Nothing.'

'Good.'

'So what's first on your agenda?' Crazy asked, gripping the wheel tightly and revving the engine.

'JJ needs a visit first. Needsa bit of geeing up, doesn't he, Mart?'

'Sure does, skimming bastard,' Marty agreed,

27

a wicked smile expanding across his mean face.

'Then after we've had some fun with him, let's really get down to business.' Ray clasped his hands behind his head. 'Because today is the day when Ray Cragg puts his foot down and steps on some shite.' He glanced at his driver. 'Let's go, Crazy.'

Joe Sherridan's court appearance was over almost before it began. It took two, maybe three minutes at most. The clerk of the court read out his name and Sherridan nodded when asked if the details were correct. He made no response to the charge against him. He then sat down in the dock, a morose expression on his face, his eyes staring unfocused at the floor.

Henry Christie watched his prisoner thoughtfully, wondering what was going through the man's mind. Turmoil, despair, Henry guessed. Remorse about what he had done – perhaps. Uncertainty about the future? His head must be spinning like a washing machine.

The defence made no application for bail. Seconds later the magistrates remanded Sherridan in custody and without a backwards glance he was led down to the holding cells below by his Group 4 jailers.

Henry stood up wearily. He chatted about the case for a few minutes with the pretty lady prosecutor from the Crown Prosecution Service, knowing it was best to keep her sweet, then left court and headed to Blackburn police station, which adjoined the court building. After ironing out what still needed to be done post-charge with

28

the local DI, such as the case file, custody remands, the inquest, reviews and family liaison, he phoned his own office to see if there was anything outstanding for him to deal with. There was nothing that needed immediate attention, so he jumped into his car and decided he fancied a trip to Blackpool.

He could do some work on the cold case he had been given to review, then he could have lunch with Kate. Surprise her.

Johnny Jacques had been in bed with Carrie, his lady friend, when the knock came on the door. He had been awake, but groggy and bleary-eyed, still sluggish from the effects of the night before's drink and drugs binge. It had not been anything too dangerous. Lots of lager, one ecstasy tab and a nose full of coke, or two or three. He'd lost count. But it was all having its hangover effect now and not for the first time. He thought that at the age of forty-five he was getting a little old for it, his body did not seem to have the resilience it once had.

The sound of hammering on the door made him roll over and pull a pillow over his head. The knocking persisted.

'Shit,' Carrie said. She was suffering equally.

The knocking went on. Carrie heard the letter-box flap open with a clatter and a voice shouted through it. She recognized it immediately.

'Fuck!' she said this time, shooting bolt up-right, shaking JJ by the shoulder. 'It's Marty Cragg,' she hissed.

'Wha—'

'It's fuckin' Marty, and if it's Marty, it's Ray too.'

'Shite.'

The knocking grew into pounding.

Carrie's breathing was short and desperate, her heart pounding. 'They must know you're here.' Suddenly, with a clear head, she jumped out of bed, grabbing her towelling dressing gown and wrapping it tightly around her. JJ stayed in bed, having removed the pillow from his head. He stared up at her, eyes wide as a bunny caught in the glare of headlights on main beam. 'I'll do my best to keep them at the front door. You get dressed and scarper out of the back window.'

'Yeah, yeah, right.' JJ twitched, but still lay there as if stunned.

Carrie leaned over him and spoke as though he was retarded. 'Get fuckin' moving,' she said, exaggerating her lip movements so he would understand.

Marty shouted something obscene through the letterbox.

JJ shot upright, jumped out of bed and began to scrabble for his scattered clothing as Carrie left the bedroom and walked into the hallway, shouting, 'Keep yer friggin' hair on.'

Dressing quickly was no picnic for JJ. He managed to find his underpants and slotted one leg through a hole, then put his second leg down the same hole, only to discover they were not his underpants at all, they were Carrie's knickers. He ripped them off as fast as he could and threw them furiously across the room. He dived for his jeans and hopped into them, pulling a grubby T-shirt on at much the same time. Picking up his trainers, he dashed through to the living room at the exact moment Carrie opened the door on the security chain.

JJ ran to the window, slid it open and peered out.

'C'mon,' he panted to himself, trying to get it together. It looked a very long way down to the ground, which was a large, asphalt kids' play area, though with no equipment left in it. It would hurt.

He heard the sound of Ray Cragg's voice at the front door. A motivator to action if ever there was one.

Ray Cragg kept the tone of his voice reasonable, calm and dangerous.

'Just let us in, Carrie,' he said. Ray could see just one fearful eye looking through the narrow gap allowed by the security chain. He knew she was bricking it. 'We just want to have a chat with him, that's all Carrie,' he said smoothly.

'No, just get to fuck. You're not coming in here, you set of twats,' she said, now wishing she had not been so foolish as to open the door in the first place because Ray was leaning on it and she doubted she had the strength to close it on him. 'Anyhow, he isn't here, so you might as well piss off and leave me in peace.'

Ray inhaled and breathed out through his nose. His temper was starting to go but he held on to it. He leaned into the gap, his face only inches away from Carrie's. He could smell her breath and the dank flat beyond: sweat, cannabis, spermicidal lubricant. 'Listen, you cunt,' he said evenly, 'if you don't open up, we'll kick this door down and then I'll get really annoyed with you. I'll smack your face in, just for fun ... and I don't have any axe to grind with you, love. It's JJ I want.'

Carrie desperately fought for time so that JJ could get out of the window, shin down the drainpipe, along windowledges, drop to the ground and leg it, even though it was four floors up. He was an agile guy and had done it before when the cops came calling.

'I said he's not here. You deaf or summat?' she stalled brazenly. 'Now piss off.'

Ray moved back quickly and with a flick of his head towards the door said, 'Crazy, Marty.' He leaned against the wall and folded his arms.

The two had been waiting for the moment with keen anticipation. Marty went first, going for the gap in the door. His hand shot through it and reached for Carrie's face, or whatever he could grab. Crazy, just behind, shouldered the door with all his weight.

Carrie was expecting the move. She slammed the door on Marty's wrist.

He howled like a demon in pain and rage, but it didn't really matter because it meant the door was still open and Crazy, who had stepped back, braced himself and flat-footed the door. It flew open on the second whack, releasing Marty's trapped limb and sending Carrie stumbling and screaming backwards as the badly fitted security chain snapped and splintered off the door frame.

And they were in.

'You cow,' Marty yelled. He went straight for Carrie's cowering form, enraged by having his wrist trapped. He powered into the hall and kicked her in the face with as much force as he could, breaking her jaw. She rolled away, blood pouring out of her mouth, trying to protect herself. Marty continued to lay into her, overcome by anger, as Ray and Crazy strode past, their minds focused on catching JJ.

JJ heard the crash, the scream, the shouts as the front door was booted in.

He had to move now.

He lifted his body and sat astride the windowledge before twisting round and lowering his feet blindly until his toes touched the ledge which jutted out from the wall about three inches, several feet below.

This was the position in which Ray and Crazy found him as they burst into the living room.

JJ panicked as Crazy strode across the room towards him, a menacing look on his countenance, Ray Cragg behind him. JJ reached out his right hand for the soil pipe, which he knew he could shimmy down if he could just get to it. But before he could even touch it, Crazy grabbed the front of his T-shirt in his fists and pushed him outwards away from the wall. JJ screamed. His arms flailed like a demented windmill but he managed to grab the window frame, though his fingers slipped as Crazy threatened to push him away again.

The two men were focused on each other's

faces, both with determined expressions. Crazy's look was one of sheer glee at what he was doing; JJ's, by total contrast, was a look of terror. The thought of hitting the ground headfirst reeled through his mind, the prospect of his skull splintering through his brain.

'This is gonna hurt you.' Crazy grinned twistedly.

JJ's fingers slipped even more on the window frame. He knew that all Crazy had to do was push and let go of his T-shirt and he would go plummeting down.

'Your head'll smash like a tomato. What d'you think, Ray?' Crazy looked back over his shoulder. 'Push the thieving fuck or what?'

'It's a tempter.' Ray leaned out of the window, judging the distance to the ground below. 'Pull him in,' he said. Crazy looked disappointed. Then with a shrug he hauled JJ back into the flat.

'I need words,' Ray Cragg said to JJ.

The murdered girl's flat was on the sort of grubby street where Henry Christie had done so much of his police work in the past. Same old story, same old people, he thought jadedly as he gazed out of the car window up at the five-storey terraced block of flats, each one probably inhabited by a dolie or a junkie or a loser. Henry prodded himself mentally for forgetting that there were also many good people caught up in it as well. It just seemed that he did not meet them that often.

The house was structurally solid, having stood the test of time on the outside. It was its innards and inhabitants that had changed.

He climbed out of the Vectra and made sure it was locked before leaving it unattended.

He wanted to get a feel for the scene of the murder. He walked up to the front of the house and stood at the bottom of the steps leading to the main door. To his left was the flight of steps which descended to the basement flat.

He looked around. The street was pretty quiet. A couple walked down the other side. A car waited at the junction to pull out. He could easily have stepped down to the flat without being seen ... or could he?

If nothing else, Henry's experience as a detective had taught him that very few crimes are committed without witnesses. Somebody always sees something. The trick was to find that somebody and bleed them white. In the nicest possible way, of course.

Henry stood where he was and rotated slowly on his heels, allowing his eyes to rove, to try and spot someone watching him. He saw no one.

It was very tempting to go down to the girl's flat, but he wanted to keep that experience for later. First things first. He would check out the owner of the property who, he remembered from the file, lived in Lytham, in a very desirable location.

He got back into the Vectra and thought seriously about going into the property rental business.

JJ made himself a roll-up. Though his hands were shaking, he put the cigarette together expertly.

Ray Cragg leaned forward eagerly with a lighted match and a smile. 'Calm down,' he said as JJ chased the flame with the end of his cigarette. 'There's no need to worry.'

'No need to worry? How d'you work that one out?' JJ retorted, inspecting the lighted end of his cigarette and blowing gently on it. He put the thin stick between his lips and drew deeply on it. Almost one half of it disappeared with the drag. 'You're gonna kick my head in and you tell me not to worry?'

JJ's narrow eyes darted nervously around the room, taking in each face, then, looking at Carrie, his face creased in pain. She was huddled in one corner, whimpering pathetically, cradling her busted face in the palms of her hands, nursing her shattered jaw.

'She needs a hospital, Ray,' JJ wheezed through a cloud of smoke.

Cragg shrugged. 'As and when.'

JJ tried to hold his eyes to Ray Cragg's, but they flinched fearfully away from the confrontation.

'So what do you want?' JJ asked.

'I think that's fairly fuckin' obvious, don't you?' Cragg grinned. 'Otherwise, why try and leg it?'

JJ shrugged his thin shoulders, looked down between his knees and flicked ash on the carpet. He took another drag on the cigarette and blew smoke out through his nose. It was all but gone now. Sitting there, head bowed, eyes blinking at the floor, his jaw rotating, JJ did not see the blow coming.

Cragg put almost all he had into it and really JJ should have expected it because he had witnessed Ray do it several times before. It was his trademark, a long, powerful, open-handed smack across the side of the face, the palm of his hand cupping over the ear. It lifted JJ off the seat and dumped him in a sprawl on the carpet. The pain in his ear was so severe, he wondered if the drum had burst. The butt of his cigarette rolled away underneath the settee.

Before JJ could react or even scream, Marty and Crazy dragged him off the floor and flung him back across the settee.

'When I ask you a question, you answer it,' Ray Cragg said mildly. 'Are you with me?'

'Yeah,' JJ answered quickly. A booming, painful sound ricocheted around his cranium.

'Right. Now we've got that settled, let's get down to business,' Ray said. 'I'll let you have it right between the eyes, figuratively speaking,' he went on. 'I don't give you much to do, do I? Bit o' this, bit o' that. Enough to pay for your dirty little habits and keep the wolf from the door – and then some. Carry this, deliver that.' He swayed forwards again. He could smell JJ's fear. It smelled dank, but he liked it. 'All in all, nothing very arduous, and I trusted you JJ.'

JJ closed his eyes for a long moment.

'Trusted you for a long time ... but why is it that people get greedy?'

'I don't know.' JJ's words were barely audible.

'Fuckin' astounds me.' Ray shook his head sadly and pulled away from the stench of JJ's terror. 'I keep tight books, JJ, and I know for a fact you've lifted two grand off me—' JJ opened his mouth to protest. 'Ah, ah, ah.' Ray wagged a warning finger at him. 'I know you have, okay? I am not stupid.'

Ray glanced at his two companions, who stood one behind each shoulder, then stared back at JJ. 'You gonna tell me about it?' Ray's head twitched in a gesture of encouragement.

JJ nodded. He felt nauseous. It was all he could do to stop fear from squeezing his entrails and forcing him to vomit.

'Good man,' Ray acknowledged.

The landlord's house was on a recently built exclusive development of executive-style homes in Lytham. There were about a dozen houses on the estate, all detached, each with five or six bedrooms and double or triple garages, but not much land for the half million or so they cost to buy. Henry, an aficionado of the property pages in the glossy *Lancashire Life* magazine, recalled reading the adverts for the development. They were very nice houses, well out of his price bracket, but he could dream.

He parked at the end of the driveway and gazed at the house, which was a far cry from the class of property the landlord rented out in Blackpool. A totally different world. Not even on the same planet. There was a canary-yellow Mercedes sports car in the driveway, which seemed slightly incongruous to Henry. Not that the car did not belong, it was just that he'd expected to see a Jaguar or a big Lexus there, as these were often the cars that the local well-heeled landlords tended to use. There was something effeminate about the neat yellow Mercedes which did not sit right with Henry's, admittedly, stereotypical view of the greedy landlords he knew and despised so much. He shrugged. Maybe it belonged to the guy's wife.

He checked his notes then climbed out of the Vectra and meandered up to the front door, past the car, his eyes missing nothing. His finger pressed the doorbell and he heard chimes inside. He waited, handed clasped behind his back, humming tunelessly to himself. After a few moments someone appeared at the other side of the door and opened it.

Henry took a step back, caught his breath, then introduced himself.

The collections were going well that day. Harry Dixon trotted away from the council house and eased himself into the passenger seat of the car waiting for him at the kerbside.

'Done,' he said to the driver. 'Next one ... should be a fun one,' he murmured under his breath.

'Yeah,' agreed the driver. 'Want me to come in with you?'

Dixon smirked. The driver was a big guy called Miller. He was as tough as anyone Dixon had ever met and, allegedly, had a certain way with a carving knife and a cheese grater, the thought of which made Dixon shiver. Miller had been driving Dixon for a couple of months on the weekly collection runs, but there had never yet been any need to call on his skills, much to the big man's disappointment as he was eager to show them off. Dixon did not want to start now. Though he was smaller in stature than Miller, Dixon preferred to use his charm and tongue as opposed to brawn. But he knew the next address would be a toughie. It always was, but he felt he could handle it himself.

'Nahh, you're okay – just be ready if I need you.'

'Sure. I will be,' said Miller.

Dixon reached for the sports bag slotted tightly behind the driver's seat and pulled it on to his knees. He unzipped it and dropped his latest collection into it. He had a wicked grin on his face as he thought about the word 'collection'. It had a kind of religious tinge to it, sounded like something done at church on Sundays. There was actually nothing religious about the £500-roll of banknotes he dropped into the bag, each one of which he knew would have traces of cocaine on it.

He totted up the total in his notebook. That made just short of five grand he had collected that morning. Dixon's heart began to beat a little faster at the thought of the amount of money he would have in his possession at the end of the day. The palms of his hands began to sweat. By 5 p.m. there would be about twelve thousand stuffed in the sports bag. He shook his head to rid his mind of impure thoughts – twelve Gs was not enough to go out on a limb for – and replaced the bag behind the driver's seat, and in so doing his eyes caught those of Miller.

Miller smiled. It was as though he had been reading Dixon's mind.

Dixon coughed and pulled himself together, swallowing nervously. 'Let's go,' he said to Miller.

As the car moved away from the roadside, Dixon leaned forwards and, for luck, touched the barrel of the sawn-off shotgun which was tucked out of sight underneath his seat.

Ray Cragg was sitting next to JJ on the settee with an arm around his shoulders, talking in little more than a whisper, almost reassuringly.

'It's always best to tell the truth, JJ, because you always get caught out when you lie, don't you?' Ray cooed.

JJ nodded his head painfully, the pounding, searing pain from Ray's open-handed blow across the side of his face was making each movement horrendous.

'So, c'mon, pal.' Ray hugged him like a brother. 'Spill the beans. We can only move forwards when we know where we're up to, can't we?'

'Yeah,' breathed JJ. He looked at Carrie, who was still curled up in a ball on the living-room floor, whimpering.

Ray glanced at her, too. 'I know you're concerned about her, but I promise that if you tell me the truth and we work this mess out, I'll take her to casualty myself. Okay?'

'Right, right,' said JJ, wondering if Ray would be good enough to do the same for him because he was certain his eardrum had exploded with

41

the impact of Ray's blow.

'So, come on, pal,' Ray said again.

'Yeah, I have been skimming a bit, Ray. But not two grand, nowhere fuckin' near two grand.'

'Well,' said Ray, 'that's a start. How much would you say you've stolen from me, then?'

'I'm looking for Jack Burrows,' Henry said to the very pretty woman who answered the door.

'That'll be me,' she said with a slightly crooked smile. 'Jacqueline Burrows, but everybody calls me Jack, even me.'

A fleeting thought crashed through Henry's mind – Am I destined to meet women with men's names? – as he remembered Danielle Furness, known as Danny, the woman he had once loved and who was now dead, murdered by the most dangerous man Henry had ever met. He cleared his mind of the last image he had of her, lying dead in an hotel room in Tenerife, her head twisted at a gruesome angle because of her broken neck. 'Do you own some flats in Cheltenham Road, Blackpool?'

She nodded. 'And Dixon Road, Coronation Street, Hornby Road, and others.'

'Oh, right,' said Henry thoughtfully. He kicked himself for expecting to have to deal with some seedy landlord. This one looked far from seedy dressed in a jogging top and a pair of black lycra shorts which looked as though they had been pasted on to her slim thighs, her blonde hair tied back in a pony tail, exposing an area of seriously touchable neck. She was sweating lightly and Henry could just smell her fragrance ... but then again, he warned himself, she might be just as seedy and deceitful as all the rest. Because she did not reek of cigar smoke and whisky, and looked terrific, did not mean she was any different from the others. Henry knew his weakness for a pretty face, but was determined not to let it cloud his judgement. 'I'm DCI Henry Christie and I'm investigating the murder of one of your tenants in those flats about a year ago ... a young girl?'

Jack Burrows' face fleetingly creased with annoyance. But Henry had noticed it and filed it away for future reference. She recovered her composure quickly and smiled that lop-sided smile, pushed a stray wisp of hair away from her face and looked at him with wide blue eyes. It was a look, Henry guessed, designed to make his stomach go flip-flop. 'I was interviewed about that ages ago, made a statement and everything. Have you caught the killer yet?'

It was at that moment she realized the conversation they were having was taking place on the doorstep. 'Ooh, sorry.' She grinned. 'Manners! Come on in and I'll make a drink or something.'

Henry followed her inside. She led him into the lounge, which was furnished in such a way that he thought it looked like it might once have been the show house. It was a through lounge and in the dining room Henry saw an exercise bike and a rowing machine side by side.

'Tea, coffee...?'

'Tea'll be great.'

'Tell you what, come through to the kitchen

43

and we can keep talking, though I doubt I'll be able to help you any more than I already did. It was a real tragedy, but it was a long time ago.'

She walked through to the spacious fitted kitchen and clicked on the kettle.

'We haven't caught the killer yet,' Henry admitted, harking back to her question at the doorway. 'I've been given the job of reviewing the case again to see if I can open up any new leads, that sort of thing, y'know?'

'Oh.' She leaned against a worktop, her hips thrusting forward. 'I always thought that if a case wasn't solved, it got closed down.'

'No, not with a murder.' He locked eyes with her – and he had to admit she had pretty eyes – but something grabbed his heart with icicle-like fingers and made him go on to say, even though he did not necessarily believe his own words, 'I think there's a good chance of rooting out the killer in this case.' He squinted thoughtfully at the ceiling and added, 'Particularly as it's been given to me to investigate. It's a matter of pride, you see. I'm very good at catching murderers.' He came eye to eye with her again.

Jack Burrows nodded. Henry thought she looked a tad uncomfortable at the news. This pleased him no end because for no other reason than she was the owner of the property in which a brutal crime had been committed, he had made her his first suspect.

'Two-fifty and certainly not more than three hundred quid at the outside,' JJ had to admit. 'Honest, that's all it was. I skimmed a bit here

44

and a bit there, and I'm sorry, but it were never two grand. Nowhere fuckin' near. That sorta figure is one you'd've noticed, Ray. That would've been stupid.'

Cragg guffawed. 'Two-fifty or three hundred is pretty bloody stupid,' he observed, 'and I think you're a stupid person, JJ. Stupid enough to have a bad habit which clouds your judgement, makes you think you can steal from me, and now you're stupid enough to expect me to believe you only took a fraction of what you really took.'

'I'm being honest with you, Ray,' JJ insisted, opening his arms.

Cragg snorted a laugh of contempt through his nose and stood up.

Carrie was still doubled up on the carpet in one corner of the room, moaning and shivering. There were streaks of blood on the wall next to her.

Marty and Crazy lounged by the door, hands in pockets, waiting for Ray to come to some sort of decision. Crazy was the more relaxed of the two, chewing gum and picking at a large spot on his face. Marty seemed restless, more eager for something to happen, his foot tapped agitatedly.

Ray crossed to the window out of which JJ had tried to escape. He folded his arms and gazed quietly out across the rooftops of a nearby housing estate, then down to the deserted play area four floors below. It was tempting to lean on the windowsill but he did not. He was always careful to leave as few traces of himself anywhere as possible.

'You could've come to me and asked for cash,' he said eventually. 'We could've sorted something and you wouldn't now find yourself in this ... pickle, would you?'

Despite the shakes and the booming sound still rattling around his cranium, JJ had managed to roll a replacement cigarette, which was now lighted and affixed to his bottom lip. 'I didn't think, man,' he wailed plaintively. 'It won't happen again. I swear it on my goddaughter's life.'

'Bloody right it won't happen again,' Marty interjected, taking a step towards JJ, who cowered back in the settee. He knew Marty was a dangerous, sometimes uncontrollable bastard.

Ray spun on his half-brother, pointed at him and shot him a stare which stopped him in his tracks. He did not have to utter a word. Marty's face creased angrily.

'Normally,' Ray said to JJ, half an eye on Marty, 'I deal very harshly with people who shit on me.'

JJ tore his eyes from Marty. 'I know.' He swallowed.

'But I'm actually feeling a bit lenient today – with you, that is.'

JJ held his breath, his lungs full of the harsh smoke from the filterless roll-up.

'You're not going to let him get away with this, are you, Ray?' Marty said. 'He needs dealing with good and proper.'

Ray ignored him and smiled briefly at JJ.

'This is the first and last time, JJ. You skim from me again and you're a dead man.'

JJ closed his eyes, relief flooding through him.

'Jesus! You're letting the twat off!' Marty wailed, shaking his head despondently. 'He's fuckin' stolen from you.'

'My money, my decision,' Ray said, 'so shut the fuck up.' He spoke to JJ again. 'If you need any extra dosh, ask me, don't just take it. We'll work something out.'

'Thanks, Ray, oh God, thanks.'

Ray sat down next to JJ again, placing an arm around his shoulders – again.

'I do not believe this,' Marty tutted.

'Y'see,' Ray said, his lips only inches away from JJ's bad ear. 'I'm not that bad.' He gave him a squeeze. 'There is one thing I'm curious about, though.'

'What's that?'

'If you didn't skim two grand off me, who did?'

Henry had followed Jack Burrows back through her house into the lounge. He sat on the expensive soft leather settee, sinking so quickly into it he was caught off balance and almost spilled his tea.

Burrows smiled. 'Always gets people, that.'

'Mm,' murmured Henry doubtfully and sipped the hot drink while studying her face carefully, but surreptitiously. There was something familiar about her. He had an exceptional mind when it came to recalling names and faces, rarely forgetting either, but his recall of her was slightly skewed and out of all context. He frowned. 'I know your face, but I'm struggling to place you,' he admitted.

'Sounds like a chat-up line.'

'If I wasn't investigating a murder, it would be,' he said. Then he made the connection in his mind: murder ... body ... death ... 'I've got it,' he said with a hint of triumph. A sudden death, two, no, three years ago ... a suicide. The deceased had taken a shed-load of pills and not been discovered for about a week or so and had started to rot nicely, thank you. Henry had gone to the death as a matter of routine, but there had been nothing for the CID. Nothing suspicious in it. Henry had happened to be at the scene when the body remover arrived. 'You're an under-taker,' he declared.

'I've had enough of this shit now,' Ray Cragg said bluntly. 'You can go.'

'You mean it?' JJ said in disbelief.

'Oh, c'mon, Ray,' Marty whined. 'You're not gonna let him go, are you? Let's break a few fuckin' fingers at least. Twat deserves it.'

Ray scowled at Marty. 'Yes, you can go, JJ,' but then he pointed to the open window. 'But you've got to go that way. I want to see you climb down the wall. You must be just like Spiderman.'

'Eh?' JJ said suspiciously.

'You heard. I said you can go, but you've got to climb out of the window, just like you were doing when we came in.'

'You're joking.'

'Never joke. If you want to go, that's the way you're going to have to do it, otherwise I'll let Marty and Crazy give you a few digs and a few

48

broken bones.'

The Adam's apple in JJ's scrawny throat rose and fell. He pushed himself slowly to his feet, stubbing out the butt of the hand-rolled cigarette in the overfilled ashtray. With a terrible sense of foreboding he approached the window, cautiously eyeing the three men, seeing if there was any possible way out past Marty and Crazy. There wasn't. They had the door blocked. No chance of doing a runner. Even Carrie had stopped her sobbing and moaning and was watching transfixed from behind her bloody fingers.

'Go on, don't dilly-dally,' Ray urged him. 'Giving me a display of your climbing prowess is the only way you're going to leave this room.'

JJ hesitated, then swung his right leg over the window and sat astride it.

'Go,' said Ray. 'I want to see you climb down.'

JJ eased his left leg over and lowered his toes down to the ledge.

Suddenly Ray crossed the room and faced JJ. 'Actually no one skims from me. Two hundred quid or two grand, it doesn't matter. Principle's the same. You stole from me, committed theft.'

On the last word, Ray's right hand shot out palm first, but landed softly on JJ's chest. JJ clung on to the window frame. His eyes pleaded with Ray's, but got nothing back in return, just ice.

'Fuck ... Ray ... Don't!'

A look of utter contempt twisted on to Ray's face. Then he pushed and said, 'Fly, you bastard.'

JJ could not hold on. His fingers lost their grip

49

and he was out in mid-air in freefall. He knew there was nothing he could do, just wait for the impact and maybe hope to survive it somehow. There was a whooshing sensation past his ears as he hurtled down. It lasted only momentarily and then he hit the ground. But there was nothing. No pain. No feeling. No blackness.

Ray had leaned out of the window to watch the fall. To him, JJ seemed to be in the air for a long, long time, it was as if everything had slowed down. JJ's arms flailed like a broken windmill, his mouth opened in a silent scream. Time then clicked back to normal and he smashed into the ground. Ray plainly heard the dull whack as the top of JJ's head struck. His body twitched a jig, his eyes came open, then he did not move anymore, his eyes staying open, staring up at Ray accusingly.

Ray pushed himself away from the window, a grim, wild look in his own eyes.

'First one of the day,' he announced. 'Let's get a move on.'

He made towards the door. Carrie, who had watched him murder her boyfriend, forgot her own fear and pain and pounced at Ray's feet, screaming, 'You bastard!'

Ray smartly side-stepped and rammed the sole of his trainer against the side of her face, kicking her away. She sprawled across the room, but wasn't finished. Jumping to her feet, she went for him again.

Marty put himself between her and Ray. He grabbed a fistful of her hair and dug his fist into her stomach. He dragged her sideways and threw her to the floor.

This time she did not move, just lay there sobbing and choking.

'No witnesses, Marty,' Ray said. 'Take care of her and see us down in the car when you've done.'

The words were bliss to Marty's ears. 'It'll be a fuckin' pleasure.'

It was a mess underneath the settee. There were discarded cigarette packets, matchboxes, a couple of pizza boxes (one with a half-eaten Margarita in it), numerous cigarette and roach ends, some scrunched-up free newspapers and a pair of knickers. All in all, a tinderbox.

The cigarette end which had fallen from JJ's fingers did the trick.

It burned slowly and almost died, but re-ignited when a waft of fresh air rolled through the flat when Marty left the premises after he had finished with Carrie. A tiny ember blew on to a rolled-up fish and chip paper and started to burn. The little flames crackled and licked the underside of the cheap settee, immediately melting the plastic-like fibre and spreading to the foam-filled insides.

In less than sixty seconds the fire had engulfed the piece of furniture and was reaching towards the curtains.

The old man who found JJ's twisted body on the playground did not think to call the police. A paramedic unit was first on the scene. Once they were certain JJ's life was extinct – not a difficult thing to work out – they called the cops and covered the body from the prying eyes of the crowd which had started to gather.

While waiting for the arrival of the boys/girls in blue, they saw the flames begin to pour out of the open window of the flat four floors above.

So they called the fire brigade.

It was going to be a full turn-out for the emergency services.

Three

'Now I remember you, too,' Jacqueline Burrows said. 'Bit of a messy suicide, wasn't it? You were one of the detectives who came to the house to have a look at the body.'

Henry nodded and raised his eyebrows. 'Mind if I ask you the question you probably always get asked?'

'The "why" question?' she said. 'Why would a girl like you want to become an undertaker? Dead bodies and all that messy stuff? The smell of death, embalming fluid, etcetera, etcetera?'

'Yeah, the "why" question,' Henry confirmed.

'Impulse,' she admitted. 'No great feel for a vocation or anything like that. I was fifteen at the time, a rebel at school, really pissed off, saw an ad in the local rag and thought I'd have a go at it. An undertaker took me on and I really enjoyed it.' She shrugged. 'Took to it like a duck to water, just loved it. Embalming, making people who'd been smashed to bits look good again so their relatives could have some decent memory of them. Spent a few years learning the trade and my dad set me up in business when I was nineteen. Got a bit bored with it a couple of years ago, so I sold up, bought an empty hotel on South Shore and converted it into flats ... done that ever since. Very lucrative. Got ten properties now.'

'Who is your father?' Henry wanted to know.

'Bill Burrows – transport.'

'Oh,' said Henry, slightly taken aback. He knew of Burrows Transport and their international fleet of haulage vehicles. It was a very successful business, rivalling the best transport companies in Europe, and Bill Burrows was one of the richest men in the north of England.

'I thought you'd know him,' she said, seeing Henry's reaction. Then she changed tack and said, 'So why did you become a cop?'

'I think I'm here to ask the questions.'

'Fair's fair,' she insisted.

'Okay,' he relented. 'Impulse. Boredom. A desire to shock my mother. And it sounded like a fun job.'

'And has it been?'

'It has its moments ... now, back to business. Somebody was murdered in one of your bedsits about a year ago.'

'Like I said before – I don't know anything about it.'

Henry paused before speaking again. He liked silence during interview situations, was never

uncomfortable with it; it was always the inter-
viewee who got twitchy – usually – but Jack
Burrows did not seem to mind. She was a very
cool customer, he thought. He hoped this was
just a veneer and that underneath she was pad-
dling like mad.

'I find that very difficult to believe.'

'It's true,' she replied without any trace of
annoyance.

'Convince me,' he urged her.

'When I started out in the rental game and had
one or two properties, I did all the day to day
stuff and I knew everybody who was in the flats.
The more properties I took on, the less time I had
to do that,' she said, tweaking her fingers. 'By
the time I'd got five places, there was just no
way I could personally know all the tenants, so I
hired a manager and opened an office in town.
He did all the routine tasks for me, including
arranging lets to clients. I simply do not know
who is in my flats now. I'm too busy buying
another block and I'm also negotiating to buy a
sea-front hotel. It's go, go, go.' She smiled. 'And
that's why I don't know anything about the girl
who was murdered. Obviously it was a tragedy,
but...' She did not finish what she was going to
say but then went on, 'So it's the manager who
knew her and let her have the flat, not me.'

Henry nodded, processing this information. He
glanced down at his notes. 'This would be
Thomas Dinsdale, would it? He's the manager?'

'Was at the time,' Burrows corrected him. 'He
quit shortly after the girl got killed.'

'Where is he now?'

'Absolutely no idea.'

'No forwarding address? Contact number? New place of work?'

She shook her head and pouted.

Henry was just about to get very annoyed with her because he knew she was lying. He opened his mouth but his words were cut short by the pager affixed to his belt, which began to ring. Frustrated he unhooked it and read the scrolling message. He sighed and fitted it back on to his belt, then looked at Jacqueline Burrows.

'Saved by the bell,' he said coldly. 'But just for the record, Miss Burrows, I don't believe you didn't know anything about the dead girl, nor do I believe you haven't got a clue as to the whereabouts of Mr Dinsdale.' He finished his tea and struggled out of the settee. 'So I'll just have to find him myself, won't I? And, as a muscular movie star once said, "I'll be back." I'll find the front door myself, thanks.'

Burrows, stony-faced, let him go without uttering a word. She watched him from the living-room window as he got into his Vectra. She was feeling very nervous, dithery almost, as though her blood sugar was low. There was something about Henry Christie which made her very wary indeed. It wasn't as though she had not been cautious of the detectives who had interviewed her initially, but she had not felt challenged by them in any way. In fact, when she had lured one of them into her bed, she had known she was completely safe. But Christie was different. There was something about him that worried her and gave her the feeling that

55

even if she could get him into bed, he would still be a danger to her.

She picked up her phone and dialled a mobile number.

Annoyingly the call was immediately transferred to the answerphone. She slammed the receiver down and swore.

They made their way to a small terraced house in South Shore, not far away from the Bloomfield Road football ground used by Blackpool FC.

Crazy dropped Ray and Marty off at the front door and parked the Astra some distance away and walked back to the house by another route, checking for any signs of surveillance by the cops. It was time to be careful because things were about to get very serious. He walked down the back alley behind the house and entered through the rear door.

Ray and Marty were already upstairs in the front bedroom where they had stripped off and were naked. They were folding their clothes into black plastic bin liners. Crazy joined them and stripped off too, placing his clothes into a third bin liner.

'It's all in the back bedroom,' came a voice from downstairs. 'When you're ready.'

The three naked men trudged down the short hallway into the room where everything was laid out on the uncarpeted floor for them.

Each man had a pair of jockey shorts to put on, a pair of black socks, a fairly tight-fitting pair of dark-blue overalls, latex gloves and a ski-mask. Their feet were to be covered by Hi-Tek trainers.

It had all been newly bought, but no two things had been purchased from the same supplier, with the exception of the latex gloves, which came in a box of a hundred pairs.

All dressed, but without the masks, they trooped downstairs to the kitchen where the man who was known as the Supplier waited patiently for them, brew in hand, a selection of handguns laid out neatly on the Formica-topped kitchen table.

'Fuckin' World War Three,' exclaimed Marty.

'Everything fit okay?' the Supplier asked, appraising the men.

'Yeah, good,' said Ray. He stared greedily at the guns.

'Got a bit of a choice for you here,' the Supplier said proudly, displaying his wares on the table with a regal waft of the hand. 'And every one is guaranteed to be as clean as a whistle.'

'How do we know that for sure?' Ray asked cynically.

'Stole them myself. Every gun here is clean and cannot be connected to any other criminal act.' The Supplier smiled. 'Guaranteed.'

Ray nodded.

The Supplier selected one of the handguns – a 9mm Glock, very light and compact. He removed the magazine, showed the three men that it wasn't loaded and handed it to Ray, butt first. 'Used by a lot of police forces in the country. Easy to use, reliable, kills people.'

Ray weighed the gun in his hand. 'Very light,' he admitted.

'Accurate, deadly,' the Supplier confirmed.

'Will it jam?'

'No,' he said with confidence.

Ray handed the weapon to Marty, who appraised it, nodded sagely and passed it to Crazy, who did the same.

'Twelve rounds in the mag, one in the chamber.'

'Unlucky for some,' smirked Ray.

'Eh?' said Marty, a quizzical expression on his face.

'Nowt,' said Ray, shaking his head. 'What else you got?' he asked the Supplier, looking down at the table full of guns.

'I think you'll like this one, too,' the Supplier said. He picked up another weapon and showed it to Ray Cragg.

By the time Henry Christie arrived it was all over. He parked some distance away from the flats and sauntered to the scene, hands thrust deep into his pockets. Now that he was a member of the 'circus' – the HQ team brought in to assist the local cops to investigate serious crime – he did not like arriving in the time-honoured traditional fashion, bursting into crime scenes, throwing his weight about like they did in days gone by. He liked to do things his way, a way that reflected his personality: quiet and sneaky. So he came on foot, approaching from an oblique angle, taking his time, letting his eyes, ears and nose do the work; coming up from below as opposed to pouncing from above as some senior investigating officers had a reputation for doing.

There was a lot of activity at the flats.

Ambulances, fire engines and police cars and all their occupants. It all looked pretty confusing, but Henry was pleased to be able to pick out one of the local jacks, Rik Dean, doing some directing and supervising, getting the uniformed branch to push back gawping members of the public and generally make some room.

Rik saw Henry approaching. He cut off from what he was doing and scurried to meet him.

Henry liked Rik. As a uniformed bobby he had been a good thief-taker with a superb nose for rooting out villains. His transfer to CID could not have come soon enough and he showed himself to be a very capable detective, having recently been promoted to sergeant.

'Hi, Henry.'

'Rik.' The DCI nodded.

'Hope you didn't mind the call ... just seemed to be a bit of an odd one, that's all.'

Henry shook his head. He never minded the call. 'What've you got?'

'I'll show you.'

He led Henry round two fire tenders, stepping over hoses which were coiled like an annual convention of boa constrictors, up a flight of steps leading to a block of flats. Henry had expected to be taken up to the fourth floor where he could see a lot of activity taking place on the landing.

'We're not going up there?' he asked.

Rik shook his head. 'Not yet.'

Henry frowned, but kept an open mind.

'Come on, John, get those kids away from there,' Rik shouted at one of the uniformed PCs

59

who was having problems keeping a bunch of youths away. He continued to walk around the perimeter of the flats, taking Henry to the back where even more things were happening. A group of people – paramedics, firefighters and cops – were gathered around an object on the ground. They all looked up as Rik and Henry came towards them, parting as they got nearer. Henry saw they were standing around a body which had been covered by a green sheet from the ambulance.

Instinctively, Henry glanced upwards, seeing smoke drifting out of a fourth-floor window.

Rik reached the covered body and pulled back the sheet for Henry to see.

At first he thought it was Ronnie Wood from the Rolling Stones, the body looked so similar, but on second thoughts he said, 'Johnny Jacques.' Henry had been a detective in Blackpool on and off for many years and he knew most of the local low-lifes. He had had some fleeting dealings with Jacques in the past, but nothing too complicated. Henry had always thought of JJ as a pathetic ageing junkie on the periphery of the drug-dealing scene in town who would, one day, wind up dead through an overdose, as opposed to flattened from a fall. 'Okay,' he said to Rik Dean, 'what's the crack?'

'Ambulance get called to a splattered JJ. They arrive and find him dead, look up and see flames shooting out of that flat.' He pointed upwards. 'The fire brigade arrive, douse the fire and find another dead body in the ashes, that of a woman, believed to be Carrie Dancing—'

'JJ's old lady,' interjected Henry. He knew Carrie, too.

'Yep.'

'Okay – hypothesis?'

'Fire gets started somehow. They get trapped, JJ jumps for his life to escape being burned to death, she bottles out and gets fried. How about that?' He sounded doubtful.

'Sounds okay, so why the hesitation?'

'Paramedics arrived and found the body here and only then did they notice the flames up above, so it doesn't look like he jumped to escape the flames, because it seems they came after the jump.'

'Suicide?'

The local detective shrugged. 'Could be.'

'But you're not convinced.'

Rik scratched his head and screwed up his facial features. 'Mm, could be. But why is she dead? Did he kill her after some domestic or other, or some suicide pact, or what? Did he set the place on fire, then jump? ... Dunno. Some things don't add up, Henry.'

Henry patted him on the shoulder in a terribly patronizing manner and smiled in a fatherly way. 'Let's go and have a chat with the fire people.'

'Home Office pathologist is up there, too. Professor Baines ... I thought it wise to get him in early.'

Henry smiled at the prospect of bumping into Baines.

They were each given a new (stolen) pay-as-you-go mobile phone just in case they needed it

61

for the job. They would be disposed of later, along with their clothing.

Ray switched his on and waited for it to register, then keyed in a number, but disguised his own number by putting '141' in front of it first. He put the phone to his ear and eyed Marty and Crazy as he waited for the connection. They were alone in the house now, the Supplier having left a few minutes before. They were drinking water from plastic bottles.

'Me,' Ray said when the call was answered. He listened intently for a few seconds, said 'Thanks' and ended the call. 'It's on,' he said to his two companions.

Crazy stayed outwardly calm. Ray knew that inwardly he would also be calm, because despite his nickname, Crazy loved action, thrived on it.

Marty twitched nervously, making Ray wonder – and not for the first time – whether or not to ditch Marty from the big scheme of things and promote Crazy into his place. He knew it would mean killing Marty if he did that, but such was the way of the world.

'Your call now.' Ray nodded to Crazy.

Crazy tapped a number into his mobile, had a short conversation then announced, 'Be here in ten minutes.'

Henry and Rik Dean met the chief fire officer at the front door of the fourth-floor flat. His name was Grant, a large, gruff man who did not really like the police but did not allow this to detract from his professionalism. Henry knew Grant of old, they had once put a serial arsonist away for

62

twelve years by working closely together.

Grant had been inspecting the scene of the fire. He had been a firefighter for as long as Henry had been a cop and he knew what he was talking about, so Henry listened carefully as they walked into the flat.

'The fire was very much contained in the living area due to the living-room door being closed,' Grant explained. 'Closing doors is a simple but effective way of holding back a fire.'

'I'll remember that,' Henry said.

Grant gave him a stern look which cracked into a little smile.

The living room was a blackened, burned, charred mess. Everything had been touched by flames. The walls were black, the TV had melted where it stood and the furniture was completely destroyed with the exception of any metal parts, such as springs.

Henry stood on the threshold, not wanting to enter and disturb evidence. He let his eyes wander. At first glance he could not distinguish a body. He looked harder and saw the outline of what had once been a living, breathing human being among the charred debris of what had once been the settee.

He gasped. Though death was his trade, it never failed to touch him somewhere inside. He could be as cold and clinical as anyone while dealing with it, but he was unable to ever quite detach himself from the thought that he was dealing with something that had once been alive.

A firefighter was still dousing down the mess

which smouldered with the possibility of re-ignition. This was okay and necessary, but it didn't half destroy evidence. Henry winced at the thought.

'Had a good look,' Grant, was saying. 'It was an extremely hot fire because of the foam in the settee, which was also the seat of the fire. Until everything has been doused down, I can't say for sure, but I'll lay my career on it being a discarded cigarette underneath the settee. Caught hold of the rubbish underneath, then whoosh!' Grant's hands explained his words with an explosive gesture. 'They don't put this sort of filling in furniture these days. It was a very old piece, to say the least – and she was lying on it, poor bugger.'

'Why didn't she get off, try to escape?' Henry asked.

'Drink? Drugs? Who the fuck knows?' said Grant. 'Post-mortem'll tell you that, no doubt.'

'Would you say the fire was accidental or deliberate?' Rik Dean asked Grant.

There was no hesitation in Grant's response. 'Accidental. You don't start a deliberate fire by discarding a cigarette and hoping it'll burn a house down.'

Henry turned up his nose doubtfully. That was unless you were a very tricky person, he thought to himself.

'Still doesn't add up,' said Rik. 'Why did JJ go out of the window?'

'Do we know for sure he went out of this window?' Henry put in. 'At the moment it's only an assumption.'

'Yeah ... but...' Rik protested.

'I know, I know.' Henry raised his hands. 'This is his girlfriend's flat and it's more than odds on he did go from here, but it's not a racing certainty as yet, not until we get our house to-house teams to knock on every door in this building.'

Rik accepted this. 'I'll get a couple of guys on to that now.'

'Good idea.'

'And I'll go and clean up,' said Grant.

They left Henry standing alone by the door of the living room. He was still amazed by the devastation that fire could bring in such a short time. It was still an assumption that the body on the settee belonged to Carrie Dancing, but he was pretty certain that subsequent examination would reveal that to be the case. Henry liked to deal with facts as opposed to supposition whenever possible. He knew that assumptions did have to be made, particularly in the early stages of an investigation into a suspicious death. The trouble was that assumptions tended to have fangs which had a nasty habit of biting you where the sun don't shine.

He sniffed. He could smell charred flesh. It turned his stomach, making him feel queasy. It was one of those aromas that once inhaled never purged.

Suddenly he was whacked between the shoulder blades. He staggered a couple of steps from the unexpected blow and spun to face his unknown adversary, ready to fight.

'Jesus!' he said, fists raised defensively.

It was just as well he did not lash out,

65

otherwise he would have punched a Home Office pathologist into next week.

'Henry, you slimy old twat.' Professor Baines beamed. 'Back in plain clothes? I knew that uniform business would not last.' He was referring to Henry's recent short but sharp time as a uniformed inspector.

'Yeah, I'm on the SIO team now,' said Henry, trying to rub his back from the friendly, but hard blow delivered by Baines.

'Oh, that's handy.'

'Why?' Henry asked suspiciously.

'Well, not being one to jump to conclusions ... but I'm pretty sure this female was dead before the fire cremated her.'

The van arrived on time and drew up in the alley at the back of the terraced house. The driver stayed behind the wheel. He did not sound the horn, just waited with the engine ticking over smoothly. He was not being paid to do anything else.

The three men left the house quietly, walked smartly across the back yard, through the gate and climbed quickly into the back of the van. Ray banged the side of the van and the driver let out the clutch gently and drove away.

A couple of minutes later another vehicle arrived at the back of the house. The man driving it parked in the alley, let himself into the house and collected the three bags of clothes which had been left in the front bedroom. He carried them to the car and threw them into the boot.

Before leaving he checked the house was

66

locked and secure. It would not be used again.

'Let's assume that JJ and Carrie were at the flat,' Henry said. He was sitting on a low wall some distance away from the block, Rik Dean next to him. Both were sitting on their hands like little lads. They were going through the hypothesis stage of the enquiry, that stage when there were few facts available to them beyond a scene of crime as yet unexamined, and two bodies, neither of which had been post-mortemed. 'So they have a barney, JJ kills her and then, in remorse leaps to his own death from the window ... and just by accident, the flat catches fire from a discarded fag.'

They pondered this for a while before turning to each other and going, 'Naaah!' simultaneously.

'I've known JJ for a long time and he's really nothing more than a sad old junkie who would not hurt a fly. He's been knocking around with Carrie for donkey's years. They doted on each other in a sort of hippyfied way. I know that anyone is capable of murder, but I can't see him whacking her, but I could be wrong. It just doesn't seem to fit.'

'Unless someone else did it and pushed him out of the window,' Rik Dean suggested.

'I like that. It's something we must bear in mind. Let's see how the PMs pan out tonight, but in the meantime let's be making some enquiries into JJ's current lifestyle. See what he's been up to recently.'

* * *

The next stage of the mission found the three men arriving at a large garage premises on the periphery of an industrial estate on the outskirts of Bispham, just north of Blackpool. The doors were already wide open and the van was driven in.

Here, they de-bussed with all their gear and transferred it to another vehicle which was waiting for them in the garage. It was a Golf GTi, stolen a couple of weeks earlier from south Manchester, given a new paint job and a set of number plates referring to a clean GTi owned by some poor soul in Derbyshire. Just enough work had been done on it to keep any inquisitive cop at bay for a few minutes at least. It had been stolen for a particular purpose and after today would be delivered to a scrap yard in Rossendale to be crushed into a square no bigger than a cardboard box.

Crazy slid into the driver's seat. He was the wheelman and wanted to get comfortable. He was wearing his latex gloves, pulled tight over his fingers, as were the other two. This would ensure that no prints belonging to them would be found in the car should the police somehow get to it before it became a cube of crushed metal. None of the men had been in physical contact with the car before today.

The garage owner, who ran a profitable sideline 'ringing' stolen cars, gave Crazy the thumbs up and said, 'It's a beast, this motor. It won't let you down.'

Crazy nodded.

'Better fuckin' not,' murmured Marty loud

enough for the man to hear. He got into the back seat.

Ray retreated to the far end of the garage, out of hearing, his mobile pressed to his ear. He had a brusque conversation, which ended as he slid his phone into his overall pocket and looked across at the others.

'It's still on,' he said. 'Let's go ... we need to meet Pete.'

With a curt nod to the garage owner, Crazy reversed the GTi out of the premises and turned back towards Blackpool. Ray and Marty slid low in their seats, keeping their chins to their chests.

All three were now beginning to feel the tension.

Henry was in no particular hurry to move Carrie's body, but he did allow JJ's corpse to be moved once it had been photographed, videoed, and given a once-over by scientific support and the pathologist. The paramedics kindly offered to remove it to the mortuary and Henry ensured that a police constable accompanied them in order to provide continuity of evidence.

He let the experts do what they had to do in the flat after he had assessed the scene himself. He was not a hundred per cent convinced there would be much for the SIO team here, other than to lend a guiding hand. If the facts seemed to point to JJ having killed Carrie and then topped himself, it would be pretty much a paper exercise which could be handled locally.

'You were close by when you got the call,' Rik Dean commented to Henry, more by way of

69

small talk than anything else.

'Mm,' said Henry. He told Dean why he had been so close and as he told him, something somersaulted into his memory. 'You were involved in that investigation, weren't you?'

'Yeah, just took a few statements, that's all.'

Henry frowned. 'Did you interview Jacqueline, alias Jack, Burrows ... you did, didn't you?' Henry now clearly recalled seeing Dean's name at the bottom of one of the statement forms in the file.

'Yeah, yeah, I did.' Rik looked a tad uncomfortable for a passing moment.

'What did you think of her?'

'Er ... who?' he asked dumbly.

'Jack Burrows,' said Henry, almost spelling the name out.

'Oh. Okay, I guess.'

'Did she tell the truth?'

'Er, I think so.'

Henry eyed Dean thoughtfully, not remotely happy with the response he was getting from the officer. He wanted something meaty, tangible, but all he was getting was the impression that Rik Dean did not want to discuss Jack Burrows. It puzzled and intrigued Henry at the same time.

They were standing on the walkway outside Carrie's flat, leaning on the balustrade overlooking the car park below. Out of the earlier chaos had emerged some sort of order. The fire service was now withdrawing having drenched the flat and probably destroyed any evidence the fire had not. The entrance to the crime scene was now being controlled by a uniformed PC,

70

who was keeping tabs on everyone coming and going, providing people with overshoes and paper overalls, but mainly ensuring that as few people as possible entered the scene in the first place.

Scenes of crime and scientific support officers were beavering away at the remains of the flat; someone from the forensic science lab was en route, so things were pretty much bottled up. Door to door enquiries had started in a limited way, to be expanded later when staffing allowed. Once Carrie's body was moved, they would soon have the result of the post-mortem.

Henry checked his watch. It was 4 p.m. already. He had missed his surprise lunch with Kate, but as it had been a surprise, she did not know any different, so there was nothing lost there.

A car drew on to the car park below. Henry half thought he recognized it.

'It's the DI,' Dean said.

The driver's door opened and the detective inspector climbed out and looked up towards Henry and Dean, acknowledging them with a little wave.

Dean waved back. Henry, however, found he could not move. He was in deep shock.

'First day back at work,' the DI said to Henry. They were walking slowly along the concrete walkway outside Carrie's flat, shoulder to shoulder, touching occasionally. 'I wasn't going to turn out to this because I knew you were here and I was busy with other things ... but then I

71

couldn't resist,' she admitted ruefully.

Jane Roscoe let her shoulders rise and fall in a gesture of submission.

'I didn't even have a clue you were coming back. I thought you were having a long career break, especially after all you went through.' Henry fell quiet for a few seconds as he thought about the fairly recent past. 'And you were trying for a child, weren't you?' Henry was quite nervous being so near Roscoe. His voice wavered slightly.

'Yeah, we were, but it never seemed to happen. I suppose it helps if you have sex.'

'Usually part of the equation.'

'Well it started off like having sex to order ... can you imagine that?'

'Bliss.' Henry laughed.

'Not in our house,' she said seriously. 'But apart from that, I got bored being at home, doing the wifey thing. It just didn't seem natural, so I asked to come back and luckily my job was still open, so ... here I am! Large as life and twice as dangerous.' They reached the end of the landing and stopped walking. Roscoe took a deep breath, which she then exhaled unsteadily. 'Things aren't right between me and Tom, which doesn't help.' She had a sad expression on her face.

Henry could feel his heart beating away, thumping away at his ribs.

'What's wrong ... why the sad face?' he asked, the words sticking slightly in his throat, afraid of the answer.

Roscoe had big eyes and they looked into Henry's.

'What's wrong?' she said. 'You really want to know?'

Henry nodded, but not with great enthusiasm.

'You,' she said. 'I can't get you out of my head. Can't stop thinking about you. I know we've never actually done anything other than kiss – and that was bloody brief.' She chuckled. 'Yeah, all we ever did was kiss, but I had to get back to work because it was the only way I could think of seeing you again.' She blinked, her eyes moist, then gave a short laugh. 'That's why.'

Henry was speechless. It had been the same for him.

'I think we can move the body now,' Professor Baines declared as he emerged from Carrie's flat. 'Done all we can here.' He caught sight of Henry and Roscoe standing face to face, inches apart. He tilted his head back and looked down his nose at the pair of them. 'Obviously I'm sorry to interrupt,' he added, 'but a murder has been committed here.'

The King's Cross public house was situated on Lytham Road, South Shore. It was a large building, double fronted, bars on either side of the front door. Its clientele was drawn mainly from the seedier side of town and much drug dealing was carried out on the premises, which were owned by a man called Rufus Callan.

Callan had four such pubs, all of a similar nature, none very upmarket, but they made him vast amounts of money, as did the drug dealing he controlled in them and which he was keen to expand. It was this desire to grow which had led

73

him to cross swords with Ray Cragg. And why, on that day, Ray Cragg had decided that Rufus Callan was going to pay the ultimate price for trying to muscle in on his territory.

Rufus Callan was going to die.

Four

Henry had met Jane Roscoe a few months earlier under very difficult circumstances. He had returned to work following a virtual nervous breakdown, expecting to return to his old position – detective inspector at Blackpool Central. He had been shocked to be told that – for his own good – he had been transferred to uniform duties and that someone else had been given his job, that someone being Jane Roscoe. He had wanted to despise her, but had found himself deeply attracted to her and she to him, although neither of them did anything about it.

In a particularly traumatic incident Jane had become the target for a deranged serial killer who had kidnapped her with the intention of murdering her. Henry had tracked him down and released her. This incident had made Jane decide to take some time off work and start a family with her husband, with whom relations had been somewhat sour.

At the same time Henry had started to try and make a permanent peace with Kate. He had

74

moved back in with her and was doing his best to make the relationship work. He was ecstatic to be back with his daughters, but things were often pretty strained between him and Kate. Not only had he found himself thinking about Jane Roscoe more than was healthy, he was not completely sure he was still in love with Kate. He told her he was, but sometimes he did not believe his own words, and without that true love, he knew the chances of their relationship working were pretty minimal.

Henry and Jane accompanied the blackened, charred body of Carrie Dancing to the mortuary at Blackpool Victoria Hospital. It was laid out on a slab next to the one with JJ's now undressed body on it. Girlfriend next to boyfriend.

In a corner of the room, Professor Baines was preparing to carry out two post-mortems back to back. He looked across at Henry, who was inspecting the two bodies. 'Y'know, it's funny, but every time I bump into you, Henry, there's never just one body to cut up. Usually I get a whole busful!' He laughed.

'It's the effect I have on people.'

'I have no doubt there'll be even more for me to do before the day is done now that you're on the scene. You seem to attract violent death.'

'Cheers ... at least it keeps you in luxury items, doesn't it?' Henry said knowing how much Baines charged for his work.

'Yes, beluga caviar and champagne tonight.' The pathologist smiled, blowing into a latex glove so it resembled a cow's udder.

75

Jane Roscoe came to the door. She and Henry caught each other's eyes. He knew they needed to talk.

'We need to nip out and get a few things sorted,' he told Baines. 'Back in about twenty minutes, half an hour or so.'

'Whatever.' Baines moved to the bodies, flexing his fingers. 'I'll be here for a good few hours I expect.'

They parked in a side street off Lytham Road. Crazy kept the engine of the GTi ticking over. He thought the car felt good and knew it would not let them down if they needed it.

All three were silent, waiting.

About a hundred metres away, around the corner and out of sight, was the King's Cross, where their business was going to be conducted very shortly.

Marty tapped his foot on the floor. It was beginning to aggravate the other two.

'Fuckin' stop that,' Ray said impatiently.

The sound ceased instantly. A short while later Marty started keeping a beat by slapping his thighs. Ray decided to let it ride. He was nervous, too, but he kept things bottled up inside, like Crazy did. Later he would allow himself an outlet for his emotions. Until then they would remain as controlled as they could be under the circumstances.

Soon they would be on the move.

A small man came round the corner from Lytham Road and approached the Golf. Ray wound his window down. Looking furtively round, the man bent down to the car window and breathed out smoke and beer fumes from which Ray recoiled slightly.

'What've you got, Pete?'

'He's in the snug. Through the door to the left. He's sat at the bar with Teddy Wright and Big Townley on either side of him. There's one bar-man and no one else inside the place when I left. It's dead quiet.'

'You a hundred per cent?'

'Yep.'

'Right. Thanks. I'll square this up with you later.'

The small man nodded and walked hurriedly away, lighting a cigarette as he went.

'Shit,' muttered Crazy.

Ray and Marty looked up quickly as a cruising police car turned into the side road and rolled slowly past them. All three tensed, but the PC at the wheel did not seem to notice them as he drove by.

Crazy, his hands gripping the steering wheel rigidly, watched the police car get smaller and smaller in his rear-view mirror.

'Gone,' he said.

All three puffed out together.

'Times like this I wish I'd been a banker,' Crazy said seriously.

'Mate,' said Ray sympathetically, 'you are a banker!'

They all laughed in a release of tension.

'Right. Let's go and do this. Remember, Marty, in and out. No fucking around. We walk in quick, up to them, guns to their heads, as little distance as possible. Bang, bang, bang, they're dead. Leave Rufus to me. Don't say a word. Shoot 'em and then we're out and away. Okay?'

Marty nodded.

'Crazy – you know what you're doing?'

He nodded.

'Right – let's go.'

Crazy pulled away from the kerb, drove to the junction with Lytham Road and into the line of sight with the King's Cross. He edged on to the busy main road and into the traffic heading south. Nice and easy. Seconds later he stopped outside the pub on the single yellow line. He did not anticipate getting a ticket. Wouldn't be there long enough.

Ray and Marty climbed out together, crossed the wide pavement and stepped into the entrance vestibule. They pulled on their ski-masks and drew their weapons.

Through the eyeholes in their masks, they appraised each other.

'Ready?' Ray asked, his voice muffled by the mask.

Marty nodded and raised his gun to show he was.

Ray put his weight against the door which led to the snug. He opened it an inch so he could see through. It was quiet, dead, even, as their small informant had said it would be. He could see the barman, but only two figures sat hunched over the bar, deep in conversation. He was unable to tell if one of them was Rufus Callan or not.

One way or another he had to do something, though.

He could not wait where he was for fear of some innocent customer coming in and tripping over them in the vestibule. He pushed the door open and walked smartly – did not run – towards the men at the bar.

'Snug' was an inappropriate term for the room because it was extremely spacious and it was perhaps thirty feet from the door to the bar. A long way to walk with a gun in your hand.

As Ray came in, Marty behind him, time seemed to move very slowly. Ray felt like he was walking through treacle, as though his hearing had been tampered with and he was wearing mufflers. Nothing seemed real – except for the realization that Rufus Callan was not sitting at the bar.

The barman was first to notice their approach. His head jerked up and he shouted something which, to Ray's ears, was loud, strange and dis-. torted. It was obviously a warning, but Ray could not distinguish the words.

Instinctively Ray raised his chosen weapon, the Glock.

The two men at the bar looked over their shoulders. Expressions of horror creased their faces as they reacted to the sight of two armed, masked men approaching.

One of the men pushed himself up and away from the bar, his stool tipping over, and turned to run, but even in the slow-motion time in which Ray was operating, he did not have a cat in hell's chance.

Ray shot him in the back, two bullets double tapped from the Glock, driving between his shoulder blades. The man's arms flew up, he pitched down on to his knees, then smack down on to his face where he squirmed on the beer-sticky carpet.

The other man at the bar belonged to Marty. He did not move, just stared rigidly at their approach and raised his hands in surrender.

Not a good enough gesture for today. Marty waltzed up to him, jammed his gun hard into the man's temple, forced his head to the bar top and pulled the trigger.

Ray stood over the man he had taken out and, shot him in the head.

Time returned to normal for Ray with a blinding flash, as though he had stepped out of a time tunnel.

'Where the fuck is Rufus, where is he?' he yelled. He jumped across to the bar and pointed his gun at the cowering barman. 'Where is he?'

'B-bog,' stuttered the terrified man. 'In the b-bog, having a shit.' He pointed to the toilet door.

Callan pulled up his trousers and flushed the toilet. He tucked his shirt into his jeans and went to wash his hands, which he dried under the hot-air machine. It was because of the combined noise of the toilet flushing and the hand drier that he did not hear any of the shots being fired in the snug. Unaware of any problem, he left the toilets and wandered back down the corridor towards the bar.

For a few vital nano-seconds, it did not even register with his brain when a masked figure appeared at the door ahead of him. It did not register because it did not seem real, because he was not expecting it. But as the gun rose in the hand of the masked man, it became all too real and he reacted.

'You keep an eye on that fucker!' Ray screamed at Marty and pointed at the barman. 'Kill him if you have to.'

He jumped over the body of the man he had shot and ran to the door leading down to the toilets. As he pushed it open he came face to face with Rufus Callan.

Ray hesitated and Callan threw himself against an emergency exit by his side, slamming the release lever down and lurching out of the door.

Ray fired, but because he was slightly off balance, he missed. The bullet gouged into the wall by the door. Then he gave chase.

Callan banged the door shut behind him. Ray booted it open again with the flat of his foot, paused, then leapt through it. It opened on to an alleyway at the back of the pub. Callan was running hard towards Duke Street. Ray fired another shot, not really expecting to hit him, but Callan screamed, staggered, clutched the back of his left leg and fell to the ground. He managed to execute a forward roll and was back on his feet straight away, holding his leg and hobbling towards what he hoped would be the safety of a public road.

Ray pursued him relentlessly. He was experiencing that sense of utter elation one feels when taking someone's life from them. It did not matter that he was going to kill someone in broad daylight, in the middle of a busy street, because he believed absolutely that he would get away with it.

Callan stumbled out of the alley, howling for help.

The first person he approached was a middle-aged woman out shopping. When he raised his blood-soaked hands to stop her, she screamed and recoiled.

'Callan,' came a voice behind him, a voice which sounded like the devil calling his name.

He twisted, the agony of his damaged leg smeared across his face. He fell over on to his backside on the pavement and Ray raised the Glock again. Callan tried to crab away backwards on all fours, bawling, 'No, no, no—'

Ray fired. The bullet rammed into Callan's right shoulder, pinning him to the ground.

The woman screamed horribly again, a car screeched to a halt, and people started to run and hide. But Ray Cragg had stepped back into his distorted time tunnel and all he could see and feel was the figure of Rufus Callan, a man he hated, a man who had dared to encroach on his drug-dealing patch, who had taunted Ray, who'd had the temerity to think about taking on the most powerful drug dealer in the north of England.

Ray hunted the crawling man. He fired another shot into him as he dragged himself into the road between two parked cars. The bullet went into Callan's thigh, but he continued to drag himself away from Ray, leaving a trail of thick blood behind him.

A car swerved, just missing him. Another car stopped with a squeal of brakes and tyres as Ray stood over Rufus Callan and shot him twice in the head.

And once again, Ray Cragg's normal world spun back into focus. He did not vacillate. Making sure that every onlooker saw his pistol waving in his hand and did not dare approach him, he turned and legged it back down the alley and into the King's Cross through the emergency exit. He burst into the bar, shouting, 'Go!' to Marty, who was still covering the barman. Ray had to hurdle the two splayed-out dead bodies to get to the door, which he yanked open. Marty was right behind him.

Seconds later Crazy was driving them away, very coolly, very sedately, not drawing any undue attention to them. Ray ripped off his ski-mask, sweat drizzling down his forehead and face. He was breathless.

A police car, sirens wailing, hurtled past them in the opposite direction, going to the scene.

Crazy kept glancing at Ray, saying nothing, but eager to know what had happened.

Ray gulped deep breaths, calming himself. Eventually he looked sideways at Crazy and smirked victoriously. 'Fuckin' good,' he snarled. 'Well done, Marty, what a fuckin' scene that was! Shot the bastard like the dog he was.'

Henry came back to the table balancing two coffees and two plates of Eccles cakes in his hands. Jane Roscoe took hers from him, their eyes catching each other fleetingly, their insides churning. Henry seated himself and took a sip of the hospital cafeteria coffee, wincing at the bitter taste.

'It was just so false, me being at home all the time,' Jane said. 'Making his breakfast and having his tea on the table when he got home, usually late. Then sex!' She snorted. 'Just to try and have a baby to keep us together. I think he thought it was wonderful, but it just wasn't ... right.' She shuddered at the thought. 'I didn't really want to conceive – even though I do want to be a mum – because deep down I don't really want to be married to him. I just don't love him,' she concluded sadly with a shake of the head. She took a bite from her Eccles cake, wiped some crumbs from her mouth and smiled. 'How did you know an Eccles cake always makes me feel so good?'

'Intuition.' Henry stared into his coffee. It was a muddy-grey colour. 'I'm back home now, you know.'

'I'd heard. How are things?'

He held out his right hand and waggled it from side to side. 'So-so. Not brilliant, but we're working at it. I suppose I should consider myself lucky to be allowed to have another chance.'

'But...?'

It was his turn to snort. He looked squarely at Jane Roscoe and wondered about himself. He had found himself deeply attracted to her during the short time they worked together, yet they had never got further than a brief kiss, not even a suggestive conversation. But there had definitely been something electric between them.

84

But she had gone back to her husband and he had gone back to Kate and was trying to get his life on to some sort of even keel. Though things were far from perfect, the comfort, lifestyle and stability Kate offered him were very real ... and yet, and yet ... here was Jane Roscoe back on the scene, obviously with some deep feelings for him and all of a sudden, here he was again, considering destroying his life ... for what?

His head told him he had to be strong here. He had made too many mistakes in his private life over the past few years and could not afford to make any more. He should tell Roscoe that he and Kate were a rock-solid item; that although things might be hard at the moment, the future looked good and he was going to stick with it.

'I've still got a couple of months' lease remaining on the flat over the vet's,' he said stupidly.

'Oh, the vet. Fiona. That was her name, wasn't it?'

'Yup.' Henry had been seeing Fiona at one stage during his separation from Kate, but it had not worked out. Somehow they had managed to resume their former formal relationship of landlady and tenant without too much acrimony.

Henry ate some cake and sipped his coffee. They did not speak for a while and then simultaneously opened their mouths, each over-talking the other. They laughed.

'You first,' said Henry.

'I think you know what I'm going to say.'

'Maybe, maybe not.'

'I haven't been able to stop thinking about you,

85

Henry. I'm confused. I want to love my husband, yet you are on my mind all the time.' She shook her head again. 'I mean, bloody hell! I'm nearly forty, been married over eleven years, never ever been unfaithful to Tom and you come into my life and all I can think about is being unfaithful with you ... ahem ... there, said it.'

'Wow,' said Henry. 'Mm,' was all he could think to add. Then, 'Bugger!'

She grinned. 'But I'll understand if you're not interested because I can see you're trying hard with Kate. I don't want to spoil that.'

Once again they held each other's gaze. Henry speculated as to why people became attracted to each other. What was it? What was the spark? Really, he knew very little about Jane Roscoe, yet he knew there was something extra special between them.

'Is it because I saved you from certain death?' he asked lightly, though he knew that she would surely have been mutilated and murdered had he not found her first. 'That sort of thing does tend to play havoc with your emotions. I know I am a hero figure to many women.'

'I knew even before that,' she said simply.

'Bugger,' he exclaimed again, feeling deep water approaching.

Jane's mobile rang. Henry was pleased to hear that the ring tone was the riff from 'Jumpin' Jack Flash'.

'Gotta go,' Roscoe said, ending the call and downing the last of her coffee and stuffing the Eccles cake into her mouth. 'Been a shooting down on South Shore,' she mumbled through a

86

mouthful of currants. She stood up and collected her belongings. 'Sounds like there might be a dead 'un ... want to come?'

Henry shook his head. 'Call us if you need us.'

'Bye ... speak later.' She left the cafeteria. Henry watched her disappear.

'Bye,' he whispered. He took his time finishing his coffee, then made his way back to the mortuary.

No one followed them, Crazy was sure of it, but only after making double sure did he drive back to the garage from where they had first collected the Golf GTi and transfer them into the back of the Transit van which was waiting for their return.

The garage owner immediately went to work on the Golf. He removed the number plates and replaced them with a fresh set for the journey to the scrap yard over in east Lancashire. The car would be crumpled metal within the day.

Ray, Marty and Crazy were driven to a new address in the van, this time to a terraced house in the north of town. Here they undressed and bagged everything up they had worn for the job. The guns and mobile phones were wrapped separately and everything was then handed to the driver of the Transit whose job it was to arrange for their complete disposal and destruction. This included the van, which would be burnt somewhere out of the county.

The three showered and changed back into their original clothes.

Crazy had ensured that there was a car waiting

for them near the house. When they were ready, they left discreetly and got into the car.

Although all three were hyped up, there was very little conversation between them. Ray intended to debrief the whole thing later to make sure that no holes were left in the way the job had been handled, that they had covered their tracks as professionally as possible.

He knew it would be impossible to stop rumour from spreading among the criminal fraternity that Ray Cragg had taken out a business rival. But he was happy for the message on the street to be read and understood by all, the message being that Ray Cragg controlled this town and if you got in his way, you suffered.

He also knew there was a good chance of being arrested, but because he believed he had left no physical evidence behind, the police would have to rely on a confession, which would not be forthcoming under any circumstances. He was absolutely certain nothing could be pinned on him and that, even if they did lock him up, he would be free within hours.

'Well I don't know about you,' Ray announced, 'but I need to fuck just now.' He eyeballed Crazy.

'Don't look at me,' the driver laughed, 'you ain't gonna bum me.'

Ray looked over his shoulder at Marty who, for some reason, looked severely infuriated.

'What's up with you, half-brother?'

'Nowt,' he snapped.

'You did fuckin' well today. We need to talk about it later, need to talk about bonuses.' He laid a hand on Crazy's left arm. 'You did good, too. Big bonus. But first I need to have some hot sex to cool me down ... you know where to drop me.'

Jane Roscoe was trying to focus on the job which lay ahead. It sounded deadly serious. A shooting. Another run of the mill job in the lovely town that was Britain's biggest, brashest holiday destination. Murders were frequent and cops were run off their feet all the time with big, nasty incidents which were ten-a-penny in this town. But even so, she was still pretty new to the post of detective inspector and sometimes the enormity of the job was a little awe-inspiring.

She drove quickly through the traffic, using skills she had picked up on an advanced driving course. She was in her own car, not equipped with a blue light or two-tones, so when she hit the backlog of standing traffic where Lytham Road joined the promenade, she could not make any further progress, stuck in a line which she assumed existed because of the incident she was attending.

She thought quickly, but did not know any way to circumnavigate the traffic, so she pulled off the road, rode her car up on to the pavement and abandoned it. She was going to have to walk the rest of the way, which was perhaps no bad thing.

The King's Cross was about quarter of a mile down the road and it took her about ten minutes to get there. When she reached it she found out why the traffic was backed up all the way to the promenade and in every other direction too:

there was a body in the road and the uniformed cops had sealed the scene. Now they were desperately trying to get the traffic moving somehow.

The inspector in charge of the scene was an old lag called Burt Norman, a wizened cop who had seen just about everything in his time. He spotted Roscoe arriving and went up to her.

He blew out his cheeks and said, 'Even I'm shocked by this one.'

Jane Roscoe did not know Burt Norman well at all, being fairly new to Blackpool division, but she knew of his reputation and for him to admit that was quite something.

'Tell me,' she said.

'Okay – this guy here was seen being chased out of the alleyway here – which backs on to the King's Cross, by the way – so it looks like he'd been chased out of the pub and gunned down in cold blood here in the street, in broad daylight. A witness says the attacker just kept shooting him as he tried to get away. There's a trail of blood which pretty much verifies that. Bloody ruthless. This town is the pits.' He almost spat.

'Let's have a look.'

Jane Roscoe inspected the scene quickly. It reminded her of a Mafia-style hit, photos of which she had often seen in Sunday supplements. The man was lying in a pool of black blood. One of his legs was drawn up, his arms splayed out almost as though he was sunbathing.

He had plenty of bullet holes in him.

Norman was at her shoulder. 'There's more ... two shot dead inside the pub.'

90

'Do we know who they are?'

'Yep – that's Rufus Callan. The two inside are his running mates. They're drug dealers and it looks like they have annoyed somebody.'

'Annoyed?' Jane said incredulously. 'Fuckin' totally pissed 'em off by the look of things.'

Henry had returned to the mortuary to find Baines engrossed in the post-mortem of Carrie Dancing, assisted by a young male mortuary technician who would not have looked out of place on a slab himself. The burnt flesh smelt terrible and seemed to claw at Henry's nose hairs and cling to his clothing. The pathologist peered over his mask as Henry entered and walked past the painfully thin body of Johnny Jacques.

The thought of the two of them dying made Henry feel sad. He had always thought of JJ as one of life's losers, a pretty harmless soul, more likely to do himself mischief than anyone else.

'Ahhh, Henry.' Baines smiled behind his surgical mask. 'Glad you could make it back. Not too smitten with the very pleasant, but homely Ms Roscoe, I hope?'

'No, I'm not,' Henry said firmly, but with a grin. Henry's up and down love life was always cause for amusement for Baines. 'What've you got?'

'I was right,' Baines said, delving into Carrie's open chest with his scalpel and cutting out her heart which he pulled out with both hands. He carried it over to the dissecting table, laid it out and sliced it open expertly, checking the arteries for any possible blockages. 'Nothing

91

much wrong with that,' he said, raising his eyes to Henry. 'Yeah, I was right ... this girl was dead before the fire. It was the line of the jaw that made me suspicious – out of line, if you will. My examination confirmed it. She had a broken jaw.'

'That wouldn't have killed her, though, would it? Even I know that.'

'No, but the severe beating about the head by some blunt instrument did. There was no smoke inhalation in her lungs.' He pointed with a gloved finger to the deep-pink mass of dissected lung tissue on the table next to Carrie's heart. 'Clean and healthy ... as much as a heavy smoker's lungs can be. Definitely beaten up and killed prior to the fire. And just out of interest,' he added, pointing to the side of Carrie's head, 'I think that could be a footwear mark, so I've asked one of your footwear experts to have a look at it.'

Henry peered at Carrie's temple and could see a couple of faint ridges. 'So, did he do it?' Henry thumbed at JJ.

'I'm not sure a post-mortem on him will give you that answer, Henry old boy. You might have to do some detective work for a change instead of continually relying on me to solve all your cases for you all the time.'

'Cheeky git,' said Henry.

The barman who witnessed the shootings in the King's Cross was in no fit state to make any sort of statement. Roscoe spoke to him for a few minutes, ascertained that he had been threatened at gunpoint and was in fear of his life, and arranged for him to be taken home with a police escort who would stay with him for the time being. Roscoe wanted to be present when he was eventually interviewed.

The pub had been closed and was now a sealed-off crime scene, being dealt with thoroughly and professionally.

She took a seat at the rear of the snug and tried to imagine the terrible thing that had happened here: two masked gunmen, three people shot to death, drugs' connections, turf war.

One thing was certain. She was dealing with some totally ruthless individuals who had coldly planned this multiple execution very carefully and precisely.

Henry had once dealt with a domestic murder where a man had killed his wife simply because she had moaned at him for smoking in bed. The guy had been drunk at the time, admittedly, but it had demonstrated to Henry that people can go 'off on one' for no particular reason and resort to murder in their rage. What Henry could not see happening in the case of Johnny Jacques and Carrie Dancing was that JJ had killed her, whatever the provocation. And he especially could not believe it when Baines peeled back the charred skin from Carrie's head to reveal the cranium underneath. The damage caused to it was beyond anything Henry thought JJ was capable of. JJ was a weak, spindly druggie and Henry just could not see him being so violent over the sustained period of time needed to inflict such injuries on the woman he'd been with for years.

Which kind of put a spoke in the wheel.

In truth, this was the sort of incident Henry knew he could write off if he so desired. He could easily surmise that JJ had murdered Carrie and then, in a fit of remorse, had leapt to his own death. He was supremely confident he could get a coroner to swallow it hook, line and sinker.

It would be a good one-for-one. A murder solved without the expense of a trial. A good one for the figures.

Except he did not believe it and his conscience would not allow this to happen, until he was totally convinced otherwise.

He bagged up JJ's clothing for forensic examination, and did the same with Carrie's burned garments too.

If JJ had killed her, Henry was sure he would be able to see blood on JJ's jeans at the very least. There was nothing.

He decided to return to the scene of the fire to see if anything had been missed or forgotten.

Before setting off he spoke to Rik Dean via mobile phone and found out he had been redeployed to the shooting incident down in South Shore. It sounded like an interesting job, but Henry was not going to poke his nose in unless asked – which he knew he would be very soon. He wasn't going to show his face before then because he trusted Jane to get a grip of everything and work the scene professionally.

He bade farewell to Baines, after warning him he was likely to be dealing with a further three bodies before the night was over.

Baines thanked him profusely for the news and said again, 'Why is it that when you're involved there's always a mass of bodies?'

'Just lucky, I guess,' said Henry.

Crazy drove Ray to his girlfriend's house. Marty, still in the back seat, looked drained and unhappy.

At the end of the driveway, Ray instructed Crazy to be back in an hour or so, not to hurry, but to be there. Crazy promised he would be and Ray got out of the car. Marty clambered over between the seats and plonked himself into the passenger seat.

Crazy put the car into first and set off, but Marty said, 'Wait!' a little too quickly, then felt he had to explain himself to Crazy. 'Er ... let's make sure he gets inside safely.'

Ray rang the doorbell. The door opened and Ray stepped inside.

Jacqueline Burrows gave a quick wave to Marty and closed the door.

Five

'Welcome to life as an SIO,' Bernie Fleming, the detective chief superintendent in charge of the team, said to Henry Christie. 'Never rains but it pours.'

Henry was unfazed. This was what he wanted. Involvement up to the hilt. To be kept busy, to be hunting down killers. He was sure he had been born to do this job – well, perhaps not – but it was certainly something he enjoyed, keeping all the plates spinning in the air, hoping to God they did not smash around his feet.

Fleming had turned out to the triple shooting, then called Henry in to see him at Blackpool nick, following a consultation with the divisional chief superintendent concerning allocation of resources, which is what murder enquiries always came down to these days.

Which is also why Fleming was slightly irritated with Henry and his view on the incident involving Johnny Jacques and his girlfriend. It would have been simpler for all concerned for Henry to write the job off, but because he believed it was not as straightforward as it appeared, it meant that a team needed to be allocated to it at the expense of the triple shooting.

Henry and Fleming were trudging up the steps

in Blackpool police station because the lift was not working. They were making their way up to the canteen. Both men were starting to sweat, and the bigger, older and less fit Fleming was wheezing as he breathed. He was also whining about costs. It was a story Henry was familiar with and the words only just registered.

'There's six ongoing murder investigations right across the county. I'm not saying they're all labour intensive by any means, but we don't really need two more.'

'Tell that to the murderers.'

'Yeah, right,' Fleming snorted gruffly. 'So obviously the shooting is going to take priority here.'

At last they reached the sixth floor and stepped into the canteen, which was about to close for the evening. Using their charm they managed to wangle two mugs of coffee from the reluctant lady behind the counter.

'How do you want to play the fire job?' Fleming asked.

'Run it as a full enquiry until it's proved otherwise,' Henry said defensively.

Fleming shook his head. He looked pained. 'Not enough people to go round.' He pondered things for a few moments, rubbing his chin. 'What about if you head up the shooting, then split your resources to look into the fire and see how it pans out?'

'I thought you were going to SIO the shooting.'

'Name only, name only. I want you to do it and as a sideline, use people as and when to look into

97

the other job.'

'Okay,' said Henry. There was no point arguing. The days had long since gone when every suspicious death was allocated a full team. Everything got prioritized these days and in these circumstances it was seen as far more important to catch someone who was dangerous enough to use a gun in public to shoot a man down, than to catch someone who may have killed someone in the confines of a council flat. Henry could not see the difference, but in a world where money counted, that's what happened. It was not unusual these days for a pair of detectives to investigate a murder – a state of affairs that had long existed in the USA.

Although Henry accepted the way of the world, he hated to see the police being driven solely by money and budgets. He believed the public did not get the service it deserved because of it.

He squinted. 'You want me to run both jobs at the same time? Is that what you're saying?'

'Henry, one day you'll make one hell of a fine detective with such a sharp mind.'

The sex had been over within a minute. Ray Cragg, still hyper after the shooting, had almost dragged Jack Burrows up the stairs, tearing her clothes off as he went. She played the part too whilst disguising the shiver which ran through her. She led him into the bedroom and pushed him on to the bed before straddling him and letting her breasts flounder over his face.

He bit and sucked at them greedily, biting her

98

large, purple nipples so she gasped, not with pleasure, but with pain.

'You really have had some kind of day.' She smiled lovingly.

'You wouldn't believe it.' He moaned then said, 'I want to do it from behind.'

'Yeah, okay babe,' she agreed.

'Like dogs,' he added.

As she slid off him and he took up his position behind her, she was glad he could not see the expression on her face.

He rammed himself in and after only a very few hard, ruthless thrusts, he came, jabbing wildly in an orgasm all of his own.

She pretended to climax, but all she felt was a cold, cold chill inside. She was relieved when he withdrew and slumped on the bed, exhausted.

'Yes, I know it's my first day back at work, love, and I'm sorry, but I can't help it that three people have been shot to death on my patch ... Yes, *my* patch, and unfortunately I have to start running an investigation immediately ... time? Er ... not sure ... when I get there...'

The door to Roscoe's office opened. Henry Christie poked his head through.

She beckoned him in, shaking her head. She did not want him to go. She mouthed the word 'husband' to Henry and raised her eyes heavenwards.

'Look, I'm not sure what time I'll be back ... There's a pizza in the fridge which you can do in the microwave ... As soon as I can, okay?' She slammed the phone down and sat heavily on the chair at her desk, brushing her hair back from her face. She looked frazzled and sighed deeply. 'Yeah,' she said, 'first day back and I'm going to be late home.'

'Goes with the territory, and you don't get overtime for it.'

'And guess what?' she said, placing both hands on the desk. 'I don't care. I'm just glad to be back at work, involved in something as meaty as this – and especially with you around.' She sat back. 'Henry, I've really missed you.'

He swallowed. She had been in his thoughts too. Not just in his thoughts, but all over his brain every waking moment. He sometimes even dreamt about her. 'I've missed you too,' he admitted. 'But we've got a bit of a job on and it needs to be done pdq.'

She smiled radiantly at the prospect of working alongside him. 'Better get on with it, then.'

'I need an alibi,' Ray said to Jack Burrows. 'For around two till four o'clock this aft. You have to say I was with you during that time, okay?'

She had returned to the bedroom from the shower, having spent a long time washing under the hot, power jets. Ray made her feel dirty. She always had to wash herself after intercourse.

'Sure, no problems.' She sat at the dressing table, a towel wrapped around her body, and started working on her hair. Suddenly, a thought came to her and she stopped brushing it. 'I can't,' she said, her mouth arid. She turned to Ray, who was spread-eagled on the bed, still naked, thin and pasty white.

'What the fuck do you mean, you can't?'

She told him about the visit she'd had from a cop that afternoon.

Henry and Jane walked side by side into the parade room on the ground-floor annexe of Blackpool police station.

The people assembled there were not the actual murder squad, but a mish-mash of people cobbled together just to get things underway. The real squad would come together for an 8 a.m. briefing in the morning when all the detectives and other specialists were brought in. Henry desperately wanted to get things moving now, but it didn't mean it would be a haphazard deployment of personnel. He had particular goals in mind for this evening, especially the rooting out of informants to bleed them of anything that might be useful.

It was 8 p.m. by the time the briefing finished. Henry and Jane returned to her office to discuss the briefing which would take place the following morning and get everything prepared for it. They had numerous phone calls to make, trying to pull a team together. It did not help that other murders were being investigated across the county and that the majority of the people Henry would have liked on his team were already gainfully employed.

After an hour, Henry hung up the phone for the last time and wiped his brow in mock exhaustion.

'Just one more call to make, if you'll excuse

me.' He stood up and took his mobile phone from his jacket pocket, leaving the room as he dialled Kate.

Out in the corridor he filled her in on what was happening. She already knew a lot because he had spoken to her earlier, but as part of the communication package between them he had felt obliged to call her again and tell her he was going to be very late coming home. Then, not really knowing why, he added that it might be better if he spent the night at his flat because it was so central, handy for the police station, and he would not disturb Kate or the girls by coming in late.

It was all rubbish, of course, but that 'certain something' had crept into Henry's brain again. He experienced a vicious stab of guilt when Kate happily accepted what he was saying at face value, told him she loved him and asked him to ring her if he could – any time.

He ended the call with an irritated frown on his face. He returned to Jane's office, replacing the expression with a more positive one.

'Ready?'

She grabbed her coat. Henry was going to take her on the town in the hunt for an informant or two. As they descended the stairs, Roscoe asked, 'Was that Kate you were talking to?'

'Yeah.'

'Oh,' she said, and clicked her tongue on the roof of her mouth.

By 9 p.m. Ray Cragg, Marty and Crazy had made their way to the counting house. When he was there, Ray always thought of himself as the king counting out his money. Or to be more accurate, overseeing while others counted out his money for him.

The counting house was in the middle of a short dead-end terraced street in the town of Rawtenstall in east Lancashire. The houses had been built towards the end of the nineteenth century to accommodate workers at the nearby cotton mill on the banks of the River Irwell. Over a hundred years later the mill and the cotton business were long since gone. After having been abandoned and allowed to decay through non-use and vandalism in the decades following the Second World War, the shell of the mill had finally been flattened in the early 1990s. The demolition of its massive chimney had made national TV news. A new industrial park had replaced the mill and the cotton trade itself had been replaced by a variety of businesses and services, none of which would last half as long as cotton had done.

But the street remained. Two rows of houses with back yards and outside toilets, clinging perilously to the side of the Rossendale Valley. Even its original cobbles remained, now shiny and worn with age, use and weather. On damp, dank, foggy days it did not take too great a leap of the imagination to visualize those bygone days when cotton ruled: clogs clattering on cobbles, the mill chimney belching plumes of unhealthy smoke into the atmosphere, cholera and typhoid.

However, it had been touch and go for the

survival of this street. Most of the surrounding streets had been demolished, grassed over, never to be rebuilt in any shape or form. The bulldozers had been ready to roll to flatten this last one. The required compulsory purchase orders had been served and all the residents, bar one stubborn old lady – ninety years old, who had lived in the street all her life and had never been further than Blackpool – had been evicted and rehoused. It was only a matter of time before the old lady popped her clogs and the bulldozers waded in. The council had been prepared to wait.

The street had been saved by Ray Cragg. He had spotted its location and potential, and had slipped some fairly hefty backhanders in the form of cash and B-list celebrity blowjobs to a couple of councillors ripe for the plucking.

It would be a crying shame to flatten the street, destroy history, wipe out our heritage ... at least that's how the councillors lobbied on Ray's behalf. The council were informed that a local businessman and general do-gooder (no name mentioned, obviously) wished to preserve the street, yet also modernize it and let out the properties to the local community at low rents.

What the council did not hear was the truth: that Ray Cragg had seen the street's potential. A nice, little nondescript location, tucked out of the way, affording the privacy he craved, close to a motorway link giving him fast access to Manchester in one direction and the whole of Lancashire in the other. It was also extremely cheap.

Neither were the council told that he wanted to

relocate his counting operation from Blackpool to Rawtenstall, somewhere easily guarded and controlled, away from the prying eyes and greedy intentions of his business rivals, where he knew who the neighbours were – somewhere like Balaclava Street, Rawtenstall.

The first job Ray had done when it became his was to ensure that the stubborn old lady died in the house she had been born in. He had enjoyed doing that himself, breaking into her house in the middle of the night, sneaking up to her bedroom, his face covered – appropriately enough – with a balaclava. His intent had been to terrify her to death, something he thought would have been easy. It did not happen as quickly as he had anticipated.

Her valiant old heart only packed in after he had dragged her from her bed, torn off her winceyette nightie, thrust the barrel of a revolver into her toothless mouth and told her he was going to rape her.

'That is, unless you die, you old bitch,' he'd growled into her hearing aid. 'Die, die, die.'

She'd complied and Ray had placed her back into bed, covered her up and left her to be discovered by relatives three weeks later. It had been one of Ray's proudest moments.

'What are you smiling at?' Crazy asked him.

'Oh, nothing.' Ray chuckled, shaking his head to rid himself of the memory of that night in the old biddy's room. He had really enjoyed making her die. And no one, not even Marty, knew he had done it. It was his little, proud, secret.

Ray's eyes roved round what had once been

the living room of one of the terraced houses, but was now where the counting took place. There was no front window any more. A large piece of hardboard had been fixed on the outside of the window to make it appear as though it had been boarded up. Behind the board was a thick sheet of steel pock-riveted into the stone window frame. The rest of the room had been gutted. Four tables had been brought in, similar to decorators' pasting tables, and one person sat at each of the tables.

Ray moved and stood behind one of these people, a woman by the name of Carmel. He watched her counting.

The week's takings were looking very healthy indeed. Spread out on the four tables were four very large piles of cash. At each of the other tables was also a woman studiously separating the notes into respective denominations, piling them neatly and then counting them.

Ray Cragg glanced appreciatively at the stacks of cash, feeling a flush of excitement. A quarter of a million, he guessed. All in used notes. Not a bad week's work by any standards. A million a month. Twelve million a year, conservative. All his hard work over the past four years had been worth it. The violence, the intimidation, the planning, the homework and the killing where necessary. He now virtually controlled the supply of drugs from Merseyside to Cumbria, and from Manchester north to Blackpool.

Sure there were a few gaps in the map, but he intended to plug them in time and become the undisputed king of the north.

And drug dealing wasn't the whole picture. It was a vast part of his empire, but the running of illegal immigrants into the UK was becoming far more lucrative and far less dangerous.

He intended to have a couple more years with the drugs, but to keep building on the people-movement side of the business for another four years on top of that, then he would retire, maybe with thirty million stashed away. That was the figure, he estimated, that would see him out. He would take his mother to Florida and live a lazy lifestyle down on the Keys. Nothing too flashy – that wasn't his style – just live off the interest, want for nothing, and chill.

He had been planning this since the age of sixteen.

He checked his watch and frowned. It was getting late and not all the money had arrived.

Marty and Crazy were sitting reading magazines by the front door, keeping a check on the CCTV monitor fixed discreetly over the front and rear doors of the premises. The street outside was deserted.

'Haven't heard from Dix, yet,' Ray said. 'He's usually pretty good.'

'Maybe he's done a runner with the loot.' Marty chuckled, not lifting his head from his magazine.

Ray grabbed Marty's face and squeezed it hard. 'Not fuckin' funny,' he snarled.

Marty jerked his head out of Ray's fingers and glared at him.

'Hey, hey, hey,' cooed Crazy soothingly. It was apparent that both brothers were still up in the sky and agitated from the day's events. Even Ray, despite having got laid, was still buzzing and could not stay still. On the way over from Blackpool he had relived the shooting time and time again for Crazy's benefit. Crazy had listened calmly, wondering if he was the only one with a cool head, even though he was called Crazy. But he did realize that he was the only one of the three with no direct blood on his hands, so he could be chilled ... to a degree.

'He'll be here soon. Dix is a good lad,' Crazy said.

'Yeah, you're right. Sorry, Mart.'

'Whatever.' The younger man's eyes returned to the magazine, but inside he was seething. Apart from the congratulation after the shooting, Ray had said nothing more to his half sibling. It was as though Ray had done all the work, and yet hadn't he, Marty, also wasted one of the miscreants? Marty's teeth grated like sandpaper, but then he glanced up from his reading and became entranced by the sight of the wads of money being counted in the room. His breath shortened, his heart raced.

An hour later all the money was counted, stacked and wrapped in thin bricks of a thousand, each wad put into a plastic wallet. Ray's earlier estimate of a quarter of a million was about right. In fact there was just over that amount, all neatly piled up, ready to be packed into one large sports bag for the next stage of its journey. The women who had done the counting were paid off, warned to keep their mouths shut – a warning received every time they counted –

and sent on their way. The only people left in the place were Marty, Crazy and Ray.

And they were still short of the money that Dix should have collected and dropped off by now. Ray strutted angrily round the room. Marty and Crazy watched him nervously. He looked as though he was about to explode.

'Where is the fuck?' he demanded.

'Ray, c'mon, cool it,' said Crazy. 'Gimme your phone.' He waggled his fingers at Ray. 'Let me call him.'

'He shouldn't need bloody calling. He should be here NOW!' Ray jabbed his finger towards the floor. 'Here.'

'Phone,' Crazy said. 'Gimme.'

Ray wrenched it out of his back pocket and tossed it over to Crazy. 'Make sure you dial one four one first.'

'Yeah, yeah, I know.' It was the first rule of making a phone call when you were a crim. Make sure your number doesn't end up on anybody else's phone. 'He'll be here,' said Crazy confidently as he dialled. 'He's with Miller anyway, so there'll be a good reason for being late ... bet you.' He put the phone to his ear and listened to it connect.

Because Jane Roscoe had only been posted to Blackpool for a short time, she'd had little opportunity to get to know any of the town's high spots. When she had been transferred there several months earlier – unwittingly taking Henry Christie's position as DI – she had been immediately embroiled in the murder enquiry

109

which had resulted in her kidnap, then had subsequently decided to take a career break. On her return to work she had been very fortunate to get straight back as a DI at Blackpool, because no guarantees were ever made to officers returning from such breaks that they would get their old jobs back.

Henry, who had spent more years than he cared to remember trawling through the jungle that was Blackpool, knew all the best places, all the best people and he saw that evening as a bit of an educational opportunity for Roscoe.

He was also on the lookout for one of his best-kept secrets – an unregistered informant by the name of Troy Costain who might be able to tell him one or two things if the price was right, or pressure was exerted where it hurt.

With those things in mind, he dragged Jane on a whistle-stop tour of the less salubrious hostels in South Shore.

Obviously Jane knew a lot of detectives, many of whom bathed in the afterglow of their reputations, real or imaginary, but Henry Christie was different from anyone else she knew because he really did have a reputation which preceded him like a fanfare, but seemed unaffected by it. She knew that he'd had to kill a man, that he had battled, and won, against the Mafia, a KGB hit man, dishonest cops and child killers, yet none of it seemed to affect the way that he was as a person. He remained quiet, unassuming and, on the face of it, very ordinary. Those were some of the qualities which attracted her to him. He was the main reason she had returned to work so quickly. There was just something about him and she had fallen in love with that 'something'. She had thought about him constantly, and her desires often made her shudder at their implications.

Now here she was, investigating a murder with him – and loving every moment.

The first pub Henry took her to in South Shore was a huge double-fronted monstrosity, with a rock band pounding out some up to date guitar music. The place was heaving and Henry had to jostle his way through to the bar where he had to shout for two halves of lager.

After he had been served, he and Roscoe seated themselves at the back of the room where there was a little space, but no chance of talking. The band was deafeningly loud.

Henry seemed to be enjoying the music, but when Roscoe surreptitiously glanced at him, she saw he was actually scanning the bar area, inspecting every face, sometimes pausing as a thought struck him.

She looked round, too, and noticed several people eyeing Henry with a mixture of suspicion and hate. They were no doubt some of his previous customers, she thought. It was as plain as day he was well known in these circles, and though this was sometimes a disadvantage and a danger, Roscoe felt safe and comfortable next to him even though some of the characters looked like they would have been happy to smash their beer glasses and grind them into his face. Henry did not seem unduly perturbed by their attention.

'Seen anybody you know?' she asked him,

being forced to repeat the question an inch from his ear as the band cranked into the latest Oasis rocker.

'Only fifty per cent of them.' He laughed. 'This is one of the big low-life hang outs, but there's never really much trouble. A bit like a watering hole in the Masai Mara. Some are hunters, some are prey, but here there's a kind of truce between them.'

There was no doubt in Jane's mind as to which category Henry fell into.

'Here – hang on to this. Just need to pay a visit.' He pushed his glass into her free hand. Before she could say anything, Henry had ducked into the crowd and was heading towards the toilets.

He had seen someone he needed to talk to.

'Ten minutes.' Crazy hung up.

'What the hell has he been up to?' Ray demanded.

'Had a few probs.' Crazy shrugged. 'He'll tell you when he gets here.'

'Well I don't know about you, but I'm effin' starvin',' declared Marty with a stretch of his limbs. 'I need some sustenance and I'm gonna get some chips. Anybody else want any?' The other two shook their heads. 'Suit yourselves.' Marty stood up. 'How's about putting the kettle on anyway?' He peered at Crazy and raised his eyebrows, hoping to galvanize him into some movement. Crazy did not move. 'We're gonna be here till Dix lands and then we've got to count the cash ... yeah?'

Crazy sighed and dragged himself out of his seat. 'Okay – get me a fish, then.'

'Ray?' He looked at his half-brother. 'Sure you don't want owt?'

Ray shook his head.

'Buzz me out, then.'

Marty went to the front door and waited while Ray pressed the buzzer release, allowing Marty to step out into the night.

It was cold, a biting draught coming down from the steep hillside. Marty shivered and hunched down into his coat, digging his hands deep into his pockets as he moved away from the door and headed towards the town centre of Rawtenstall. He knew there was a fish and chip shop about five minutes away.

Suddenly he felt very nervous, yet undeniably elated.

The gents' toilets were at the back of the pub. Henry followed his man into them, about fifteen seconds later. When Henry pushed the door open, he was not surprised that the other man was nowhere to be seen and that the toilets appeared to be empty. Henry had long since ceased wearing leather-soled shoes. They creaked and announced arrival. He preferred man-made because they allowed him to sneak up on people.

There was a low murmur of voices about half-way down the toilets, coming from one of the cubicles. Henry smiled and his heart moved up a gear. He loved times like these.

The sound of voices remained indistinct, but grew slightly louder as Henry slid along from

113

cubicle to cubicle, holding his breath. He reached the occupied cubicle just as the door swung
open and a small man he did not recognize
stepped out, then froze at the sight of the detective soaring over him.

Henry smiled wickedly. In a hoarse whisper he
rasped, 'Police – scram!' The little man paused
uncertainly. Henry added, 'Before I change my
mind.'

The man needed no further prompting.

Henry swung into the cubicle, rammed his
hand against Troy Costain's chest and forced
him down on to the grey, cracked toilet, the seat
of which was not down, ensuring that Costain's
bottom hovered only inches above the surface of
the water and whatever happened to be floating
about in it.

Costain struggled, but he was no contest for
the six-foot-two Henry, who grabbed his denim
jacket and said, 'I'll push your arse all the way
down this bog if you don't stop.'

If was only then Costain actually realized who
his assailant was.

'Oh, shit,' he breathed, 'it's you. I thought I
was going to get hammered.'

'Yeah, it's me. I want to talk to you and if you
don't tell me what I want to know, you will get
hammered.'

'God, Henry – I can't talk here,' Costain pleaded. 'Please, not here.'

'Okay.' Henry stood back. 'Car park. Five
minutes. And if you're not there, I'll be round
knocking at the family home, letting the rest of
your criminal tribe know what a helpful little

114

soul you've been to me over the past ten years.'

'Henry,' Costain said seriously, 'you're a real twat.'

Henry patted Costain's cheek and gave him a winning smile. 'I know.'

Dix hated being late, but he also hated not doing his job properly and doing the job properly meant turning up with all the money that was owed to Ray Cragg, not just eighty per cent of it. He was fuming and not a little nervous as Miller, his driver, powered the car across the county.

Ray would be angry because of his tardiness, but he would have been even angrier if all the money wasn't there. At least Dix had good reason to be late – and maybe Ray would do something constructive about the reason now.

Miller cooled it as he drove into Rawtenstall, past the magistrates' court building on the left, then around the fire station roundabout, left into Bocholt Way past Asda, the river Irwell running parallel to the road on their right.

Miller wound his way through some terraced streets and stopped at the top of Balaclava Street to let Dix out to walk the last 100 metres. Ray did not like to see any cars coming down the cobbles. He preferred to see people approaching on foot.

'Give me fifteen minutes,' Dix said as he swung his legs out of the car.

'Sure. I'll go and juice up at Asda.'

He drove away and Dix, holdall in hand, trotted down towards the counting house.

Miller yawned and rubbed his eyes as he drove

115

away. It had been a long, tiring day and he was looking forward to getting back to Blackpool and hitting the sack with his girlfriend. Exhausted as he was, though, he still managed to glimpse the two cars parked at the end of a nearby street, containing two guys each.

They looked out of place. The hairs on Miller's neck crinkled as they rose.

It was a low-walled car park just off the busy main road. It was poorly lit and over the years there had been many crimes committed in it, ranging from car theft to rape, from mugging to manslaughter. The proximity of the pub, people passing by on foot and in vehicles, did not prevent the commission of offences.

Henry and Jane sat in Henry's car, engine idling, heater blowing.

'Now I don't want you to tell on me,' Henry said quietly, 'but this guy is an unregistered informant.'

'Tut tut.' She grinned.

'And last time I spoke to him was when you went AWOL.'

'Was he any use?'

'Naah,' drawled Henry, 'not much.' He failed to mention that during that particular encounter, his frustration had so boiled over that he had splattered Costain in a heap on the road leading up to Blackpool Zoo. The recollection did not make him smile.

From where they were parked they had a view of the side door of the pub, but not the front. If Costain chose to be uncooperative he could easily have legged it without Henry knowing, but Henry firmly believed his informant would decide to have a cosy chat instead.

Costain was one of several sons in a family of gypsies who had been settled for a couple of generations on the Shoreside estate in Blackpool. They terrorized the inhabitants and made their living mainly through intimidation and theft. Troy Costain had come to Henry's notice over ten years earlier when he had arrested him for theft. On his arrival at the police station, Troy's hard man image had cracked immediately and his fear of incarceration in a pokey cell was apparent when he begged Henry not to lock him up. He promised to tell Henry anything he wanted to know, which was music to a cop's ears. A good informant on Shoreside was like gold dust. Most folk on the estate kept their mouths shut and told the police nothing.

The side door opened. A blast of rock music shot out and the furtive figure of Troy Costain sneaked out.

'Here he is,' whispered Henry.

Costain stood on the steps and peered out at the dark car park. Henry flashed his headlights once. Costain started to zigzag his way around the other parked vehicles.

'It's Troy Costain,' Henry said to Jane before the informant reached them. The significance of the surname was not lost on her. Troy's brother had been the victim of the killer who had kidnapped her. She shifted with discomfort. 'But he won't know who you are,' Henry reassured her.

117

As Costain reached the car, Henry opened his window. 'In the back.'

Costain slid in, shaking his head. 'Fuck me, Henry, you don't half put me in some shite positions,' he moaned. 'One day someone'll find out about us and I'll be a dead man.' His voice was jittery. Only then did he notice Jane slumped low into the front passenger seat. 'Oh fuck!' he groaned. 'Who the shit is this?'

'No one you need worry about.' Henry adjusted his rear-view mirror so he could observe his man without having to twist around. Costain closed his eyes and slammed his head back on to the seat. 'The noose tightens,' he said, blowing out long and hard.

'So what were you doing in the bogs?' Henry enquired.

'I'm saying nowt.' Costain's lips went tight as piano wire.

Henry shrugged. 'Just want to know what I'm turning a blind eye to.'

'Just some nicked property. Nothing really.'

'You sure?'

Costain paused. 'Just put him on to a good shoplifter that's all.'

'Okay,' Henry said accepting this. 'Whatever.'

'So why the hassle?'

'I've hassled you, have I?' Henry said, affronted. 'Just run that one by me, Troy?'

'You know what I mean. Turnin' up at my waterin' hole and puttin' me in a ... a situation which I've got to explain to some very nasty people.'

'You'll think of something,' Henry said with

118

certainty. 'Go on, have a guess why I'm here.'

'Doh – let me think about that one.' Costain put a finger to his lips in a dumb gesture.

'You don't have to be the Brain of Britain to get it right, Troy.' The car was beginning to steam up. Henry flicked the fan heater up a notch and readjusted the rear-view mirror for a better view of his informant.

'Yeah, right ... Rufus and his two cronies blasted to smithereens not too far down the road.'

'Correct. One point.'

'How much is this gonna be worth?' Troy asked. 'Because I'll tell you now, whoever grasses on whoever pulled those triggers is gonna need some dosh to lie low, get out of the country or whatever. It's not gonna be cheap information, Henry.'

'I take it you already know something, then?'

'Not saying that.' Costain became cagey. 'But if I did' – he opened his palms – 'it would be expensive. Big drugs people involved there, I'd say.'

'No!' exclaimed Henry. 'I would never have guessed.' He paused, then for the first time turned in his seat and looked squarely at Costain, who shrank a little deeper into the upholstery. 'I'll make it worth your while, but you'd better get something quick. Slow won't do.'

'I'll see.'

'Good man. Hey, just an afterthought, you knew Johnny Jacques, didn't you?'

The words penetrated Costain's cranium quite slowly. He said, 'What d'you mean, knew?'

119

'I take it from that reaction he used to be a bit of a buddy of yours?'

'Bit of a buddy? Bloody good mate ... what's all this "knew him" and "used to be" crap?'

'You haven't heard? He's been taking flying lessons, only his wings didn't flap fast enough. Splat!' Henry clapped his hands once to reinforce the last word.

'Jesus! Dead?'

'Dead as a pancake, I think the expression goes. So who would want to hoik him out of a window?'

'His bird? He was always messing her around.'

'She got burned to death in her flat, Troy, the same flat JJ took a leap from.'

Costain reached for the door handle. 'I'll be back to you soon.'

'You know my mobile number,' Henry called out to Costain's retreating back.

'It's Dix,' Crazy said watching the CCTV monitor. He pressed the door release button and Dix went out of sight as he stepped into the counting house, reappearing a couple of seconds later in the living room, sports bag in hand, humble in his body language.

'Sorry about the lateness,' he apologized. He gave the bag to Crazy who immediately unzipped it and tipped the contents out on to a table top.

'You'd better explain. We should be out of here by now,' said Ray.

'It's that idiot, Zog. He's just one lazy twat. Doesn't want to hand any money over, can't be

120

arsed to collect it in the first place. I had to shove the shotgun up his shitter and go round all his people to collect his debts. Took time, Ray, but at least it's all there.' Dix nodded at the pile of cash. 'Eleven grand.'

Ray sighed. Zog had been getting to be a nuisance. The only problem was that his string of contacts was second to none and his infrastructure of drug selling in Fleetwood was excellent. He was just very lazy, reluctant to pay up and a user himself. 'We'll have to see about him,' Ray said. 'Later.'

'Yep – it's all here,' Crazy said, leaning back from the task of counting the money. It had been easy to do because Dix always presented it in neat bundles anyway. Crazy picked up one of the bundles and tossed it to Dix, who caught it expertly. His week's pay.

'Cheers.'

'Okay, Dix, you can get going and we'll see you in a week's time,' said Ray. 'Meanwhile I'll have a think about Zog.'

'Sure.' Dix checked his watch. Miller should have filled up by now, should be pulling up at the top of the street to take Dix back to the coast. 'See you guys.' He folded his money and tucked it into his jeans' pocket, collected his now-empty sports bag and turned to the door. 'Give me a buzz out,' he told Crazy.

Crazy watched him walk out of the room into the short hallway. He glanced at the CCTV monitor, saw nothing untoward on the street and pressed the electronic door release. At the same time the screen went blank. Puzzled, but still with his finger on the door release button, Crazy smacked the side of the monitor in the hope that this tried and tested method of repair would work. It had no effect.

'Strange,' he said.

'What is?' said Ray, who had been transferring the recently counted cash into the big holdall. Crazy directed Ray's eyes to the blank screen. Then both men looked up as Dix walked back into the room. His face was a veil of fear, his eyes terrified and pleading because there was a massive revolver skewered into the back of his neck, held there by a large man wearing a stocking mask pulled down over his face, distorting his features. Three other men, similarly attired and armed, crowded in behind him.

'There was nothing I could do, Ray,' Dix wailed plaintively.

The man pushed Dix hard away from him, making him stumble towards Ray. The three other men fanned out into the room, brandishing their guns with cool menace.

The one who had herded Dix into the room pointed his gun at Ray. 'Hard or easy,' his voice rasped behind the stocking. 'That's always the choice. Just hand the money over, nice 'n' easy and there'll be no problem at all.'

Miller had been in the business long enough to know when something wasn't quite right and the dark shapes huddled in the parked cars only a matter of yards away from the counting house put his senses on a high. He drove past as though he had not seen them and pulled in a few streets away where he sat and inhaled deep breaths.

Then he leaned over to the passenger side where Dix had been sitting and reached into the footwell. His fingers curled round the barrel of the pump-action sawn-off shotgun Dix always took with him on collection days. Miller knew the weapon was fully loaded and ready to fire.

There was a very uneasy silence between request and response. Both parties weighed up each other's strengths and weaknesses. There was no contest here. Ray and Crazy, even if Dix was included in the reckoning, were outnumbered, outgunned and outmanoeuvred and they knew it.

'Looks like it's all yours,' Ray said, admitting defeat.

The biggest of the four intruders, the one who had done the talking so far, said, 'Good speech. You' – he pointed to Dix – 'pick up the bag nice and careful.'

Dix shot Ray an anxious glance.

'Do it,' Ray confirmed the instruction. He was standing still, his nostrils flaring, assessing the situation continually, looking for an advantage.

With a tremulous hand, Dix reached for the holdall containing the week's takings. His fingers closed around the handle loops.

Ray said, 'You don't really think you're going to walk out of here with my money, do you?' His voice was soft.

'Yes we do.' Their spokesman raised his weapon, a Star Model 30M, 9mm, originating from Spain. He pointed it at Ray's chest. 'Oh aye, we do.'

Miller came down the street, his back tight to the building line, staying deep in shadow, the sawn-off held diagonally across his chest, ready for instantaneous use.

He was a former soldier. Nothing special, just an infantryman, but he had done time in a few of the world's hot spots in his younger days. This situation reminded him of Northern Ireland, a semi-derelict Belfast street of the 1970s. He had been up and down numerous of them and even now he expected a sniper to have him in his sights.

He was at the door of the counting house only seconds after he had watched the four masked men force Dix back inside ahead of them at gunpoint. With his back to the wall by the front door he reached out and pushed with his left hand, hoping the door would be open. It was.

The masked man held his gun steady, pointing unwaveringly at Ray Cragg's upper body. Very briefly, Ray thought about the impact of the slug into his small frame: it would shatter him. Then he dismissed the thought because it wasn't going to happen. No one was going to shoot him because he was invincible. This was merely a battle and he would live to fight another day and annihilate the people who dared to be so brazen as to steal from him.

He glanced at Crazy, still seated by the dead TV monitor. He had not moved, just sat there quietly, taking everything in. One hell of a cool bastard, Ray thought. Didn't even look worried.

And where was Marty? Typical of him to choose the wrong moment to go for chips.

Next he looked at Dix, his hand grasping the handles of the holdall with close to £270,000 in it, all counted, all sorted.

Ray's mind flashed: was Dix up to some scam or other?

No. The expression on his trusted gofer's face told its own story.

'It's okay, Dix, pick up the bag. Do as they say,' Ray told him.

Ray turned back to the masked man who seemed to be the leader. 'Take the money and fuck off,' he said, 'but don't think for one second I won't find out who you are.'

The man laughed behind his mask. 'Don't count on it.' He gestured for Dix to come. All four men, plus Dix, began to reverse out of the room, into the hallway, leading to the front door.

The first of the men backing into the hall turned towards the front door and stopped dead. The last word to leave his mouth was, 'Shit!'

Miller stood there on the threshold of the front door like an avenging devil. His face was hard but deadpan, almost lacking expression. The shotgun was held with the sawn-off butt to his groin, ready to fire.

The one thing Miller's military training had taught him was that to hesitate is to die. Miller did not feel like dying on that particular night.

The shotgun came up, fast. He pulled the trigger and the man staggered backwards into one of his colleagues. The shot had whacked him right in the middle of his chest, causing his sternum to disintegrate with massive damage to his heart and lungs. His arms flailed and his gun flew out of his hand. He died before he hit the floor.

One down, three to go.

Miller twisted out of the door, standing with his back pressed tight to the wall, and racked the shotgun. The action was smooth and well-oiled. The spent cartridge ejected and a new one slid easily into the breech to replace it and those few seconds were as long as Miller was prepared to give them. He spun back into the doorway faster than ever and saw the three remaining men in disarray, shocked at having been ambushed so spectacularly, stunned and unready for Miller's next onslaught.

He came round at a crouch, as low as a shadow.

The shotgun roared again and he gritted his teeth as his body jerked against the kickback.

Another masked man went down with a scream, this time hit in the belly and the groin area. He continued to scream horribly.

The remaining two men dragged their unwilling hostage, Dix, into the kitchen, slamming the door behind them just as Miller reloaded and loosed his third, and penultimate, shot into the closing door.

He racked the final shell into the breech and flung himself against the wall as a bullet was fired back through the kitchen door, down the hall, whizzing dangerously close to his head. Another bullet splintered through the door, then another.

Miller dived low through the living-room door and came up into a crouch, breathing heavy.

Ray and Crazy stood stock still for a frozen moment, then seemed to come to life.

'Well done,' Ray said. 'Let's get these fuckers, Crazy.'

Crazy jumped out of his seat, crawling underneath the table on which the TV monitor was positioned, tearing away at the tape which held three guns to the underside. He tossed a revolver to Ray, kept one for himself.

The remaining two men were not about to wait. Things had gone wrong and they knew time was against them, that the odds had changed. They bundled Dix out through the kitchen door into the backyard, then out into the alley where they did a right turn towards the Irwell, pushing, prodding, forcing Dix ahead of them.

One was definitely dead. The other would probably die sooner rather than later. Ray yanked the stockings off their heads, firstly to see if he recognized them – he didn't – and secondly to ask the living one some quick questions. It was obvious that the pain he was in made him impervious to any quizzing. After a few yelled questions, Ray dropped the man's head hard on the floor and left him to die.

Miller picked up a discarded gun – another Star revolver – and tucked it into his waistband, then took up position at one side of the kitchen door with Crazy at the opposite side. Ray Cragg hung back.

Miller counted to three, then twisted to face the door. Crazy reached across, pulled down the handle, then stood back as Miller booted the door open. It flew back on its hinges revealing the empty kitchen.

'You don't need me, let me go,' Dix pleaded. 'Here's the money, just take it and run.'

'Shut it,' the lead masked man snapped, and pushed his gun into the small of Dix's back, urging him forwards.

They had run across a grassed area and over a low fence taking them to the steep river bank. They had been hoping to loop back to where they had left their cars, but in their panic to escape, they had become disorientated. At the point where they reached the Irwell it was perhaps only twenty feet wide. Normally it was quite shallow and easily crossable. But the river was running heavily following torrential rain on the moors high above. On the opposite bank was a road and more terraced housing.

'Down there – and keep hold of the bag,' the man ordered Dix. 'We go across the water.'

Dix peered down the almost perpendicular bank. The rise and fall of his throat made the sound like that of the mouse in the *Tom and Jerry* cartoons. 'It looks a bit dangerous to me,' he said.

'It's either that or a bullet in your spine.'

Ah, certain death either way, Dix thought. 'I'll go for drowning, then,' he said. He took a firmer grip on the holdall and dug his heels into the bank as he stumbled, tripped and fell towards the water, accompanied by his two captors.

One shot a glance back. 'They're coming,' he said, spotting the low approach of Ray, Miller and Crazy. 'Move it,' he urged.

Dix stepped gingerly into the fast-running water. Its bitter coldness immediately took his breath away. He gasped.

'Get across.' He felt a jab in the back from the gun muzzle.

Dix stepped further in, expecting it to be fairly shallow. Instead, his right leg went in as far as the knee and he had to fight to keep balanced.

'This is friggin' dangerous,' he shouted.

'Just get across and keep hold of the money.'

Only just keeping on his two feet, Dix heaved the cash-laden holdall on to his back, putting his arms through the handles and wearing it as though it was a haversack.

He put another foot into the water, feeling for a steady place to put it down. The water was freezing cold, so cold it burnt his legs. He wobbled unsteadily.

'Go, you fucker,' one of the men shouted and pushed him hard.

'Right, I'm going,' he said, stepped into the current and lost his balance completely. It was as though the river was practising its judo throws as it swept his legs away from under him. He toppled over, caught his right ankle between some rocks on the river bed and fell sideways.

He had expected to be able to stand up again, but the strength and depth of the water were too much for him. Before he could surface properly, he was sucked under and dragged downstream.

Now he was sure he was going to drown.

Henry and Jane spent a further couple of hours in the hostelries of South Shore, but Henry could not weed out any more of his informants, registered or otherwise. Obviously word had got round he was out on the prowl. Just after 11.30 he suggested that they drive back to central so he could drop her off at her car. She agreed and they headed back north up the promenade in companionable silence. He drove to the police station and she directed him to her car, a neat little Toyota.

With her fingers looped around the door handle, she hesitated. 'It's been nice to see you again, Henry. I'm glad we're working together.'

'Me too.'

'You'd better be getting home to the missus.' Jane smiled painfully. 'She'll be wondering where you are.'

'Not tonight. I'm going to crash out at the flat so I'm nearer to the action. She's not expecting me home.'

'Oh. Anyway, good night, Henry, see you in the morning.'

'Yeah. Bye.'

He waited until she was in her car before driving away with a quick salute. He drew up outside the flat a few minutes later and called Kate on the mobile. She was in bed, sleepy, and the conversation was short. When it was over, he sat at the wheel of his car, mulling things over and sighing occasionally.

He nearly jumped out of his skin when

someone tapped on the window.

'Jane,' he said, surprised, or maybe not so surprised, as he wound down the window.

She leaned in and, without a word, kissed him full on the lips. Their mouths seemed to be a perfect fit. She was wonderful to kiss and Henry wanted it to go on for ever. She bit his bottom lip, then slowly drew away, her hand on his face, her eyes fixed on his.

'Take me to the flat,' she said quietly. 'You can do anything you want to me, so long as you wear something.'

Henry was stunned. 'Okay ... I'll keep my socks on,' he said with a squeak. They both burst into a fit of giggles which lasted all the way up the back stairs to the flat.

Six

'And you' – Ray pointed with a forefinger, which, if it had been a dagger, would have shot through the air like a missile – 'you come waltzing back carrying fish and chips as though nothing had happened. Ffff...!' he hissed and shook his head irately at his half-brother, who hung his head in shame. 'Fish and chips! You'd gone for fish and chips and four armed men come in and rob me of a week's takings. So there's two stiffs that need taking care of, two bastards who got away and my money washed down the bleedin' river.'

'It's not my fault,' Marty bleated plaintively.

'No, maybe not, but somehow it feels like it.'

'Yeah, well, it always does, doesn't it? I can't do anything right – except shoot somebody for you, y'know? Murder somebody, something you seem to forget so very bloody easily, Brother.'

'Yeah, yeah, right. I need to think.'

They had left the counting house and were parked in a picnic area on the Grane Road, the winding A-class road which snakes across the moors from Haslingden to Blackburn. It was pitch black and very cold. Sleet had started to slant across the sky.

Ray got out of the car and paced round the car park before climbing into Miller's motor. The heater was turned well up.

'You did well, Miller,' Ray admitted.

'Still got away, though, didn't they?'

'Only two of the four of them, though, and' – Ray laughed frostily – 'they didn't get the money, did they? That's somewhere down the river attached to a probably very drowned Dix. Little hope of getting that back.'

'You never know.' Miller shrugged. 'He might've got out alive. But, just a bit more pressing, what're we going to do about the two bodies?'

'Good question. Dispose of them – we'll sort it. And in the meantime I want you and Crazy to do some asking around. I want to find the people behind the people who dared to rob me. I reckon it's too big a job for four knuckleheads to take on

132

alone. They must have a backer.'

'You don't recognize the two dead 'uns?' Miller asked.

'Nope. I'll bet they're from Manchester or further south.' He thought for a while. 'I wonder ... maybe the Midlands would be a good starting point. I want you two to do the digging for me. I'll pay, and pay good.'

'Okay, I'm game,' Miller said.

'Me too,' Crazy concurred.

'You and Crazy'd be a good team, I reckon, having just seen you in action. I'm annoyed I didn't see it before...' Ray paused for a few more moments of thought, then pulled his mobile out and looked at his two men. 'Those two bodies – had a thought – we might not know who they are, but the cops would find out for us, wouldn't they? If we make sure they get dumped somewhere a bit public, we could wait for the cops to ID them. That'd give you something to work on, wouldn't it? You know, I'm full of good ideas.'

Henry stopped what he was doing and gazed down into Jane's face beneath him.

'Oh God, that feels good,' Roscoe breathed, her jaw line rotating.

'Feels wonderful.'

'Oh God.' – She said 'Oh God' quite a lot during lovemaking, Henry observed. 'We fit together very well.' She smiled with a depraved curl of the lips and dug her nails into his flesh just hard enough to send something very sensational through him.

'Oh God!' he uttered, falling into her trap, 'not

133

long now ... oh ... ohh.'

'Yes,' she said and bit his neck. 'Come on. It feels fantastic.'

Henry lost it then. All semblance of technique and coolness went right out the window as his primitive urge took over. Underneath him, Jane responded with a wild passion she had never known before as the feeling inside her exploded with an unbelievable relaxing warmth.

They lay quiet for a long time, breathing heavily, their hearts pounding.

Eventually he propped himself up on his arms, kissed her neck, ran his tongue across her breasts, then rolled off, but still held on to her, hugging her close so he could feel her body from top to toe.

'That felt so right,' she said quietly and bit his earlobe.

'It did.'

'I'm glad you decided to take your socks off.' She grinned, tickling his feet with her toes. 'It wouldn't quite have had the same magic.'

'No, true.'

'I've never been unfaithful,' Roscoe admitted.

Henry said nothing.

'It was wonderful,' she said.

'Yes, it was,' he agreed and kissed her slowly on the lips, not wanting to admit how many times he had been unfaithful to his wife in his life. Too many.

Harry Dixon had been convinced he was going to drown. The irony of it was that it would be in a river less than twenty feet wide and three feet

134

deep and he had a bag with him containing a small fortune. Yet the surging flow was so powerful, it constantly knocked his legs from under him so he could not stand up and wade to the bank. Every time he thought he was getting somewhere, he was toppled over again and sent spinning downriver like a twig. The weight of the bag strapped to his back did not help matters, but something would not let him let go of it.

Eventually he found he could no longer fight the current. The sheer cold, the power of the water, sapped all his energy. He decided that the icy river could have him.

'Suppose I'd better go,' Roscoe declared sleepily. She sat up and stretched. It was 1 a.m. and the bedroom was still nippy even though Henry had turned the central heating on as soon as they had come in.

Henry looked at her body and thought it was wonderful. He rolled on to his side and laid his hand on her tummy between her belly button and pubic hair. She juddered at his touch.

'Think you can make love to me again?' she asked.

Henry glanced down. When he saw his penis as erect as it had ever been, he thought he was nineteen years old again.

'It'd be rude not to,' he said, and put his mouth around one of her hard, dark, purple nipples.

The River Irwell begins life as a trickle in the wind-ravaged moors high above Bacup in east Lancashire. It flows through the Rossendale

Valley, never more than a few feet wide or deep, then meanders through some picturesque landscapes and villages as it makes its way to Greater Manchester. Sometimes it widens out, but never by very much.

The rushing waters, forced through the narrow gorge, washed Dix about a mile downstream, often crashing him against mid-stream boulders and various other bits of debris, like broken prams and bedsteads, until, near the area known as New Hall Hey, it slowed dramatically before pouring down a weir.

Dix could not believe he was still alive: he had swallowed what seemed like gallons of foul-tasting, ice-cold water, and retched much of it back; he had been bashed to hell. Suddenly the strength of the river weakened and he found himself close to the bank, near overhanging trees.

Exhausted though he was, his innate survival instinct was reborn. He paddled desperately to the side, feeling weaker with each movement. He caught and hung grimly on to a branch and started to tremble.

He saw a footbridge fifty metres ahead and the lights of houses and street lamps.

Still holding the branch for support, he dragged himself to his feet and lurched up the bank, out of the water, slipping and sliding in the mud and grass. He forced his way through bushes which tore at his skin and clothing, but he was so chilled he did not feel the snags and cuts. He tumbled over a low fence on to a narrow, muddy path, which he followed towards the lights. It brought him out by the bridge and into New Hall Hey. It was quiet. Nothing moved.

Sodden and shaking, he made his way to a telephone box.

'Have to let 'em know I'm okay,' he wheezed desperately.

Once inside the phone box, he began to dial a number which would eventually connect him to Ray Cragg.

He was on the last digit of the dial when he stopped to think.

His exact thoughts were: I've got a quarter of a million pounds strapped to my back ... There's a very good chance people now think I'm dead, drowned ... Now there's a thing. He hung up the phone with a dithering hand. Whatever, he thought, I need to get dry otherwise I will die ... of pneumonia.

He pushed himself out of the phone box and looked up and down the street. He needed to get inside somewhere warm, fast, before hypothermia set in.

Jane and Henry separated, bathed in sweat, shattered, breathing heavily. They lay staring at the ceiling, legs and arms splayed out across each other.

'You know, I really wanted to hate you when I met you ... but as soon as I saw you, I knew deep down that you'd change my life.'

Henry said nothing. A slight feeling of trepidation in his guts.

'I've been in love with you from the first,' Jane

whispered.

Still he said nothing, but his mind was racing. He thought, She's married, I'm trying to get my life together – oh God!

Her mobile phone rang. With a rumble of annoyance, she fumbled for it among her discarded clothing and studied the display.

'Hubby,' she said thinly and pressed a button.

Henry lay back, hands clasped behind his head while she talked to her obviously irate spouse, who was wondering where the hell she was. She kept her composure, raising her eyes at Henry as she talked him down from the heights and assured him she would be home soon. Things had got very hectic and it looked like being a long, involved investigation, this last bit being news her husband did not take well.

'Yes, a long one. Comes with the territory ... Right, fine! I'll be home soon but I've got to be back at work by half seven, so I'm going straight to bed ... What? Well if that's your attitude, I will.' She pressed the 'end-call' button, scowled at the mobile as though it was its fault and tossed it back on her clothing, shaking her head. 'He said I might as well find a hotel cos it's not worth me going home – so I'll do just that,' she said haughtily, tossing her fine mane of hair back, 'I'll stay here if you'll let me.'

Henry had been secretly hoping she would go, but he said, 'Sure, no problem, but we'd better get some sleep. It'll be a long day tomorrow.'

It was an end-terraced cottage, up for sale and unoccupied by the looks of it. Dix was shivering

138

badly, unstoppably. He needed to get out of his clothes and get warmed up. The cottage was an ideal place.

The street was deserted. Dix went round the back, expecting to find that each cottage in the row would have a separate walled yard which would have provided him with some sort of cover from snooping neighbours. Instead, all the yard walls had been demolished long ago and each house now had a lawned back garden, divided by low stone walls.

Dix cursed, but then had some luck. There was a clothes-line next door with jeans, T-shirts, socks and underpants strung across it. They appeared to be about his size. He unhooked the holdall from his shoulders and deposited it by the back door of the empty house and stepped slowly across the garden walls until he reached the line, then helped himself. They felt cold and damp, but at least they were not drenched like his own clothes.

He was inside the empty cottage within moments. Having been a prolific housebreaker in his younger days, burglary was a skill that had never left him.

The house was completely empty, but had the ambience of having been recently habited. It was warm and cosy and even warmer and cosier when he lit the gas fire in the living room and turned it up full. The curtains had been left open, so he drew them and stripped off, then stood in front of the fire, turning himself round as though he was a pig on a barbecue. The heat permeated his body very slowly.

Ten minutes thawed him out. Fifteen minutes and he was glowing.

He dressed in the stolen clothes, which fitted nicely, and stayed by the fire, taking the damp and chill out of them, trying to dry his zip-up jacket. The worst things were his feet and his sodden trainers. He sat on his backside and toasted his soles on the gas fire, wriggling his toes like mad, trying to get full circulation back.

Half an hour found him in the right frame of mind to unzip the holdall and inspect the cash. Drawing back the zip he wondered if the water had done much damage to the contents.

He almost did a jig when he saw that each block of one thousand pounds was in its own plastic wallet. The money was safe and sound. He'd had visions of having to dry it out, plastering it all over radiators and heaters. Now no such problem existed.

His only remaining problem was what to do with the cash.

Dressed in overalls and wellingtons, Ray, Crazy, Marty and Miller dragged the two bodies out of the house, leaving a slippery trail of blood behind each, and heaved them into the back of a van. They drove up on to the high moorland between Rawtenstall and Rochdale where they threw the dead men into a flooded quarry known as the Blue Lagoon – as were so many across the country. This particular one had been the disposal place for a number of bodies in the past. Ray Cragg knew it would not be long before the men were found and subsequently identified by

140

the police.

They returned to the counting house where they began a clean-up operation with mops, buckets, bleach and detergents. About an hour later they had finished their ghastly task and dispatched Marty to the Irwell to fling the equipment they had used into the river. He threw the blood-soaked items into the fast flow and watched them disappear into the night, just like that idiot Dix had done with the money – got washed away.

Marty was feeling very depressed. He sat down on a stone and pulled out his mobile phone, dialling a well-remembered number.

It rang for a while before being answered by a sleepy voice.

'It's me,' he said. 'We're back to square one ... not good, not good,' he whined. He watched the river in front of him. 'We're right up shit creek now,' he observed, looking at the murky water of the Irwell.

Henry slept fitfully, unused to having a stranger in bed with him who, when she fell asleep did not move at all. He, on the other hand, could not get comfortable, finding himself right on the edge of the bed, half-in, half-out of the covers, half-hot, half-cold.

He nodded off about 4 a.m., then sprang back to life when his mobile phone rang on the bedside cabinet. Next to him, Jane did not stir.

The display said 'Anonymous Caller'.

'Yeah,' Henry said groggily.

'It's me,' said a voice.

Henry rubbed his eyes. 'You'll have to do better than that.'

'Troy.'

'And why are you phoning at this time?'

'Got some gen, need to see you, can't tell you on the phone.'

'Where and when?' said Henry, abruptly fully awake. 'And how much?'

'Somewhere there's no bloody CCTV cameras for a start – how about the White Café in St Anne's? Say twenty minutes? I'll talk dosh when I see you ... but it won't be cheap.'

Henry swung his legs out of bed and started to dress in the dark, not wishing to disturb Jane. As he crawled around the edge of the bed on his hands and knees, searching by touch for his underpants and socks, he heard her move and groan. He looked up and saw her face peering over the bedside. She was smirking.

'Doing a runner?' she asked.

He laughed as his hand found the item of clothing he needed. He stood up and pulled on his white Marks & Spencer Y-fronts. 'Just got a call from Costain. Says he's got some info, but wants to see me now.'

'Can I come?'

'No.'

Dawn was still a long way away as Henry drove on to the car park adjacent to the White Café on the beach in St Anne's. Jane huddled down in her coat in the passenger seat next to him, shivering, even though the heater was blowing hot.

Henry had wanted to speak to Troy Costain

142

alone, but Jane had insisted on accompanying him. It was her case and she had a right to keep her finger on the pulse, she argued as she dressed herself. Henry was too weary and shell-shocked by his recent sexual encounter to put up much of a fight. She was ready before he was.

He drove to the far side of the car park and stopped near the lifeboat station, doused the lights and sat there with the engine ticking over. He reclined his seat, closed his eyes and waited. Jane did the same, letting her right hand rest on his thigh, her little finger slotted into a fold in his trousers just by his groin. She squeezed his leg and despite himself, Henry began to harden.

A tap on the window by his ear made him jerk. Costain's face pressed up to the glass almost made him scream. He opened the window.

'What's she doing here?' Costain demanded.

'Same as before – it's her case.'

'I talk to you, no one else, Henry, that's the deal.'

Henry gave Jane a look. She got the message. 'I'll go for a walk,' she said and got out of the car. Costain walked round and dropped into her warmed-up seat. In silence, the two men watched her amble away.

'You tommin' her?' Costain grinned.

'Nope,' said Henry shortly.

'She's worth one ... a bit motherly, maybe, could do wi' losin' a bit o' weight, but nice tits 'n' arse.' Costain's face curled up lustfully.

'What've you got for me, Troy? I hope it's good because I hate getting up for nothing. Know what I mean?'

'I've been working me socks off for you over the last few hours and all you do is whinge about being woken up – great!'

'Just get on with it,' Henry snapped, aware of Jane tramping around the car park, getting cold.

'Okay, okay, but it'll cost – a lot.'

'I'll decide how much it's worth. I've always paid well for good value.'

Troy Costain took a deep breath, tipped his head back against the headrest and gazed at the car roof. 'Johnny Jacques was a good mate of mine. We go back a long time. He used to be clean, well, sort of, but then he got into crack and it screwed his head.'

'My heart bleeds.'

Costain turned sharply on Henry. 'Look, you twat, he was a mate, okay? Maybe not like your middle-class friends, but he was still a mate and he meant a lot to me.' Chastened a little, but not much, Henry shrugged. 'You might think we're pond life, you stuck up git, but we do have mates and feelings – I don't think I want to talk to you now.' Costain's hand went to the door handle.

'Sorry,' said Henry. 'Come on, tell me what you've got.' His voice had become soft and encouraging. 'I'm just tired.'

'Yeah, well,' murmured Costain. 'JJ kept his head above water, financially, that is, by doing a bit of dealing here and there. Not much, just pocket money. But his living wage came from being a delivery boy. He ran errands. Dropped things off, picked things up for people.'

'Like a white-van man?'

'Summat like that.'

144

'What sort of things did he pick up and drop off, as you so eloquently phrase it?'

'You name it – mainly drugs, sometimes guns, often money.' Costain twisted his lips. 'Thing is, I know JJ had a bit of a bad habit. Sometimes he helped himself to his packages.'

'Ooh, bad boy ... what did he help himself to?'

'Some junk, and he used to peel off the occasional tenner here and there. Not much, not regularly, but it must've built up over time, maybe into hundreds.'

'So you're saying he skimmed from the people he worked for?'

'That pretty much sums it up. I saw him about a week ago and he was getting worried about it, said he was going to stop doing it – as if,' Costain said sardonically.

'Who did he run for?'

'I haven't finished my story yet. Saving that to last.'

Their faces turned to the front of the car. Jane had done a couple of circuits of the car park and was now standing at the radiator of the car with her palms out. She said, 'Will you please fucking hurry up. I'm freezing my balls off out here.'

Dix was warm and dry. He was almost back to normal apart from having just counted out £267,000 in hard cash. He unwrapped two of the plastic wallets and stuffed two grand into his pockets, which would be his operating money. The rest he carefully stashed back into the hold-all which he had dried in front of the gas fire.

145

Two hundred and sixty-five thousand pounds left.

Nice.

All he had to do now was get away with it. Make some plans. Change the money. Get out of the country. Never come back. Let people think he was dead.

He left the house as secure as he had found it and turned out on to the early morning streets of New Hall Hey where a cold, snow-threatening wind was starting to blow. He chose an easy car to steal, an old F-registered Ford Escort. He was into it within seconds, had hot-wired it seconds later. It started first time and he was away. He had no intention of keeping the car for long. He just wanted to be somewhere that was populated, where he was not well known and where he could choose a form of transport to get him away.

Jane wrenched open the back door of Henry's Vectra and got in.

'I tell you what,' she said. 'You two go walkies and I'll stay here.'

Costain glared furiously at Henry.

'She's all right,' Henry said. 'Honestly. Trust her.'

Unenthusiastically, Costain nodded.

'So who did he run for?' Henry probed again.

'Not finished. The shooting yesterday?'

'That has something to do with JJ?'

'It was a drugs thing.'

'We've already sussed that.'

'The dead guys were muscling into some

hallowed territory.'

'Whose?'

'Listen, Henry, these guys are very bad people and I'd better be able to trust you two because when I say this name, I'll get a bullet in my brain if they ever find out.'

Just at that moment it clicked and suddenly Henry knew who Costain was going to finger.

'I don't know who pulled the triggers, I don't know if they are responsible for JJ's death, but I do know that JJ thought they were on to him for his skimming.'

'Say the name,' Henry urged. 'Say the name and we'll do the rest. You don't have to worry. No one'll ever know you talked to us and I will make it worth your while.'

Costain took a deep, frightened gulp, then blurted out the names, 'Ray and Marty Cragg.'

The exact same names Henry was thinking of.

By 5 a.m. Ray, Marty, Crazy and Miller were back on the coast at a flat in South Shore, one of several Ray owned in the resort. It was nothing more than a bedsit, but was well equipped with everything needed to lie low for a few days: food in the fridge and freezer, tins of food, cooker, microwave, toaster, kettle, satellite TV and video, a settee and a half-decent bed with clean sheets. He had flats like this all over the resort and in other places around the county. He ensured they were always well maintained and serviced because you never knew when you would have to go to ground.

However, that morning, Ray had no intention

of lying low.

He had taken enough trouble to cover his tracks all day long and believed himself to be safe. All he wanted to do was get home and climb into bed and sleep. He gave the others keys to similar flats should they want to use them. But whatever they chose, he wanted them back in action by noon. Particularly Crazy and Miller. He wanted them to start hunting down the people who had tried to rob him and had survived the shooting.

The last thing he did before going home that morning was to telephone Lancashire police and tip them off about two bodies which could be found in a flooded quarry in Greater Manchester. He knew the message would be passed on immediately. He needed to know the names of the two dead men and the sooner the cops were on the case, the sooner he would find out.

They went their separate ways. Miller drove himself home while Crazy dropped Ray off at his home and then Marty at his own flat. Marty gave him a wave and watched him drive away. When he was sure he had gone, he called a number on his mobile. A groggy voice answered.

'Can I come round?' he asked.

'Now?'

'Yes – now.'

'Will it be safe?'

'Yeah, he's gone to bed and I need to see you.'

'Come round then.'

'Be there soon.'

* * *

Henry handed over the contents of his wallet to Troy Costain. Fifty pounds was all he had, but he promised him more soon. Costain took the money grudgingly and got out of the car. He disappeared over the sand dunes into the dull grey morning. Roscoe climbed across from the back seat and plonked herself down.

'Use of unregistered informants is against Home Office guidelines,' she said disapprovingly. She was feeling mean and crusty. Henry looked at her stonily.

'I wouldn't register him if he was the last informant on earth,' he said. 'When I was on CID here and then on RCS as it was, he gave me more run of the mill prisoners on Shoreside than anyone else. It would ruin him if he was registered and if you blab on me I'll never ever speak to you again.' He stuck his tongue out.

She leaned over and kissed him. 'Your secret's safe with me.'

Marty left his car on the outskirts of the small estate and walked the last quarter of a mile or so to the house, skulking round to the back door so he would not be kept waiting at the front door in open view.

A woman opened the door. She was wearing a short dressing gown, exposing her long, tapering legs.

'Come on in.' He stepped into the kitchen and they fell into each other's arms, kissing greedily. Her gown fell open, revealing a lithe, tanned body. She pulled his shirt out of his trousers and expertly flicked open the buttons, her hands

149

going to Marty's hairless chest, pinching his nipples hard. A moment later her hands were at his belt buckle, unfastening it, zipping his jeans open. She eased the jeans and underpants over his backside and erect penis, then slid to her knees in front of him. She looked up dirtily as she took his member in her hand and eased it away from his belly.

Seven

'If you ask me, it's bloody odd,' said Ray Cragg. 'That river's nothing more than a stream, even if it was swelled up by the rain. Four days and nothing!'

'He'll turn up,' said Marty. 'Dead as a duck.'

They were sitting in a restaurant on the seafront at Lytham, a premises which Ray had no connection with, which he had never tried to muscle in on and never would. There had to be some places left untouched. They were in the dining room, overlooking the wide green towards the windmill and the Ribble Estuary.

Jack Burrows was sat with them, snuggling up to Ray.

Marty had his girlfriend with him. He had not really spoken to her or even acknowledged her presence since coming into the restaurant. She did not seem to mind. She ate and drank what-

150

ever was placed in front of her and spent the rest of the time, long thin legs crossed, filing her already perfect nails. Her name was Kylie and she was seventeen.

'And what about all that money?' Ray whined pitifully, very depressed.

'You can kiss that goodbye,' Marty said. It was said without humour, more with an air of despair.

'Are we sure Dix is dead?' Ray asked. 'He could easily have got out the river and done a runner with the cash.'

'Course he's dead,' said Marty. 'If he wasn't, he'd have brought the money back.'

'I don't know ... unless it was him that set the whole thing up, unless he got tempted. Even the best of us get tempted, Marty.'

'I need to go and powder my nose,' Jack Burrows announced.

'Have a slash, you mean?' said Ray in an ungentlemanly manner.

'If you like,' she said, very pissed off. She stood up, her eyes catching Marty's for a split second.

'Dix has a bird, hasn't he?' Ray asked.

'Yes, she lives in Fleetwood,' Marty said.

'Can you find her? Ask if she's heard from him? Put some pressure on her?'

'Pleasure.' Marty's eyes sparkled at the prospect.

'Wonder how Crazy and Miller are getting on?' Ray pondered, changing the subject slightly.

Marty's insides churned. 'Dunno ... I need a

151

piss too.' He patted Kylie's exposed knee and headed for the toilets.

'You're gonna file your fucking fingers away,' Ray said to Kylie with a sour, disdainful look on his face. He looked out towards the windmill.

The police in Greater Manchester announced the identities of the two murdered men found floating in a flooded quarry just inside their boundary three days after discovering them. They had identified them quite quickly, actually, but had wanted to give themselves a couple of days' uninterrupted investigation before telling the world at large who they were.

It was as a result of that public announcement that Crazy and Miller travelled to and began to trawl the streets of Stockport, the home town of the two men.

Their plan was extremely simple: go in feet first, annoy people, ruffle feathers and see what bugs came skittering out.

Marty came face to face with Jack Burrows in the corridor leading down to the toilets. 'Is there anybody in there?' Marty nodded towards the ladies' toilet.

'It's empty,' she said.

Marty took her by the hand and yanked her to the door. On his right he saw a disabled person's toilet.

'Even better,' he said gleefully, opening the door. 'More room.'

He swung her into the room and locked the door behind them.

'Marty, we don't have time for this,' she warned him, aware of the danger. However, there was a look of mischief on her face.

He winked at her. Suddenly they were in an embrace, kissing passionately, their hands running up and down each other's bodies.

'I'd rather have sixty seconds of this than nothing,' he breathed, his lips slavering up and down her neck.

'What are we going to do, Marty?'

'Don't know, don't know,' he said, his mouth moving up and down her sweet-smelling neck. 'I'll figure something out.' He pushed her away from him reluctantly. 'We'd better get back.'

'Yeah, yeah,' she said, smoothing her skirt down.

Marty went to unlock the door, but Burrows put a hand over his and stopped him, throwing her arms around his neck. 'I fucking love you,' she said and kissed him hard on the mouth.

'That was a long piss,' Ray remarked as the two unruffled people came back from the loo, chatting amicably and sharing what appeared to be an innocent laugh. Burrows gave Ray a nice peck and sat down next to him. Marty sat next to Kylie and she smiled thickly at him, then returned to the more important subject of her fingernails, which were superb examples of a blank intellect.

'I've been thinking,' Ray said. 'I think you should definitely go and visit Dix's bit of stuff. See if she's heard anything from him. I'm not convinced he's dead until I see his body on a

153

slab. And in the meantime I'll have a chat with my friend on the force.'

The Murder Incident Room (MIR) was up and running smoothly under the auspices of Temporary Detective Chief Inspector Henry Christie. There was a lot of information and intelligence coming in and being dealt with. All in all, Henry was content with the way things were progressing. The room was buzzing, a sign that everyone in the team was feeling confident.

But in spite of everything he suspected, there was very little coming in that pointed in the direction of Ray and Marty Cragg, the chief, but unofficial, suspects of the shootings and maybe also of the deaths of Johnny Jacques and his girlfriend. The latter investigation, though, was being kept fairly low key.

Henry had moved into Jane Roscoe's office and they shared it between them. Jane was out following some leads and Henry was in the office becoming frustrated by the lack of stuff coming in about the Cragg brothers. It was pretty apparent that their reputation as hard men was keeping people at bay.

He was taking a breather from the hubbub of the MIR just to skim through and review a wide range of material from Victim Association Charts to Sequence of Events Charts and the policy log in which he had to document all decisions made and the reasons for them.

One of the tasks he had asked the intelligence cell to undertake was to research the history and associations of the Craggs and to distil the information down into a brief, readable format.

For the umpteenth time he sat and read a précis of the life and times of Ray and Marty Cragg.

The Craggs were born of the same mother but two different fathers. Ray was thirty and Marty was twenty-seven. Ray had been making a living from crime since the age of ten. He had started off as a petty thief, graduating to burglary and street robbery. By the time he was thirteen he was well known for selling stolen goods throughout the Fylde coast and further afield. Information had once come in that he had been dealing in stolen VCRs in Manchester, showing that even at such a young age he had a good strategic mind on his shoulders. It also showed that he had the intelligence to distance himself, whenever possible, from the actual act of committing first-line crimes. He had become a middleman, dealing profitably with stolen property, but not having the risks associated with actually stealing the gear in the first place.

It was during these early years that, in spite of his small stature, he developed a reputation as a hard case. Very willing to fight dirty. He was known to have stabbed at least two people, though his follow-up intimidatory tactics ensured that he was never prosecuted for them.

By the age of fourteen he was dealing drugs and pimping for teenage girls.

At twenty he was believed to have established connections with the Colombian drug cartels, Eastern European drug traffickers and Asian heroin exporters. He was reported to be a millionaire several times over, though he remained living with his mother, moving to a detached house with her in Poulton-le-Fylde. He did not indulge in a flamboyant lifestyle which would keep him in the public eye, and this helped him to keep his businesses going for so long.

He had later become involved in a turf war in north Lancashire over drugs. Two people had been shot dead and Ray and Marty were the main suspects, but nothing was ever proven against them. They had walked even before they reached court and the police had found out how very forensically aware Ray was. Add that to his uncompromising reputation and here was a man who could evade the law.

Ray was also believed to have some police officers on his payroll.

Marty, it seemed, just followed in Ray's wake, trying to emulate him, but never quite succeeding in doing so.

Henry skimmed through the rest of the summary, then moved on to the Association Charts. He decided he needed a coffee to assist his concentration.

Dix's girlfriend, Debbie Goldman, lived in a small terraced house in Fleetwood, well maintained, quite pleasant and near to the seafront, within the sound of waves and the Isle of Man ferry. Marty called round that afternoon on the off chance he would find her in. There was no reply to his knock. He was about to turn away from the front door when he heard the telephone in the hall begin to ring. It rang for a very long time, then stopped.

* * *

As part of the work carried out by the analysts, they had photocopied any custody records relating to the Cragg brothers as a tool to increase their knowledge about them and in case there was anything of value to be gleaned from them.

There were four custody records for Ray. One related to the shootings in Lancaster when he had been arrested on suspicion of murder, two related to assault charges that were never substantiated and another to a public order offence committed when he stupidly became embroiled in a drunken fracas outside a pub in South Shore a year before. He had been cautioned for it.

Marty had eight custody records. One was for the shootings. Three related to him beating up his girlfriends, all of whom had called the police in terror when he had been knocking them around. Four more related to public order and drink-related incidents. He had been charged with two of them, had appeared in court and been fined.

Both brothers, it seemed, had a penchant for violence.

Henry skimmed through the documents, his head bursting with an overload of information. He had reached his limit for the day and stacked the papers up neatly. As he was doing this, something made him crease his brow. A name. He had read a name on one of the custody records, but could not remember which one and in what context.

His mind cleared and he started to read the

157

records again. This time he did it very carefully and very methodically.

Dix's girlfriend was back at her home just after 5 p.m. Marty was not far behind, knocking on the door before she had chance to take her coat off. The door was already chained and she opened it slowly, peering out at Marty. He stood there with a friendly grin on his face.

'Hi.'

'Hello,' she said dubiously, not taken in by his appearance.

'I'm Marty Cragg,' he introduced himself.

'I know,' she said frigidly.

'You're Debbie, aren't you? Harry's girl-friend?'

She nodded unsurely.

'Look ... do you think I could come in and have a chat? Won't take long.'

She nearly unlatched the chain, but thought better of it. She knew of Marty's character, but had never actually met him before. Dix had often talked about his instability, particularly with woman.

'We can talk here.'

Marty shrugged. 'Okay, no probs ... it's just that—' He burst into violent action and flung his whole bodyweight against the door. The chain did not have a chance. It's tiny screws were no match for Marty's power as they were dragged out of the door frame. Marty stepped menacingly into the hall and seized Debbie, twirling her round and hauling her into him, one hand covering her face, the other securing her squirm-

158

ing body.

'Nobody keeps me waiting outside,' he growled into her ear. He threw her against the wall and crushed his body up against hers, pinning her there, twisting and contorting her face against the wallpaper. 'Now then, love, I want to know where that shit of a boyfriend of yours is.'

'I don't know,' her warped voice came out.

'What do you mean, you don't know? He shags you, doesn't he?'

'I haven't seen him for days.'

'You must have heard from him.'

'No I haven't,' she pleaded. 'Let me go, you're hurting me.'

Marty spun her round so they were face to face, still holding her tight against the wall. He crushed her body, feeling himself begin to harden. He held her chin in the crook between his thumb and forefinger, squeezing her cheeks and forcing her lips out into a misshapen pucker.

'I will hurt you ... where is he?'

'I tell you, I don't know.' Her eyes were wide with dread.

Marty backed off, released his grip. Debbie sobbed. 'I haven't seen him for days,' she insisted.

But Marty hadn't finished. He smacked her hard across the face, whipping her head round and sending her spinning to the floor where she landed in a messy heap. He dropped to his haunches, his knees cracking. 'You hear from him, or see him, or have any contact with him at all, I want to know. Understand, girl?'

She nodded.

Then the telephone rang.

Both looked up at it on the wall near to the kitchen door.

'Answer it,' he instructed her. He pulled her to her feet and propelled her down the hallway towards the kitchen. Her hand dithered over the instrument.

'Pick the fucker up,' Marty said, emphasizing each word. He took hold of her hair at the back of her head and tilted her face backwards. 'Do it or you are dead.' He released his grip with a flick.

She picked it up and held it to her ear. 'Hello.' Her voice trembled.

Harry Dixon did not know why he phoned Debbie. It was a crass, stupid thing to do. The best thing would have been to skip the country, maybe contacting her in a couple of months' time when it had all died down. Dix knew it was a very foolish thing and had real danger to it, but the fact of the matter was that Debbie had been the backbone of his life for the last eighteen months and, though he would not admit it to anyone, he loved her like mad. That was why he contacted her. He needed to hear the comfort of her voice and to reassure her he hadn't just done a runner and was not dead.

He realized immediately on that first faltering word of hers that he had made a very big mistake in contacting her. He should have slammed the phone down. He should have said nothing. He should have run away. But that frightened tone touched something deep inside him and he had to respond to it.

'Debs, it's me, Harry.'

It was a conditioned response. Just as Dix could not help himself, Debbie could not stop herself from saying, 'Harry!'

Marty tore the phone out of her hand. 'Dix, you twat, where the fuck are you? You'd better show with that money or you're fucking dead—'

The phone was slammed down at the other end. Marty immediately dialled 1471, but the number was not known.

He turned slowly to Debbie, as she cowered by the kitchen door. 'You tell him to speak to me on my mobile. Me. No one else. Me – okay?'

He gave her a pat on the cheek and left her quivering in the hallway, her legs buckling under her as she folded down into a heap.

Ray Cragg had been busy that afternoon. As soon as Marty had left to try and track down Harry Dixon's girlfriend, he had immediately got on the phone and made arrangements to meet a contact at Skipool Creek on the River Wyre, near to Fleetwood.

Cragg arrived first and parked his car – a clean, very unremarkable Ford Escort which he used for business such as this – in the picnic area, which was otherwise deserted. The tide was in and the river was up and very brown-looking. A few small boats and yachts were moored mid-stream, bobbing up and down in the strong wind that was beginning to gust.

In due course another car pulled up alongside

and a middle aged woman got out and joined Ray in his car.

'It's very difficult for me to get out just like that,' she complained.

'I know, love,' he commiserated, 'but I keep you sweet, don't I?' He handed her a wodge of ten-pound notes. 'Two fifty,' he said. 'Double if you come up with the goods.'

Edina Trotter worked in a civilian capacity at Blackpool police station as an admin clerk in the intelligence unit. She had gone to the same school as Ray's mother and fallen pregnant at much the same time. The difference was that Edina had lost her baby and Ray had been born alive and kicking. The two young girls kept in contact with each other over the years, but Edina had stayed on the straight and narrow while Ray's mother had deviated somewhat. Edina had found herself in dire financial straits several years earlier when her husband dumped her and their two kids. That was when Ray came to her rescue with a proposition. As a member of the intelligence unit Edina had access to a great deal of sensitive information and also to the computer networks of Lancashire Constabulary, very useful for someone like Ray Cragg.

'Well,' she said doubtfully, riffling through some sheets of paper she had brought with her, printouts from computers. 'I've looked through all the logs relating to Rawtenstall and no body has been seen or recovered from the Irwell, nor has any large amount of cash been found either. I discreetly spoke to a friend of mine who works for Greater Manchester police in Bury, the

162

division which adjoins Lancashire, and they haven't found a body washed down the river either.'

'Okay, anything else?'

'As I was checking the computerized incident logs I noticed a couple of odd things in New Hall Hey, a little sort of village next to the river, just down from Rawtenstall.' She shuffled the papers. 'Three crimes reported on the same night you are on about. Pretty unusual, I'd say.'

Ray waited.

'One was theft of clothing from a washing line – a pair of jeans and a T-shirt; another was the owner of a house reporting damage to his door. It looks like someone's been in the house, which is up for sale and unoccupied, but nothing was stolen from it. Thirdly, there was a car stolen from the village.'

'Did the car turn up?'

'Yes, on the multi-storey in Preston.'

Ray scratched his chin thoughtfully. 'Could be,' he mumbled. 'Right, thanks, Edina.' He separated some more notes from a roll in his pocket and handed them to her. 'An extra hundred. Keep an eye on stolen cars, will you? Particularly those which either don't turn up, or those which get abandoned a long way away.'

After she had gone, Ray sat in the car for several hours, just watching the river and the boats bouncing around on the waves which were whipping up in the wind. His mobile rang.

'Ray? Me.'

'Hello.'

'He's definitely alive.'

'Yeah, thought so ... how do you know?'

'Talked to him on the phone. Let me find him, will you? I'd like to teach the little shit a lesson.'

'Marty, little half-brother, he's all yours.'

It had been a frustrating day for Crazy and Miller. They had drifted through Stockport, going from pub to pub, dropping into likely-looking corner shops on council estates, betting offices, sleazy clubs, trying to flush out any information concerning the friends of the two men they had shot to death a few days before. It was not a subtle approach, but one designed to make people angry and come out fighting. It did not seem to be working. Most people clammed up tight, said nothing and looked away; others went pale and shaky with fear. However, although they did not unearth anything of great use, they knew they had made their mark on the underworld of Stockport.

At seven that evening, they decided to call it quits and head back to Blackpool. It was motor-way all the way, M60, M61 westbound, M6 and M55. They were in Miller's ageing, but wonder-ful Mercedes Coupé, a real gangster's car. It purred easily down the motorway at 80–85 mph. Both men listened to Radio 2 and argued about the merits of sixties music as opposed to today's trash. They did not know each other very well, but found themselves quite liking each other.

Throughout the journey Miller kept a regular eye on his mirrors.

As they left the M6 and joined the M55 on the last ten miles or so of their journey, Miller turned the radio down.

'I've changed my mind,' he said grimly. 'I think we have rattled a few cages. It's been with us ever since we came out of Stockport.'

'Yeah, I know,' said Crazy. He had been using the big mirror on his door to keep tabs on following traffic. 'I was just waiting for you to notice it.'

'Kept the same distance all the way. Slowed down when we did, speeded up when we did.'

'Yep.'

'Let's just carry on as normal for a while.'

'Yep.'

Dix had considered stealing a car from the multi-storey car park in Preston but decided against it. He knew Ray Cragg had police contacts and that, above all, Ray would not be fooled into thinking that he, Dix, was dead. He even regretted nicking the car from New Hall Hey because it was likely that, via his informants, Ray would put two and two together. So to steal a car from Preston town centre as a follow-on to abandoning the one he had stolen from Rossendale would be the start of a trail which Ray and his cronies would soon follow. Working on the worst-case scenario, Dix knew he had to start covering his tracks now. To do that he jumped into a taxi in Preston and took a short journey to Bamber Bridge. From being dropped off at Sainsbury's, he crossed over to the Premier Lodge, both establishments close to junction 30 of the M6. He booked into the motel, no trouble, paid cash, gave a false name and address and retreated to his room and lay low for a few days to think.

It was on the fourth day that he went to Sainsbury's and bought himself a new pay-as-you-go mobile phone. Twenty minutes later he was logged on to the network and it was from his new phone that he contacted Debbie, disguising his new number before dialling.

The sound of Marty's smug and nasty voice rattled him. They were moving quickly to find him, so he knew he had to move even quicker.

He sat in his room, eating a prawn mayo sandwich bought from the supermarket, swigging bottled water with it and considering his options.

By eight that evening he had pretty much decided on his plan of action. There was nothing clever about it, but he thought it best to keep it as simple as possible. The only real problem was that there were certain risks to be taken. The other alternative was to hand the money back to Ray, claim concussion or something equally ridiculous and beg for mercy. Naah!

Dix wanted the money for himself. But before he could quit the country, he needed to realize his assets.

The car was still with them as the M55 narrowed to become Yeadon Way and threaded into Blackpool.

'Fancy a burger?' Crazy asked Miller.

'Why not?'

Miller checked the rear-view mirror. He allowed himself a grim smile of anticipation and wondered if there would be any chance to ask questions. He hoped so, because the job Ray had given him was to find out information and Miller hated being unable to deliver.

But what will be, will be, he thought philosophically.

Other than at the daily briefings, Henry and Jane Roscoe had barely seen each other for days. They were both working long shifts, none less than fourteen hours a day, and somehow had managed to avoid – or evade – one another. This was much to Henry's relief. Now that the very obvious attraction between them had been consummated, Henry was beginning to feel that things had moved on far too quickly for his liking, almost as though he had been ambushed by the act of sex. He was having regrets and did not want to be embroiled in another affair which seemed to be a repeating pattern in his life.

At least that's what he thought.

Just after 8 p.m. Roscoe came into the office. She looked exhausted, but was smiling broadly. Henry caught his breath because it suddenly hit him that to him, she was a stunningly beautiful woman. He could not take his eyes off her face, and she could not stop looking at him either.

'Phew,' she said sitting on a low chair by the office door. She crossed her legs and Henry noticed something else about her: objectively it could never be argued that she had wonderful, shapely legs; they were a little too flabby around the thigh and her feet were too big, but to Henry they were the most wonderful pair of legs he had ever seen in his life. He swallowed and felt very

167

hollow inside as though he had not eaten for days. She breathed out and shook her head. 'Lots of info coming in,' she said. 'I think it's time we made some sort of move on the Cragg brothers.'

'Sorry, what?' asked Henry, only just tuning in.

'Are you listening to me?' she demanded sternly. She licked her lips and glared seriously at him.

'To be honest, no.'

'Why not?'

'You don't want to know ... go on, I'm listening now.'

She paused, holding his gaze for longer than necessary. 'I think it's time we moved in on the Craggs – but only after I've taken you back to your flat and fucked your brains out. How does that sound for a strategy?'

'Well, speaking as a tactician, I always like to be told where I'm headed, then I can get on and do it.'

'So you want to know where you're headed, eh?' She became severe. 'To oblivion, I expect, so hold on tight, Henry Christie, because it's going to be one hell of a ride.'

Miller pulled the Merc into McDonald's car park, just off Yeadon Way, close to the newly built stadium belonging to Blackpool Football Club. He and Crazy moseyed across to the restaurant, both aware of the car which had followed them from Stockport driving past the car-park entrance, towards Blackpool.

They each 'went large' on a quarter-pounder meal, then sat at one of the tables near to the toilets and an emergency exit. Each man un-wrapped his meal with delight. They had eaten little that day and were ravenous, coffee and cola being the only things which had kept them going.

'God, I love these,' Crazy said. He bit into the slippery burger, which he had trouble keeping together.

'More a KFC man, me.' Miller bit into his and through a mouthful said, 'But it's not bad – just crap food.'

'Junk,' agreed Crazy. He folded four long, salty chips into his mouth and slurped them down with Tango.

Miller could see over Crazy's shoulder into the car park. His steel-grey eyes narrowed. 'They're pulling in now.'

Crazy nodded. He opened his burger and extracted the gherkin, which he put to one side. 'I'll save that for later.'

Miller sipped his coffee, which tasted bitter and was scorching hot. He maintained a little commentary, 'Two guys getting out ... jeans, trainers, wind-jammers ... just have a quick peek, Craze, then you'll know who they are.'

Crazy glanced round, focused on the two men and quickly returned his attention to his chips.

'Coming in now,' Miller relayed. 'Mid-twenties, short cropped hair ... up and coming young buckos, out to make their mark, I'd say.'

'Let's not let them make it on us.' Crazy wiped his fingers and lips on a serviette. He took a deep breath, feeling his heart rate increase with the expectation of conflict.

169

'Little or no chance of that,' Miller said quietly.

The two young men entered the restaurant, trying to look cool, calm and dangerous, their body language buzzing. They could not keep still, were jittering with nerves and finding it impossible to keep their eyes off Crazy and Miller sitting in the corner.

'You ready for this?' Miller asked.

Crazy smiled. 'Got to be.'

Miller watched the two men join the end of the short queue to the counter. They pretended to inspect the menu and to discuss their preferred choices.

'I think they're going to go large, too,' Miller said.

Crazy nodded. He could see them in the reflection from the large window behind Miller. 'They must only have handguns,' he guessed.

'Yeah,' Miller agreed. The ex-military man was cold and comfortable. Very much in control of himself and pleased to see that the younger man, Crazy, was keeping chilled as well. 'Having said that,' Miller went on, 'there might be nothing in this. Just coincidence, maybe.'

They smirked at each other, knowing the truth.

'If they don't get a move on, they'll have to buy something,' Miller said. 'Oh-oh, here it comes!'

The two men went into a kind of huddle, then sprang away from each other, spun round and revealed they had each put on a mask, similar to the Hannibal Lector face guard worn by Anthony Hopkins in the *Silence of the Lambs*, designed to prevent him from biting the throats out of unsuspecting people. The masks made them look frightening and dangerous. Each pulled a gun out of his waistband and ran towards Miller and Crazy, kicking stools out of the way, scattering other customers.

Crazy saw it all happening in reflection.

He and Miller rose together, their chairs tipping backwards.

Crazy twisted round low, smoothly extracting the pump action sawn-off which had been concealed under his jacket. Miller had a Glock 9mm in his hand. They moved rapidly and precisely. Crazy dropped to one knee, Miller stayed high, tactics they had determined at the beginning of the day.

Their two adversaries were openly startled by this concerted movement and both hesitated. Something not wise to do.

Other customers watched the unfolding scene with open mouthed astonishment and disbelief. Some dived for cover. Some simply stood there. The staff all ducked behind the counter. There was a scream.

Crazy pulled the trigger on the shotgun. The boom was ear-shattering in the confines of the building.

The first man went down clutching his groin and thigh as the shot blasted into him. He staggered against a pot plant, dragging it crashing to the floor, writhing in agony on top of the scattered leaves and soil.

The second man stopped in his tracks. More fatal hesitation.

171

Crazy racked the shotgun.

Miller shot the man in the chest. The 9mm slug drove into his right lung. Miller had shot people before and was always amazed by the different effect taking a bullet had on folk: some toppled over like skittles; one man he shot in Northern Ireland, a suspected IRA terrorist, just walked to a nearby seat, sat on it and started to cry while nursing his wound. This man, today, did not even stagger back. He looked down at his chest, looked up accusingly at Miller and opened his arms in a gesture which seemed to ask, 'Why me?' His gun dropped to the floor and he sank to his knees, both hands now covering the hole in his upper chest from which pumped blood.

Without a word, Miller and Crazy headed for the exit. They walked purposefully, not too quickly, not in any sort of panic. They shouldered their way past people, did not touch anything, stared ahead of themselves, making no eye contact with anyone. Once outside, their walk turned into a brisk sprint to the Mercedes.

By the time they were out of the car park, the first public spirited member of the public ran out and tried to take their registration number, but she was too late. They were gone.

Their lovemaking was long and slow. Afterwards they held each other tight. Henry could not stop kissing her, nor she him.

'You're pretty good at bonking,' he told her.

She grinned. 'Only with the right person.' She kissed him and sucked his bottom lip and sank her teeth into it. He gasped and squeezed her

172

bottom hard. 'And you feel like the right person.'

'Mmm,' he agreed, was about to kiss her again when the inevitable happened: her mobile rang. 'Hate those things,' he said. She clambered across him, ensuring her breasts brushed across his chest, then lay at an angle over him and answered the phone. Henry did not take much heed of the conversation. He was too engrossed in running his fingertips up and down her spine, caressing her buttocks and rubbing her shoulders. She ended the call then lay unmoving, revelling in Henry's touch.

At length she said, 'That was the office. There's been some sort of shooting incident at McDonald's, Yeadon Way ... Ahhh,' she breathed as Henry slid his hand between her legs and into her cunt. 'They want me to turn out to it ... I said I'd be there asap.' She dragged herself up, straddled him, kissed him and reached for his cock, slowly easing herself down the shaft. 'I'm not sure what asap means, though,' she confessed.

Dix took a chance. He phoned Debbie again on the new mobile, this time calling her mobile number. She answered and he could tell from her voice that she was now more in control than she had been earlier.

'Are you alone?'

'Yes ... look, Harry, what's going on?'

'Don't talk – listen,' he said firmly.

For the moment Marty was being patient. Under

the present circumstances there was no point in being otherwise. It was the only way. He had to stay focused and cool. No need to panic. Just play things nice 'n' easy. Wait for the moment and pounce. Dix was sure to show himself and the best way to get him, Marty believed, was through the sweet Debbie.

Marty was parked two streets away from her house, waiting for her to make a move. She had to drive past the end of the street he was on in order to get to the main road, so he was certain he would not miss her when she set off to meet her beau.

It was just a matter of time.

He was fiddling with the in-car CD when she whizzed past him. He gave her a few seconds, then followed. Marty concentrated hard on keeping on Debbie's tail, ensuring he was always a few cars back, trying not to spook her. Unfortunately for him, he was so wrapped up in this that he forgot the first rule of survival in the world of the professional criminal: 'Always look over your shoulder.'

Eight

Although Dix had warned Debbie to be on guard, to check if she was being followed, she really did not know what she should do, or what she should be looking for. There were cars behind her, but how could she tell if any one of them was after her? She had no idea about anti-surveillance techniques. It never entered her head to loop round roundabouts or to stop in lay-bys or to retrace her steps. All she could think of doing was to look in her rear-view mirror.

In truth she knew little about what Dix did for a living. She had an idea that he operated on the fringes of criminality, but his reassurances that he was only a debt collector – or taxman, the term used in his circles – always calmed her down. They calmed her down because she loved him, couldn't get enough of him and truly believed that when they got married, as surely they would, she could change him and his ways.

She checked the mirror. Two cars behind her at the moment. Had one of them been there before? She could not be sure.

Suddenly and painfully she had started to learn something more about Dix and his world. She knew about Marty Cragg. Dix had taken her to a nightclub in Blackpool once where he had bumped into Marty and a few hangers-on. After

175

a few drinks had loosened his tongue, Dix had told her that Marty was a drug dealer and a pimp and that he enjoyed knocking women round. Marty had frightened her. His eyes, fuelled with alcohol admittedly, looked wild. It worried her when Dix told her he worked for Marty and his brother, Ray, who was far meaner than Marty. How could that be? she wondered naively.

That had been a while ago. Dix had never mentioned Marty since and she had stopped thinking about him. Now she could not erase him from her mind.

What the hell had Dix done?

He had refused to tell her anything over the phone. He just made her listen to some instructions which, when the phone call ended, she began to follow with a feeling of incredulity.

She had gone into her kitchen as instructed and emptied the cupboard underneath the sink. With shaking hands she lifted the bottom shelf out and peered into the dark space below, reached in cautiously and pulled out a plastic carrier bag. She replaced the shelf and the items from the cupboard before turning her attention to the bag, one from Safeway's supermarket.

'Just get it, keep your eyes and fingers out of it,' Dix had warned her. 'And bring it to me.'

Red rag to a bull. There was no way she could resist a peek. At first she could see nothing to make her afraid. There was something wrapped in an oily cloth, and a small biscuit tin which used to contain shortcakes. She extracted the biscuit tin and flicked it open with her nails. Her jaw dropped.

176

It was packed full of wads of Bank of England notes. There was also a Halifax Building Society passbook on top of the money. She opened the book slowly. Her jaw sagged a little further when she saw the balance of twenty-two grand, plus change.

She replaced the book and closed the tin. Next she pulled out the object wrapped in the grubby rag and placed it reverentially on the kitchen floor.

Without unwrapping it, she instinctively knew what it was. A horrible, nasty, dirty feeling overcame her.

She peeled back one corner of the rag, then another, then another until the contents were revealed.

A handgun and some bullets. She knew nothing about weapons. Did not know it was a two-inch barrelled Smith & Wesson Model 10 revolver, .38 calibre. All she knew was that her boyfriend, whom she loved and trusted, was keeping a gun and some very suspicious amounts of cash on her premises without her knowing about it.

She slowly re-wrapped the gun and placed it back in the carrier, terrified it would go bang at any moment, then breathed out.

She knew she should have called the police there and then, but for some unaccountable reason a frisson of excitement buzzed through her belly. Shortly after she was on her way to see Dix.

Another check in the rear-view mirror: still two cars behind.

* * *

Debbie drove towards the M55, joining the motorway at junction 3 and travelling east towards Preston. She cruised along at sixty, making it quite hard for Marty because not many people drive at such slow speed and it felt odd to hang in there behind her, but he did not have much choice.

He tailed her on to the M6. She came off at junction 29 and drove towards Bamber Bridge on the A6. He was behind her when she turned right towards Sainsbury's, then immediately left on to the Premier Lodge car park. He drove past and pulled into Sainsbury's, a smirk on his face. So that's where you're holed up, he thought.

Dix was in room 34. Debbie walked straight past reception, up the stairs and along the corridor to the room. She knocked quietly. The door opened after a delay and Dix drew her in, checking the corridor before closing the door.

She dropped the carrier bag on the wide double bed. 'Dix ... what the hell is happening?'

Before she could finish her remonstration, he grabbed her and kissed her hard on the mouth. There was a modicum of resistance for a few fleeting moments before Debbie's legs turned to jelly. Her hands went to the back of his neck and she inserted her tongue into his mouth. They kissed and held each other for a long time. Then she pushed him away, brushed back her hair and decided to get down to business.

'I want to know what the hell—' she blurted again. He stopped her mid-stride by placing a fingertip over her mouth.

'Were you followed?'

She shrugged uncertainly. 'I don't know ... I don't think so.'

'Mm,' he said sceptically. 'You got all my stuff?' He nodded at the carrier bag on the bed.

'And I looked.' She folded her arms.

'Thought you would,' Dix said lightly.

'How dare you keep a gun in my house?' she said indignantly.

'Shush.' He smiled. 'Have a look at this.'

He beckoned her to follow him across the room and picked up the holdall from underneath the dressing table. Slowly he unzipped it and revealed the contents. 'Voilà!'

Somehow she managed to keep her face straight.

'How much?'

'With what I've got in there,' he pointed to the carrier bag, 'about three hundred thousand give or take a few gs.' He re-zipped the bag.

'Who does it belong to? Marty Cragg?'

'Sort of,' he answered vaguely.

'You absolute nut case,' she said and sat down on the edge of the bed, shaking her head despairingly.

'No, no, no – not if we go, get out of here ... Spain or summat.'

'We? I can't just leave,' she said. 'I've got a house, a job, me mum and dad.'

'You could come eventually though, couldn't you?' His eyes pleaded. 'I love you like mad.'

She softened. 'We need to sit and talk this one out, Harry ... I mean, is there enough to live on

179

for the rest of our lives? Because that's what this means, you know. The rest of our lives.'

There was a sharp knock on the door. Both froze, staring at each other. A feeling of dread rushed through Dix, from his teeth right down to his toes.

Marty rapped on the door again, feeling very confident that things were going to turn out right for him at last.

'Come on, Dixie,' he called softly, 'I'm not going anywhere and nor are you.'

He could feel Dix's single eye on him through the peephole. He smiled and raised his right hand so Dix would have a clear view of the gun he was holding in it. The door unlocked and Dix opened it slowly and had the muzzle of the gun pushed against his forehead.

'Back into the room,' Marty said.

Dix walked back, a pained and very pissed-off expression on his face. Debbie was sitting on the bed shaking visibly. Marty smiled at her. 'We meet again, Debs. You sit next to her,' he told Dix. 'I fervently hope you've got my dosh, Dix my boy.'

'In the bag ... and it's not your money,' Dix said. 'It's Ray's.'

'No, you're wrong there. It's mine – all mine.' Marty perched a cheek of his bottom on the edge of the dressing table and pulled the holdall to him. 'So you didn't drown then?'

Dix remained silent.

'Just decided to keep my money instead. Naughty boy. How can you live with yourself

180

being so dishonest?'

'Same as you, I guess.'

Marty tipped his head back and roared with laughter. 'Nice one. Always liked your sense of humour.' His jocularity faded as quickly as it had arrived. His face became hard and uncompromising. Keeping an eye on Dix and Debbie, the gun pointed loosely in their direction, he unzipped the bag and glanced in. 'Is it all there?' He inserted his hand and it came back out with a few packs of money. 'Or have you bought yourself a Roller yet?'

'It's all there,' Dix confirmed, 'less some expenses.'

Marty pouted. 'And what's in that bag?' He gestured to the Safeway's carrier on the bed.

'It's mine, nothing to do with you.'

Marty snorted. 'Bring it to me,' he told Debbie. She did not shift. 'Now, please,' he reiterated and pointed his gun at Dix, 'or I'll just blow this fuck away here and now.'

Debbie and Dix exchanged a glance. He gave her a reluctant nod. She picked up the bag and placed it on the dressing table next to the holdall. Marty reached in and prised the lid off the tin. His face glowed with pleasure. 'Your nest egg, I presume. How much?'

'About fifteen,' muttered Dix.

'And a gun as well, if I'm not mistaken.' He unwrapped a couple of corners of the rag to confirm his suspicion. His hand emerged from the bag with Dix's Halifax Building Society passbook in it. He manipulated it open with one hand. When he saw the balance, his eyes opened

181

wide. 'Twenty-two— Bloody hell, Dix, you're a rich man. Sadly, you've made some very unwise investments and you've lost all your money – to me.' Marty was thinking quickly. This was too good an opportunity to miss. 'For all the trouble you've caused, this is the cost of it.' He shook the Halifax book.

'No,' said Dix.

'No what? Actually, yes – every penny. All this cash and the balance in the Halifax. That's the price you pay, Dix, when you get greedy. Think yourself lucky, you could be dead as well. So what we're going to do is this, we're going to settle down here for the night, all three of us. Cosy, eh? Then in the morning you're going to go to the Halifax and cause all that money to be transferred into another account in another bank, the details of which I'll give you – then I'll see how I feel. How does that sound?'

Neither spoke.

'Knew you'd like it.' He winked. 'I'll stay here with the delicious Debbie while you do it and if you don't come back, I'll rape her then kill her. Sound okay?'

'Nothing to say, either of them.' Jane Roscoe, looking red and flushed even two hours after making love with Henry Christie, was talking to him in a more professional capacity in the A&E department at Blackpool Victoria Hospital. 'One's been shot in the chest, the other's been blasted by a shotgun in the groin. Both are stable, but the one with the chest wound can't speak yet. It's the one who nearly had his cock

182

shot off who told me to piss off. But they aren't going anywhere. From witnesses at the scene, these two went for two other guys sitting down eating a meal.'

'And they came off worse.'

'Very much so. The other two legged it unharmed. Drove off in a Mercedes sports, an old one, but no registration number taken.'

'Any connection with the shooting at the King's Cross?'

'Dunno. It's a bit of a coincidence if it isn't.'

'Let's just keep an eye on how it progresses – have you got someone capable of dealing with it properly?'

'I thought Rik Dean could sort it.'

'Yeah, he's pretty thorough,' said Henry.

By 2 a.m. Debbie had fallen into a difficult sleep, fully clothed on the wide double bed in the motel room. Dix lay beside her, completely awake, his hands clasped behind his head, staring at the ceiling. Marty sat in one of the uncomfortable easy chairs, feet up on the other, watching a soft-porn film on the video channel, sound turned down. His gun was laid across his crotch. His head kept nodding and lolling as he endeavoured to keep awake. Dix monitored him through the corner of his eye, hoping he would nod off properly and give him the chance to grab the gun and blow his head off.

At least that's what he'd like to do. Whether he would have the courage to attempt something so foolhardy and dangerous was another matter. He closed his eyes and breathed deeply, regretting ever contacting Debbie and dragging her into this situation. Not that he could blame her for his current predicament. She was just a bit naive – and maybe he was too, and now they were both paying the price.

He opened his eyes and looked lovingly at Debbie, curled up next to him. She had been very good for him, had made him think twice about his life and had promised him something more fulfilling. Perversely, that was one of the reasons he had stolen the money. A new start, away from all the shit. It had backfired badly.

Marty struggled to sit upright, yawned and stretched his arms upwards and outwards. The gun slid off his lap on to the floor with a thud. Marty ignored it and rolled his shoulders and rubbed his aching neck, his mouth opening and closing with a clicking noise.

'Need a brew ... make one, Dix.'

'Yeah, right.'

The gun was still on the floor at Marty's feet.

Dix sat up. He saw it. He could go for it now. It was about 60–40 in Marty's favour, but he could still go for it. He tensed.

'Go on, have a go. Try it,' Marty urged.

'Try what?' Dix's shoulders sagged.

'Don't tell me you weren't thinking about it.' The gun remained on the carpet.

'Thinking about what?' Dix swung his legs off the bed and rubbed his eyes, feigning innocence.

'You know.' Marty placed a foot on the gun.

Debbie stirred and rolled over. She started to snore quietly.

'Is she a good fuck?'

'I'll make that brew.' Dix stood up.

The door blew open with a huge crash and four men, hooded, all dressed in black, all wielding Uzi machine pistols, poured into the room in a well-planned well-thought-out manoeuvre. They came in in single file, past the bathroom, then spread across the room where it widened. They came in screaming – loud, noisy and disorientating.

Dix turned to face them, kettle in hand.

Marty was caught mid-way to retrieving his gun from the floor.

Debbie woke groggily to the noise, confused and woozy.

'You do not move,' the first one through the door shouted. The two behind him rushed past and pointed their weapons at Marty. The last man of the four covered Dix and Debbie, his gun constantly waving from one to the other.

'On your feet,' the first one ordered Marty.

'Me?' he said in disbelief.

The masked man shoved his gun right up into Marty's face. 'You.'

Marty rose unsteadily. His foot was still on top of his gun on the floor.

'Let's deal,' Marty said quickly. 'I've got money. I can give it to you.'

'My job is to deliver you,' the man said. 'So shut up.'

'Shit,' blabbed Marty, 'shit, shit.'

'Come with us,' the man beckoned Marty.

'Where are we going?'

'To a rendezvous.'

One of the men covering Marty grabbed his

185

shirtfront and pulled him across the room, propelling him towards the door.

One by one they withdrew, leaving Dix and Debbie standing motionless and shocked. Dix was first to move.

'Fucking hell,' he cried. He stepped across to the window and looked out through the curtains to the car park below. A van of some sort was drawn up on the tarmac near the front of the motel, its registration number obscured. He watched the four men bundle Marty into the back. Three leapt in with him, the fourth got in the front passenger seat next to a driver and the van sped away, up the road. The night porter ran out behind the van and stood there arms wide, flabbergasted by events.

'We'd better move,' said Dix. 'I have a bad feeling about those men, can't think why. We need to lie very low.'

Debbie, totally out of her league, dropped back on to the bed and did the only thing she was capable of doing at that moment. She cried.

The three men pinned Marty face down on the floor of the van. One of them knelt on him, his knee pressed between Marty's shoulder blades and his gun pressed into his neck. As soon as the back doors slammed shut, the van moved off. Marty closed his eyes and did not struggle because he knew it would be useless. He said nothing and tried to stay calm.

They travelled only a very short distance. The van slowed, turned, slowed more and stopped. Marty opened his eyes as the doors were pulled open. The gun was jammed harder into his neck and the man holding it leaned into Marty's face, huffing garlic-scented breath over him.

'You get out here. If you struggle you'll die. Nod if you understand.'

Marty nodded.

'Come.' The man eased his knee off Marty's spine, took hold of his collar and, keeping the muzzle pressed into Marty's neck, pulled him out of the van. They were in a dark car park which Marty did not recognize. Away to his left, high up, was a motorway he could not place. Either the M6 or M65, but he was too disorientated to work out which.

He was pushed round to the side of the van and down a short pathway. Ahead of him he could see a group of figures in the darkness. He was prodded hard and staggered. He did not complain. He was not in a position to do so.

As the figures got closer, they became more defined in the night.

Four men were standing in a circle, looking at something. The circle parted as Marty reached them and revealed what they were inspecting. It was a man. He was on his knees. His wrists were bound around his back with duct tape, there was a blindfold of the same tape covering his eyes and a strip of it gagged his mouth.

One of the men switched on a torch. He shone the beam into Marty's eyes, making him flinch.

'Glad you could come,' the man said. He turned the beam on to himself and held the torch under his chin, casting the light upwards, casting long eerie shadows up his face. Marty recog-

187

nized him immediately.

'Mendoza,' said Marty.

'Correct,' he said, 'and I don't often make house calls.' His voice was deep and slow and heavily accented. 'But in your case I have made an exception.' His English was excellent. 'There is something I would like you to see.'

Mendoza took a step back and shone the torch at the kneeling figure on the ground. 'Okay.'

Another man stepped behind the man and put a silenced pistol at the base of his skull, angling it upwards slightly.

'Okay,' Mendoza said again.

The trigger was pulled. The bullet entered the kneeling man's head and exited through his left eye socket, taking that side of his face with it. He pitched headlong, writhing and jerking.

The killer stood over him and shot him twice more in the head, making him still.

Mendoza's big head turned. He smiled at Marty. He had a big mouth, full of white, even teeth. 'I want you to kneel down.'

'Oh, Jesus, no,' Marty gasped. He twisted away and tried to run. Hands held him tight and forced him down to the ground.

Debbie was feeling so weak she could not move. Her limbs would not respond. She felt as though she had been turned into frog spawn, or blubber, or something which had no form or substance. She was caught in a nightmare. In one way it did not feel real, in that, surely, this could not be happening to her. For God's sake, she was a hairdresser. In another way, she knew that it was real, that she was here and that these events were definitely happening to her.

'Harry, I feel sick,' she moaned.

'Yeah, me too,' he responded. He had waited long enough to motivate her to move and was becoming irritated by her inaction. He pulled on his jacket and went to the window to look down at the car park. 'But we need to move, get on, get out of here,' he pleaded.

'I know, I know – just give me a moment.' Debbie rolled on the bed and drew her knees up into a foetal position. 'I can't stand up. I feel like I want to spew.'

Dix closed his eyes. He sighed and sat next to her. She grabbed one of his hands between hers and held it tight, transmitting her tremors to him. He stroked her hair.

'It'll be all right. We'll just put a bit of space between them and us, chill out somewhere, make some plans, then go for it. How does that sound?'

'I don't know, I don't know,' she said weakly.

'I love you, y'know,' he told her.

She nodded numbly.

Dix tensed. He'd heard a vehicle coming into the car park. He sped back to the window and peered out through the gap in the curtains. It was the van which had taken Marty away. It had returned.

'Shit, they're back.' He picked up the holdall, grabbed her arm and dragged her roughly off the bed. She whinged and he shook her. 'We've got to move – now!'

He started for the door.

189

She made no attempt to follow him.

'Now!' he yelled.

The expression on her face changed as a dawning realization jarred her into action.

'Come on,' he urged her.

At the door he turned right down the corridor and headed for the fire escape at the far end. He burst through on to the steps outside, Debbie now right behind him. He closed the door and ducked down out of sight as four hooded men appeared at the far end of the corridor and crashed into room 34.

Ten minutes later the van was back on the car park where Marty was still being held down on his knees. The men climbed out and went over to Mendoza. Marty closed his eyes in desperation when he saw that none of them was carrying the holdall. It meant they had missed Dix. It also meant something far more fundamental.

Mendoza and the men from the van talked in hushed tones.

Marty looked at the body of the man who had been executed. A surge of fear corkscrewed through his intestines. His breath shortened and he swallowed back an urge to vomit.

Mendoza moved away from the men. Marty heard him say, '*Gracias*.' He squatted down by Marty and lifted his chin up gently with the tip of his forefinger, so they were eye to eye.

'Your friends have gone.' There was a sort of sadness in his voice.

'Give me a chance. He has the money. I can find him and I can pay you.' Marty was frantic.

Mendoza shook his head. 'Too late. Too many promises broken. Too much debt.' Mendoza placed his hands on his thighs and pushed himself up. Marty's eyes rose with him, pleading. Mendoza nodded at someone standing behind Marty.

The last thing Marty Cragg felt before his brain exploded was the muzzle of a gun being pushed into the back of his neck.

Nine

Henry Christie re-read through the photocopy of the custody records relating to Marty Cragg which had caught his interest previously. Every time a prisoner is brought into custody, they are allowed certain rights which can be delayed, but never totally withheld except under certain circumstances, for example, if the custody sergeant believes the prisoner is too drunk to understand what is being said, or is too violent, or both.

This had been the case on the night about six months earlier when Marty Cragg had been arrested for a fairly minor public order offence outside a Blackpool nightclub. According to the custody record, Cragg had been brought in and had been very drunk and abusive towards the arresting officers and also to the custody sergeant. Most detainees do not realize, particularly

191

when under the influence of alcohol, that to be abusive to the sergeant is a bad move.

In Marty's case, his behaviour resulted in him spending very little time chatting to the sergeant. He was forcibly restrained and searched and immediately heaved into a cell, the door slamming shut behind him, and he did not get his rights. He banged continually on the cell door and shouted verbal abuse for at least another hour. He urinated on the door, followed this by vomiting around the cell and then fell asleep. He had been arrested at 2.05 a.m. and was deemed to be fit enough to receive his rights, after mopping up his cell, some nine hours later at 11.15. The notes on the custody record said that he was compliant, quiet and apologetic. He was released an hour later following a written caution given by the sergeant. Because of the minor nature of the offence for which he was arrested, he did not have to provide fingerprints or a DNA sample.

Henry shook his head.

How things had changed, he pondered sadly. In his formative years as a young PC, everyone arrested would be charged and go to court and get fined at least. Not these days. Everybody got cautioned to death, or referred to some agency or other. Getting locked up meant little to people and a caution was just a piece of paper to blow your nose on. They only ended up in court for persistent offending.

And Marty Cragg had been fortunate. He had only been arrested once before for that particular offence, so he got cautioned and kicked out.

Henry's face showed its displeasure. The criminal justice system, he thought bleakly, is fucked.

He re-read Marty's list of previous convictions, which included several assaults. Henry decided he needed to know more about these, so he phoned down to the brainy people in the intelligence unit and asked the woman who answered to do a bit of research for him. She muttered about how busy they were, but Henry had no qualms in pulling rank for once, moaning bitch.

Then he returned to the custody record and the point at which Marty had been given his rights.

Then he had a thought and picked up his newly issued, state of the art, cancer-inducing (if reports were to be believed) TETRA radio. These new-fangled things enabled any officers in the force to talk to any other officer by simply dialling in their collar number. It did all sorts of other wonderful things, too, except tell you how to do the job. On the off chance that the officer who arrested Cragg was on duty, Henry dialled the number. He got an immediate reply.

'Hi,' said Henry affably and introduced himself. 'Are you anywhere near the nick at the moment?'

'Having breakfast upstairs.'

'Can I come and see you?'

'Have I done something wrong?' the officer wanted to know.

'No, no – just want a word with you about a job you dealt with a while back.'

Henry smiled. Bobbies always thought it was

bad news when a senior officer wanted to talk to them. The thing was, he thought, that he felt exactly the same when a more senior officer beckoned him in, so things didn't change, no matter what rank you got to, unless you got to the top – but then again, you got the police authority and Home Office on your back, so no escape.

Before leaving the office Henry dialled another number on the TETRA on the off chance and also got through. Wonders were never going to cease, he mused.

'Rik, it's me, Henry Christie – I need a chat about something.'

'I'm up at Blackpool Victoria Hospital re the incident at McDonald's at the moment,' Rik Dean said. 'I'll be up here another hour at least, I reckon, boss.'

'Okay. I might come up and see you if I get chance.'

Henry stood up, slung on his jacket and made his way to the canteen where he found PC Dave Watts tucking into a full, very unhealthy-looking breakfast. Henry knew him by sight. He paid for a mug of decaf coffee and joined him at the table.

'Hello, sir,' the PC said. He eyed Henry with suspicion and seemed to lose his appetite.

Henry hated being called 'sir', but he let it ride. Sometimes it was too much trouble to put folk right.

'You're not in any sort of bother,' he reiterated.

The young man breathed a sigh of relief, took

a sip of his tea and pulled his plate back towards him.

'About six months ago you arrested someone for a public order offence outside the Palace nightclub?'

Watts' eyebrows knitted together. 'Did I?'

'Probably one of dozens you've arrested,' Henry conceded. 'His name was Marty Cragg.'

'Yeah, I remember him. Very hard work, bit of a bastard. A hard nut.'

'What were the circumstances of the arrest?'

'He rolled out of the club arguing with a woman. Right in front of us, he was. We were stood outside the club. They walked away, still arguing, then suddenly he turned on her and knocked her to the ground and started kicking her. We intervened and locked him up. He should've been done for assault, but she wouldn't make a complaint, so we ended up doing him for public order.'

'Do you know who Marty Cragg is?'

The officer nodded. 'Big time. Unfortunately he's got a small-time temperament.'

'Who was the girl?'

'Dunno, she refused to give us details. She spoke with a strange accent, bit like Russians do in James Bond films.'

'Okay, thanks.' Henry finished his decaf.

'That it?'

'That's it,' Henry said. 'Cheers.'

Karl Donaldson had once been a brilliant FBI field agent, working mainly in Florida from the Miami Field Office. His investigations had resulted in numerous convictions of top-flight felons as well as serial killers, bombers and rapists. He had enjoyed pitting his wits and skills against such people. But for over four years, Donaldson had not officially been on the streets, other than for occasional forays into the front line. Instead he had been ensconced in the American embassy in Grosvenor Square in London where he worked on the Legal Attaché Program, created to help foster goodwill and gain greater cooperation with international police partners. The FBI believes it is essential to station highly skilled special agents in countries other than America to help prevent terrorism and crime from reaching across borders and harming Americans in their homes and workplaces.

It was a wonderful job, very fulfilling and rewarding. Donaldson was settled, married to an English woman with two young children, and commuting every day into London from a little village in Hampshire called Hartley Wintney. He loved his work. He met many interesting people, got involved in many wide-ranging investigations which crossed international boundaries, but spent lots of time behind a desk, pushing paper.

In truth, he did miss working in the field. Sometimes he hankered for it so much it drove his wife, who was a police officer based at the Police Staff College in Bramshill, bananas.

So what he did to alleviate this hankering was get his hands dirty from time to time, though theoretically this was a no-no.

One of the tasks he had taken on, so as to keep himself as close as possible to the sharp end, was to coordinate the activities of undercover FBI field agents operating in Europe. The general public would have been surprised by the number of agents working across the continent, but following the terrible terrorist incidents in America, the FBI had become more pro-active in infiltrating terrorist organizations worldwide. But their work was not solely focused on the terrorist, they also had a number of agents in criminal gangs in Europe too.

Donaldson enjoyed his time briefing, debriefing and staying in contact with his agents. He thought they were fantastically brave people who, without exception, made light of the dangers they faced each and every day, without, of course, underestimating them.

There were currently four agents in organized criminal gangs and Donaldson had responsibility for all of them, including an agent whose code name was Zeke.

Donaldson was a big, burly guy. Six-three, fifteen stone but with not an ounce of excess fat on him. He kept himself fit by daily runs and gym visits three times a week, as well as expending an equal amount of energy chasing his two young sons round his garden and his wife round the bedroom.

He was standing by the window in his office, sipping water from a disposable conical paper cup, looking out across Grosvenor Square but his mind was not on the view.

He smiled absently at one of the secretaries

who walked past him. She was a very pretty English lady, secretly crazy about Donaldson, but his mind was not on her swaying ass.

Although no longer a field agent, Donaldson prided himself on the fact that his sharp instincts had not been blunted by desk work and sexual harassment from the staff. He knew he was as keen as ever in the brain department. Which is why, as he tossed the paper cup into the waste bin, he knew something was wrong.

Very wrong.

Henry was doing his best to avoid bumping into Jane Roscoe, although he knew it was inevitable they would soon come face to face. He resolved to tell her that their fling was over and that from now on the relationship would be purely professional and platonic. Yeah, he could do that. After all, it was only words, wasn't it? One of the best things that could happen to him was to be taken off the Blackpool jobs and given something else to deal with at the far end of the county which would consume him for about six months. A mass murder, or something. He found himself praying for something like this to happen on the Lancashire–Yorkshire border.

Back in the office, he logged into his e-mail and found that the intelligence unit had sent him details of Marty Cragg's convictions and the stories behind them. He printed them off and looked round, realizing that, in hindsight, it had been a mistake to share an office with Jane. He used his TETRA radio to contact Rik Dean to tell him he would be with him within quarter of

198

an hour.

Henry left quickly to avoid meeting Jane. He was running scared.

Karl Donaldson had worked with Zeke before when both had been field agents in Miami. Zeke's real name was Carlos Hiero. His parents had emigrated from Spain and settled in Florida in the early 1960s and had developed a fairly successful flower-selling business with about six shops dotted around the Miami/Fort Lauderdale area. They were not ultra-wealthy, but were well off and comfortable. On leaving university Zeke had become a lawyer, then joined the FBI at the age of twenty-six, when his Spanish origins meant he was used to great effect in combating Hispanic crime gangs.

He and Donaldson, although never working partners, had colluded closely on a number of cases with some good results.

Donaldson was back at his desk in the embassy, leafing through a mountain of paperwork which came with the job. His mind was not concentrating on what was in front of him. He checked his watch constantly and glanced at the mobile phone propped up on his desk. His eyes stopped at a photograph of his wife and two sons and he could not keep himself from grinning at them even though his mind was harbouring dark thoughts.

It was four days since he had heard from Zeke.

'You know, sometimes you can't please anybody,' DS Rik Dean said to Henry. 'I mean, we give 'em all the protection they can possible want, mollycoddle 'em and yet they still maintain they've nothing to tell us.'

The two men were standing outside Blackpool Victoria Hospital, near to the entrance to A&E. Henry had driven up from the police station and found Dean in a small private ward where the two shooting victims from McDonald's were being guarded by armed cops. Both men were now out of danger, medically speaking, but neither seemed to have any great desire to talk to the police, not surprising as they were deep in the mire themselves anyway.

'Doesn't really matter, though,' Dean was saying. 'Witnesses put them down as the instigators of the shoot-out and they just came off worst.' Dean shook his head. 'Blackpool, what a bloody place!'

'Yeah,' said Henry thoughtfully, 'in more ways than one.' He took a breath. 'One thing, though – keep them separated. Not only so they don't have contact with each other, but also so that they're not in the same place if anyone chooses to pay them a return match. It'll make it more difficult if they're apart from each other.'

'Good point,' said Dean. 'I'll sort that. For now they're under guard and as soon as the quacks say they're fit enough, we'll haul their backsides down to the station and start kicking their wounds.'

Henry laughed. 'Yeah, good.' He had no qualms about Rik Dean, trusting him to take care of business professionally. 'I've come about something else, actually.'

'Oh, what?'

'I told you I was investigating a cold case, reviewing the murder of that unidentified female in the flat in North Shore last year, remember?'

'How could I forget?'

'What d'you mean?'

'Nothing, nothing – you just don't forget murders, do you?'

'No, suppose not. Well, I've unearthed an interesting connection between that murder and the shooting down at King's Cross, I think.'

'Yeah?' Dean drawled, his eyes narrowed, wondering why Henry was sharing this with him.

'Thought I'd run it past you.'

'I'm intrigued.'

'You know there's a good chance the Cragg brothers are involved in that, yeah? I've been trawling through all the stuff we have on them both. Very little on Ray, he's a cool, very aware dude, but we've a bit more on Marty, much more volatile publicly, as you know. He got locked up for a bit of a fracas a few months ago outside the Palace.'

'I didn't know.' Dean still had no idea where this was going.

'Looking through the custody record I found an interesting connection, left there by mistake by Marty. I wondered if you had any observations on it.'

'And the connection is?'

'Jacqueline Burrows, aka Jack Burrows. You remember, the woman who owned the flats in which the girl was murdered?' Henry watched

Dean's face carefully. Last time he had mentioned Burrows' name to him, Dean had gone a white shade of pale. 'You took a statement from her, remember?'

'I recall,' Dean croaked. He was eyeing Henry suspiciously and once again had lost all colour. Henry could not fathom why. Dean tried to shrug off his discomfort. 'So what're you asking me?'

'Well, it might be something and nothing. I'm just chasing shadows, maybe – it's just that when Marty was arrested for the public order offence – which was for beating up a female, by the way – he was given his rights when he sobered up...' He did not complete what he was going to say. He did not know why, but he was playing Dean like a fish, for some reason.

'And...?' Dean almost demanded.

'When asked who he wished to be told of his arrest, he nominated Burrows.' Dean looked perplexed.

'An interesting connection, don't you think?'

'Fascinating.'

'I wondered if you'd come across that connection when you took that statement from her?'

'No.'

'Because the other interesting thing is that Marty has convictions on his record for beating up women.'

'Oh, right,' Dean said, nodding wisely. 'So if we'd known of the connection between him and her, he would've been worth a pull. Is that what you mean?' Henry nodded. 'No, never came up,' said Dean.

'Mm, okay... anyway, he's still worth a pull and when I get time, I'll be doing the pulling.' Henry drew his head back and looked down his nose at Dean, then leaned in close to him. 'I want you to know one thing, Rik: any time you want, you can come and have a chat with me, in confidence, about anything, because I've been a cop long enough to know one thing.'

'What's that?'

'I know when there's more going on than meets the eye.' He tapped his nose and left it at that.

Karl Donaldson had never worked undercover. Never wanted to. It took a special kind of person to do it, one with many qualities Donaldson knew he did not possess. Being undercover is not a glamorous job. It is often exciting in a sphincter-curdling way and it is always danger-ous because, every hour of every day, the life of an undercover agent is under threat. Donaldson, though a brave and courageous man, knew he could never live life like that. He did not mind putting in the necessary hours or days, but at the end of it he liked to be able to relax and forget about work.

An undercover agent could never do that because he or she could never be a hundred per cent certain they had not been grassed-up or their cover blown. At any time they could receive that fatal visit from a disgruntled felon, angry at having been taken in, deceived and cheated, and therefore determined to track down the person responsible for his downfall.

Donaldson had nothing but admiration for undercover agents. But he never wanted to be one.

Four days, he was thinking. Had not heard from Zeke in four days.

Keep calm, he instructed himself. There are no hard and fast rules about contact, but it was just so out of character for Zeke. He made some sort of contact each day, either by phone or text message. To go so long with nothing worried Donaldson.

Particularly in view of the job Zeke was doing at that moment, because he had taken the place of an undercover FBI agent who had been murdered.

'Are you harassing me? Do I need to call my solicitor? Or is this just a friendly, social visit?'

Jack Burrows stood resolutely at her front door, looking, Henry had to admit, very desirable indeed. She was dressed in a rather severe business suit, hair swept back into a tight ponytail, face made up expertly. She did not look as though she had ever been, or could be, an undertaker. She spoke lightly, with steel undertones.

'If asking a few questions about a murder committed on one of your properties is deemed to be harassment, then yes, I'm harassing you.' Henry smiled winningly.

She had been tense, but her shoulders relaxed.

'Come in,' she said, relenting, and led him into the lounge. 'What can I do for you?' She indicated for him to sit, which he did. She remained standing, affording Henry a great view of her long, tapering legs.

'Couple of things. Firstly, I haven't been able to trace Thomas Dinsdale yet, your ex-manager. I wonder if you could help?' He actually hadn't tried, but that wasn't the point.

'He left no forwarding address, but I'll see what I can do.'

'I really do need to speak to him,' Henry said, laying it on thick. 'I reckon he'll know more than he said. I'd like to sweat him a little.'

'Is that allowed these days? Interrogation?'

'I'll do it in the nicest possible way.' Henry's face indicated otherwise, bringing a glimmer of a smile to Burrows' lips.

'What else?'

'I'd like your permission to search the flat again.'

'Wasn't that done at the time?' Henry nodded. 'Surely there won't be anything to find – it's been so long. There can't be any value in another search.'

'I'll be the judge of that,' he said haughtily. 'I think it would be worth it, so I take it your permission is granted?'

She nodded, but not happily.

'Thanks. That's about it.' Henry stood up and headed for the door. Burrows followed him. He paused, turned and did his impression of Columbo. 'There is one more thing...'

'And that is?'

'What's your relationship with Marty Cragg?' he asked bluntly, going straight for the jugular. She shifted slightly as the question hit her, but stayed casual. Henry was impressed by her composure.

'I don't know any Marty Cragg.'

'How come he phoned you when he was in custody last year?'

She shook her head. 'You must be mistaken.'

Henry took a piece of paper from his jacket pocket and unfolded it. He read a telephone number out. 'That's yours, isn't it?'

'Yes.' Her face became tight and unpleasant.

'That was the number on the custody record with your name next to it. One hell of a mistake, wouldn't you say? Marty dictated the number to the custody sergeant.'

She remained silent and shook her head, shrugging innocently. Henry waited impassively, his hand resting on the inner door handle. He enjoyed these difficult silences and rarely broke them. He raised his eyebrows. Again she shook her head and would not be drawn to say anything. Henry admired her fortitude under pressure, but wondered why she was denying this relationship. For a split second it looked like she was about to say something, then she checked herself, coughed and said, 'No further comment.'

'Okay.' Henry relented, but only for that one word. 'Maybe next time we'll be talking into a tape recorder, eh?'

'I doubt it,' she responded crisply.

Henry turned the door handle as the pager on his belt bleeped. He pulled it off and read the scrolling display, then re-read it.

'Another murder?' Burrows asked brightly.

'No, just my wife telling me my dinner'll be in

the oven.' He opened the door. 'Oh, key for the flat?'

'The house manager has one. You can get it from the office in Hornby Road. I'll make sure he knows you're coming for it sometime. As far as I know, the flat is unoccupied at the moment.'

'You've been a great help,' he said, reverting to the lowest form of wit. 'No doubt we'll meet again soon.'

'Can't wait.' She closed the door behind him, then leaned on to it to stop herself falling over. 'Shit,' she breathed through clenched teeth.

In the Vectra, Henry switched his mobile phone on and called into the force control room as instructed by his pager message.

Burrows watched Henry surreptitiously through the living room window, then picked up her phone and called a number. It rang on, and on, until eventually that nice metallic lady on the answerphone service interrupted. Burrows ended the call and threw the cordless phone across the room, smashing it against the wall.

Karl Donaldson sat opposite his steely-eyed boss, Philippa Bottram, who headed the legation in London. He told her of his concerns about Zeke. She listened intently, very much aware that for Karl to be so bothered about anything meant that it was deadly serious.

She liked having him in her office. She was single, having divorced last year, living in a flat in London and she wished Donaldson would respond to her less than subtle approaches. So

207

far he had been a brick wall, but never took umbrage at her passes. She thought this was because such things like women throwing themselves at him was such an integral part of his life, him being such a goddam handsome SOB. Bottram despised Donaldson's wife and was madly jealous of her.

For his part, Donaldson was very wary of getting involved with his boss, even if he had been single and free. He had heard that Bottram batted for both sides and if he got involved with any woman, he wanted her to be all for him and none for her, as it were.

'I find it unusual and unsettling,' he was saying. 'Zeke is very good, very punctual and always makes back-up contact if he misses for any reason.'

'It's not rocket science, Karl. There could be any number of reasons for non-contact.'

'Yeah, it's just...'

'Gut instinct?'

'Something like that. I know it sounds a bit weak.'

'No, not where you're concerned.' She smiled seductively, something that was lost on Donaldson, who was far too deeply engrossed thinking about his undercover agent. He checked his watch. It was approaching midday. 'I'll give him another hour, then I make contact.'

It was a relief to Henry to be leaving the environs of Blackpool. It was as though he was leaving behind a world of chaos of which he had been the instigator. He was desperately trying not to get embroiled in another personal mess, but the thought of Jane Roscoe was starting to overpower him.

He wondered if he just liked falling in love. Was that what it was all about? The euphoric feeling of first love combined with lust? The feeling that disappeared with the solid routine of marriage?

He headed east along the M55, south on the M6 and came off at junction 29, the Bamber Bridge exit. At the first set of traffic lights he did a left towards Euxton and less than quarter of a mile down the road went under a motorway bridge and turned left into a car park; from here the Cuerden Valley Park could be accessed by cycle and on foot. He could not drive on to the car park because it had been cordoned off. He had to reverse back on to the road and find somewhere to park about quarter of a mile away. He did not mind the inconvenience.

It showed him that as much of the scene as possible was being preserved and it gave him the opportunity to saunter up, using his eyes, ears and nose to get a real sense of the place. The entrance to the car park was being strictly controlled by two uniformed PCs who logged every arrival and departure. Henry showed his ID and signed in. He was directed to another PC who was in charge of paper clothing. He doled out a paper suit and slip-over shoes to Henry, which he pulled on over his suit. He signed for these items.

Snazzily dressed, he looked across the car park to a cycleway which led to a footbridge spanning the M6, then into Cuerden Valley Park proper. Most of the police activity centred on the cycleway, just before the bridge. A support unit team was searching the car park itself, moving in a line, halting when something of interest was found, or when one of the officers cracked a joke and they all needed to laugh.

A route to the scene had been marked by cordon tape.

Henry began to walk along it slowly.

All he knew was that there had been a double murder. A shooting. Two bodies. Nothing more. He was happy with that because it gave him the opportunity to consider the scene without any preconceptions, although he had already begun to form ideas as soon as he began the walk to the centre of police activity.

Already he was assuming that the dead people had arrived by some sort of vehicular transport at the car park and from there been dumped on the path. Had they been killed here, or somewhere else?

'Morning, Henry – sorry, afternoon.' Detective Chief Superintendent Bernie Fleming broke away from a cluster of four local detectives and welcomed the newcomer.

'Hi, Bernie, what's the crack?'

A screen had been erected around the corpses, preventing onlookers from getting an eyeful and allowing the experts to work without interruption.

'Two dead men, both in their twenties, both shot in the back of the head.'

'Executed?'

'You could say that.'

Fleming belched, then broke wind. 'Sorry,' he said, 'too much of everything last night.'

'Any identification?'

Fleming shook his head. 'Not yet. Looks like an out of town job. Professional hit. We may struggle with this one.'

Henry opened his eyes wide in surprise. He made it a rule never to kick off a murder investigation by thinking he would have to struggle with it. If you think it, you do it, he believed.

'Can I have a look?'

'Be my guest.' Fleming made a sweeping gesture and Henry approached the screen, which reminded him of a beach windbreak. Behind it there was some concentrated activity going on, including the presence of the Home Office pathologist, Professor Baines, who looked up from his grisly task and smiled with great pleasure at Henry.

'Nice to see you again so soon.' He had been bent over, but stood up and backed away from what he was doing, giving Henry his first proper view. A scenes of crime photographer snapped away for the family album. 'Voilà!' said Baines.

Henry folded his arms.

Two bodies, both male, face down on the ground, one lying across the other. Both with massive head wounds to the base of the skull. Henry pouted as his experienced eyes clinically took in the horrific tableau.

'Both killed in the same manner. A gun placed to the base of the skull, angled upwards, shot through the brain, exit wounds through the

211

forehead. Very effective and instantaneous. They wouln't have suffered.'

'That's reassuring.'

A movement in the corner of his eye caused Henry to glance towards the car park. A hearse had been allowed to pull in. Two dark-suited individuals climbed out and chatted to a constable. They reclined on the long black vehicle, waiting for their turn in proceedings.

'Both killed in situ,' Baines said confidently.

'Not killed elsewhere and dumped here?'

'No – shot here.'

'Time of death?'

Baines guffawed, then shrugged. 'How long is a piece of string? You know as well as I do it would be an educated guess.'

'Guess then,' Henry prompted him.

'They've been here about ten hours, give or take a couple either side.'

'So anywhere between eight and twelve hours? Brilliant.'

'Fuck off, Henry.' Baines laughed. 'Shall we have a look at what's left of their faces?'

'Why not?'

The policy was that undercover agents always made contact with their controllers, not the other way around, unless in extenuating circumstances. This was sound common sense as a poorly thought out phone call from a worried controller could easily compromise an agent. That was why Karl Donaldson was reluctant to pick up the phone and call Zeke. He dithered over his phone's key pad, telling himself that there must be a very good reason for Zeke's lack of contact and all that he would do by contacting him would be to compromise him.

But four days was a long time. Too long.

'Right,' he said to himself. He dialled Zeke's number.

'Get this on video, please,' Baines instructed the SOCO. The officer prepared his camera, then nodded his readiness. Baines squatted down and took hold of the shoulder of the dead man who was lying on top of the other dead man. He supported the man's shattered head, then checked to see if everyone was ready. Henry was, Fleming was, the local DI was. 'Okay, I'm going to move this man now.' Gently he eased the man's shoulders back with one hand, held his head with the other and turned him slowly. The body rolled gently off and the face twisted up to the sky. The whole left side of the forehead had been blown away in a massive raggedy hole.

Henry breathed out, not realizing he had been holding on to a lungful of air.

'What a mess,' Fleming said for everyone. 'Any idea who it is?' he asked Henry and the local DI.

Both men peered to look.

'No,' said the DI

Henry froze. A mobile phone started to ring.

'Where is that?' the DI said.

'It's under this guy's leg,' Baines said. 'Someone want to get it?'

The two detectives looked at each other. Henry bent down and lifted up the dead man's leg and

213

found the phone. He picked it up carefully. The display read, 'Anonymous – answer?' He pressed okay and said, 'Hi?'

A voice he recognized immediately said, 'Is that you?'

'Yep,' he said shortly.

There was a silent moment, then the line went dead as the call ended.

'I wonder which one of these it belongs to?' the DI asked.

Henry did not answer. He looked at the murdered face of the dead man that Baines was propping up. Part of the left eye was missing. The right eye was open, sightless and blank. His mouth gaped, coagulated blood congealed around it and around his nostrils. Even so, Henry was in no doubt.

'Hello, Marty,' he said, 'long time, no see.'

Donaldson let the phone ring out until the answering service cut in, then hung up without leaving a message. He tried the number of another phone to which he knew Zeke had access and got the same result.

They stood back to allow Baines and the SOCO to carry out the necessary preliminary work on the body which had been lying under Marty Cragg. This gave Henry a little time to apply his mind to a crime scene assessment, consciously subjecting himself to a mental process of reconstructing what had happened. It was a disciplined process, concentrating on the various elements which constitute a crime scene – location, victim, offender, scene forensics, followed by post-mortem – and then considering the links between them. Though this was early in the enquiry, Henry knew he had to begin a good crime scene analysis because there was only ever one chance to do it.

He discussed the matter with the local DI and appointed him the Crime Scene Manager.

As Henry was telling the DI exactly what he wanted to happen, Baines looked up from his task and called, 'You can come closer now.'

Henry finished what he was saying and walked over.

'I'm going to turn this man over,' he said and nodded to the SOCO, who was ready with the video camera for take two. Henry watched, wondering if he would recognize the second victim. But he did not. Nor did the DI, nor did Fleming.

'They were both murdered here, I'm sure of that,' the pathologist reconfirmed. 'This man first' – he indicated the body he had just turned over – 'then this one.' He jerked his thumb at Marty. 'Both killed the same way, gun to the back of the neck, etcetera, etcetera.'

Although Henry was pleased that one of the victims had been identified quickly, giving him an immediate starting point, he had a feeling in the pit of his stomach that this shooting was intertwined, somehow, with recent events in Blackpool. There had to be a connection. It smacked of gangland. It stank of professionalism. It meant he would be working very long hours for the foreseeable future and it also meant, on a personal note, he would be going

215

back to Blackpool and, ultimately, Jane Roscoe.

Fucking tangled web, he thought, then turned his mind to more pressing matters.

Why here? Why was one man killed before the other? Was there a reason for the order of their deaths?

'DCI Christie!' Someone was shouting his name from the car park – a uniformed PC who clearly did not want to approach the scene. He eagerly beckoned Henry to come to him. Henry obliged.

'Sir, I'm PC Garry from Bamber Bridge.'

'Yeah?'

'Just been to a job at the Premier Lodge near to Sainsbury's. I think it's connected with this.'

'I was, like, shell-shocked,' the man said defensively. 'I didn't know what to do.'

'If you'd phoned the police at the time, they could have advised you one way or the other,' Henry told the Premier Lodge night porter, deciding whether or not to let the man off the hook. As far as Henry was concerned, the man had not performed his duty by phoning the police immediately. If he had, he might have saved a life. 'Four armed and masked men abduct one of your guests, then return twenty minutes later to revisit the room...' Henry's voice trailed off.

'He wasn't a guest,' the night porter bleated, 'he was visiting a couple who were in the room.'

'You should have called us.' Henry was going to lay it on thicker than butter, then thought better of it. It was plain that the night porter

216

wasn't the brightest star in the constellation and that he was petrified and very tired. Henry relented. 'We need to speak to you in detail about what happened, before you go to bed, if possible.'

'Why, has something else happened?'

'Yes.' Henry nodded, but did not elaborate. 'I want details of the couple who were in the room.' He glanced hopefully at the duty manager.

They were crammed into a small office behind reception, Henry, PC Garry, the night porter and the duty manager, a Mr Bendix – who had been the one who had called the police on behalf of the reluctant night porter.

'We only have details of the male guest. Here.' Bendix handed Henry the reservation form filled in on arrival. He snorted when he saw the name, John Smith, and tutted when he read that it had been a cash transaction, and that no vehicle details were recorded.

'Has the room been cleaned yet?'

'No – I told the ladies to hang fire with that one.'

Henry turned to the PC. 'Get up there now and don't let anyone in. I'll arrange for a team to come and dust the place.'

The PC stood up and left.

'Okay,' Henry said, rubbing his hands. 'I need you to be interviewed and I'd also like to get a statement from the receptionist who booked the couple in. We'll need a good description of them. They could be a key to this incident.'

'Do you think this has anything to do with the

bodies discovered near to the park?' the manager asked.

'How do you know about that?'

'Radio Lancashire.'

Exasperated, Henry stood up and pointed at the night porter. 'You stay here. Someone'll be along very soon to speak to you. If you need a kip, use one of the rooms.'

Only when he was satisfied that everything had been done correctly at the scene did Henry finally allow the two bodies to be conveyed to the mortuary at Chorley. He followed the hearse and its body-bagged contents all the way so as to ensure continuity of evidence. He was already thinking of the possible future court case, even at this early stage. All bases had to be covered from the word go because he knew that defence lawyers would systematically try to tear the prosecution evidence to pieces. It was his job, as SIO, to put together a case which was built on solid foundations, which included the simple things that are often forgotten in the aftermath of a spectacular death and which are often the chink in the armour of a good case.

The bodies went to the mortuary at Chorley hospital, deposited side by side on metal trolleys. Henry stayed while all their clothing was removed, listed and bagged up by a local DC.

Marty Cragg had some ID on him: a driving licence and credit card; his wallet contained £135 in assorted notes. Henry included the mobile phone in Marty's property. It was an Orange, pay-as-you-go type. Henry checked it carefully to see what the last ten calls made and received were. It revealed nothing, nor did its phone book, which was empty. Henry was not surprised.

Once the corpse had been stripped, Henry inspected Marty for anything more unusual than gunshot wounds. All he could see was an old scald mark on his right forearm. He thought nothing of this and slid him into a fridge.

Henry supervised the stripping of the second, unknown man. He had nothing on him to ID him, which Henry found peculiar. It was as though the man travelled incognito, unless he had been made to hand over all forms of identity before being blasted.

Once stripped, the unknown man was finger-printed and photographed, then slid into the fridge alongside Marty.

The post-mortems were scheduled to start at seven that evening and Henry wanted to be there for them if possible. First, he had to do some more mundane things, such as contact the coroner, arrange resources – if any – and get a murder investigation up and running. And there was something else he wanted to do, too.

Ten

Henry was back in Blackpool within the hour, pushing the police Vectra hard and fast, braking dramatically at each roadside speed camera, crawling through at the required speed and then hitting the gas once he was beyond the white markers. It was an advantage being a cop who travelled around the whole of the county: you got to know where each and every speed trap was.

He hurried to Jane's office, knocked and entered without waiting for a reply. She was going through some paperwork with Rik Dean.

'Need to speak,' Henry said briskly, noting her big smile on seeing him.

'Okay, Rik, we'll finish this later.' She handed the detective a binder. He stood up and left, nodding warily to Henry as the two men passed one another. Henry closed the office door. Jane stayed seated at the desk, resting her chin on her forefinger. 'Have you been trying to avoid me, Henry?' she asked reproachfully.

'Naah.' He dismissed the notion with a wave of the hand. 'Just dead busy.'

'Right,' she said, drawing out the word. 'Okay.' She was not satisfied but realized from the tone of his voice that the subject was going no further ... yet. 'What do you want?' Her voice had an icy edge to it now.

Henry sat down opposite and explained what he had actually been doing that day. Roscoe listened intently, the personal baggage stored away for the time being.

He kept the juicy news until the very last.

'Whuh!' she said. 'Marty Cragg? You sure?'

He nodded. 'I'm good at identifying dead bodies.'

'So Marty Cragg is dead? We were just beginning to think that he and his brother, Ray, were responsible for the King's Cross shootings, weren't we? Are we into some turf war, or something?'

'Could be.' Henry squinted at the thought of it. The only thing that did not sit straight with him about this possibility was the incident at the Premier Lodge. What was all that about? And who was the unknown body? What was that connection?

'I think it is a turf war,' Jane said forcefully, 'because something else has turned up which is pretty interesting – that's why Rik was in here. The shooting incident at McDonald's?' Henry nodded he knew what she was talking about. 'The two guys in the hospital are running partners with another couple of Manchester low-lifes who were found shotgun blasted in a flooded quarry just over the border. The two in hospital could have come looking for retribution. Maybe they had something to do with Marty's death?'

'Not them personally, because the time frame

221

doesn't fit. They were definitely in hospital, under guard, when Marty got whacked, but their other connections could have done Marty and the unidentified guy. We need to get close with Greater Manchester on this, I suspect.' Henry checked his watch. 'I need to get a move on. The PMs will start soon. How are you fixed to deliver a death message?'

Evening was fast approaching as Henry and Jane drove out to see Ray Cragg at his detached house in Poulton-le-Fylde. It was going to be a cold night and a bitter wind gusted over the incoming tide.

They rode silently, but there was a palpable and electric tension between them. Henry could tell she wanted to talk. She could tell he wanted to avoid it. Eventually she could stand it no more.

'Are we going to discuss us?' she blurted.

Us? Oh shit! Henry thought. 'I'm lost for words,' he said.

'I'm not. Just tell me if what we did was a big mistake. If it was I'll pull up my bloomers and get on with things. If it wasn't a mistake, I'd like to know.'

Henry's heart thudded noisily, his mouth went dry.

'Er, I enjoyed it ... no regrets there,' he said feebly.

Roscoe's eyes burned like lasers into his temple. He really could feel their heat.

'Right,' she said, tearing them away and folding her arms. 'I get the message. How many people have you bragged to that you've shagged me?'

'Hey, look,' he began to protest just as he caught sight of a car with four dark shapes on board, pulled into the kerbside. They were just a couple of turnings away from the avenue in Poulton on which Ray resided. 'Interesting,' he said, smoothly changing the subject. He slowed and clocked the registration number.

'Yeah, sure,' said Roscoe.

'No – that car,' he said.

She saw it too and it aroused her cop instincts. 'Four up,' she noted.

Moments later they were outside Ray's house. Henry pulled his nearside wheels on to the grass verge which formed part of Ray's front garden. Lights were on in the house, the curtains drawn.

'Looks like a normal house,' remarked Roscoe.

'Mmm, not much protection evident – double bluff. C' mon, let's see if his lordship is in.'

They were in luck. Ray himself answered the door, beer in hand, looking slovenly. Henry shoved his warrant card and badge up into his face and introduced himself and asked to come in. He stepped over the threshold.

'Get the fuck back,' Cragg said, holding the door. 'If you've got a warrant, you can come in, otherwise we do business here. This is my family home.'

'Ray, this is a personal matter, best dealt with inside,' Henry cooed. 'I promise not to go through any of your drawers, but you really should let us in.' Henry peered past Ray's shoulder and saw someone in the kitchen. 'We need a heart to heart – seriously.'

Ray relented. 'Make it quick.'

He led Henry through to the lounge. There was a huge TV in one corner, surrounded by equally huge speakers. The cartoon channel was on, that very famous canine detective Hong Kong Phooey was strutting his stuff. One person was watching TV. Henry recognized him immediately as Julian Brindle, otherwise known as Crazy or JCB. Crazy shifted uncomfortably.

'What is it? Do I need my brief?' Ray wanted to know.

'You people – now why should you need a solicitor?' Jane Roscoe said. 'Been a bad boy?'

Crazy sat upright, a cautious expression on his face. Henry saw him swallowing repeatedly, a nervous gesture.

Ray licked his lips.

Henry found himself in a quandary. He felt an urge to do some verbal jousting with Cragg, just to get a feel for the man, to sound him out and play with him, and to get him worried. On the other hand his brother was lying on a mortuary slab with a bullet having entered and exited his brain and probably a couple of others still in there. Henry's main concern should have been to deliver the message and deal with Ray as a grieving relative. Against all his natural instinct, Henry plumped for the latter approach. He guessed it would not be long before he was doing the former anyway – glaring at each other across an interview room table with a tape recorder between them.

'Is your mother in?' he asked Ray.

'No, why?'

'Where is she and when will she be back?'

'Why, what's this about? Why do you want to speak to my mum?'

'Ray, would you like to take a seat?' Jane said. 'I'm afraid we have some bad news.'

Puzzled, but still wary of two cops in his house, Ray sat down and Jane Roscoe sat next to him, giving him one of her best and most professional funeral looks.

'It's about Marty,' she began softly and informed him gently but fairly bluntly so that he would be under no misapprehension that his half-brother had been murdered. As she finished, there was an unworldly wail from the kitchen. Henry stepped out of the lounge and spun into the kitchen where he found Jack Burrows collapsed in a ragged heap on the wooden floor, head buried in her hands, just on the verge of hyperventilation.

The car with four dark shapes on board was still there when they drove away from Ray Cragg's house. Henry clocked the registration number again to reinforce his memory for later checking on the Police National Computer.

Behind him Ray Cragg was being driven by Crazy, accompanied by Burrows in a BMW which had been in the garage attached to Ray's house.

In convoy they headed to the M55.

'How do you think he took it?' Henry asked Jane.

225

'Didn't actually seem too concerned. More annoyed than anything, especially when he told us he didn't want a family liaison officer attached to him.'

'Yes, I got that impression.'

'However, Jack Burrows was just a bit the opposite. A bit strange considering that she appears to be Ray's bit of fluff. Unless...'

'Well, I didn't know she was Ray's girlfriend until now, because she'd denied any knowledge of the Craggs to me, but I'm pretty sure she was seeing Marty on the side.'

'Fact or fantasy?'

'Something I've unearthed.' Henry explained the custody records and Burrows' reaction to his questions about Marty.

'Do you think there is anything to suggest that Ray might have killed Marty? Could he have found out about the liaison and got a teeny bit jealous?'

'I won't rule it out, but I think it's unlikely.' Henry relaxed into his driving as he joined the motorway, taking the Vectra up to a steady seventy, ensuring the car behind stayed in touch. 'What have we got here?' he mused. 'Fill me in. Speculate.'

'I'd love to fill you in,' she responded.

'About the job, not personally,' he said hastily.

'Okay.' She marshalled her thoughts. 'Johnny Jacques and his girlfriend, both dead. Johnny worked as a messenger boy for Ray and could have been ripping him off. Next we have three drug dealers shot to death on the same day at the King's Cross by two masked gunmen and one

226

getaway driver. The drug dealers are known to have been poaching on Ray's territory. Two bodies are then found dumped in a quarry in Manchester and their two mates show up in Blackpool and order more than a double cheese-burger from McDonald's. And finally, poor old Marty gets shot, together with a John Doe, as they say in America.'

'And there's also the cold case I'm investigating?' Jane nodded. 'Which has Jackie Burrows' connections, who is sleeping with Ray and Marty, but not with Marty any more because he'll never get an erection again ... and Ray does not seem too upset that his brother is dead meat.'

'But Jack Burrows is.'

'And maybe therein lies a way in to Ray Cragg.' He looked at Roscoe and raised his eyebrows. 'You thinking what I'm thinking?'

'She could be a chink in Ray's armour.'

Eleven

Crazy drove away from the mortuary, concentrating on the road ahead, his hands gripping the wheel tightly. Ray sat next to him, staring frozenly through the windscreen, teeth grinding, jaw pumping.

It was not far to the motorway and soon they were speeding north up the M6. It was only as the speedo touched seventy that Ray inhaled deeply, then slowly swivelled his head round like something from a horror film and looked at Jack Burrows in the back seat. Initially, she did not know she was being stared at. Her eyes were fixed on her knees and her tightly interlocked fingers on her lap. She slowly became aware that Ray was looking at her and raised tear-stained eyes to his. She swallowed when she saw the expression on his face, the sneer of his lips, the red of his eyes.

'What was all that shit about?' he whispered loud enough so she could hear above the drone of the engine.

She shook her head slightly and frowned. 'All what shit?'

'All that fucking weeping and wailing and gnashing of teeth. Why?'

'He's your brother. The news upset me.' She

228

folded her arms.

Ray glared at her then twisted forwards. 'When I get back I need a chat with you and Miller. That bastard Dix must have done this. I want him hunted down like a dog. I want him dead and I want my money back, but most of all, I want my money back.'

There was a second interior rear-view mirror for use by front-seat passengers. Ray adjusted it so he could see Burrows. His mean face was tight and ferret-like as he watched her.

'It'd be a pleasure,' said Crazy. 'He won't take too much finding.'

'Good.' Ray continued to watch Burrows. 'OTT,' he said.

'Eh?' said Crazy.

'I'm talking to that bitch in the back – so over the top. How come? I want to know how come.'

'I don't know what you're getting at,' she said. 'He was your brother and I liked him, that's all. The news has upset me, but it obviously hasn't upset you.'

'I want to know why,' he insisted.

They had reached junction 32. Crazy peeled off on to the M55. The road was quiet and he was making good progress.

'Give me your mobile phone.' Ray held out his hand to Burrows.

'I haven't got it with me.'

'Yes you have, now give it to me.'

'Why?'

'Jack, just give it to me or I'll climb over these seats and lace you.'

Her shaking hand reached into her shoulder

229

bag. She handed the phone to Ray, who switched it on and waited for it to connect. Then he went straight into the record of the last ten calls she had made. He stared at the display and snorted. 'Why have you been calling him?'

She closed her eyes and dropped her chin. 'To talk,' she said meekly.

'What about?'

'Oh just things ... nothing really.'

'You have never had any reason to call him, Jack.' Ray released his seat belt and fed it slowly back on to the inertia reel. 'No reason at all.' He lowered his voice and said, 'Keep driving,' to Crazy.

Suddenly he spun out of his seat, found a foothold on the dash board and propelled himself back through the gap in the seats and hit Burrows hard across the side of the face with the phone, knocking her head against the side window. Then he was on top of her. He discarded the phone and set about her, pummelling her with his fists, slapping her, grabbing her hair and smacking her head against the door frame, while under his breath he growled the word, 'Bitch, bitch, bitch,' with each blow.

In front, Crazy concentrated on keeping the car in a straight line while at the same time enjoying watching the action behind through his appropriately adjusted rear-view mirror.

Crazy pulled on to the driveway outside Ray's house. He killed the engine and lights. Ray climbed out of the back seat and stood to one side while Burrows crawled out, her face a battered and bleeding red pulp. She tried to stand, but her legs were weak and would not take her weight. She staggered against the car, sucking desperately for breath through her bloody nose and cut lip.

Ray watched her coldly, not attempting to assist her.

'Get in the house,' he said.

She held on to the car, smearing blood across the roof. 'Can't.'

Ray drove his fist into the small of her back, punching her kidneys as hard as he could. She emitted a long moan of pain and sank to her knees. Ray picked her up by the collar and threw her to the ground, stamping on her head.

'Shit, boss,' Crazy intervened. 'Not here, not in public.'

Cragg was breathing heavily, the look on his face murderous, but he saw the wisdom of Crazy's words.

'Drag her in and dump her in a bedroom.'

Henry and Jane had stayed for the post-mortems after Ray had formally identified his brother. Both detectives had carefully watched his reaction. Ray had been icy and clinical, showing no emotion whatsoever. They had accompanied him back to his car, which he had got into, and nodded at both occupants. Crazy was as impassive as Ray, but Burrows was deeply affected by the fact that Marty was a goner.

Henry leaned into the car and told Ray that a detective would be calling round to see him to obtain a statement regarding the identification. Some time later, Henry would also want to interview Ray himself to get more information about Marty, his movements, friends, acquaintances and bad habits. Ray did not seem too pleased by this news and Henry already knew that very little would be forthcoming from that particular conversation.

The post-mortems were long and detailed, carried out thoroughly and painstakingly by Professor Baines.

It was 1 a.m. when Henry and Roscoe landed back at Blackpool.

He dropped her off and drove straight home. He saw her in his rear-view mirror, watching him leave.

'Bugger,' he said and kept going.

Henry was exhausted when he reached home, but even so he took a little time in the front room, accompanied by a large Jack Daniel's to review the day he'd had and to plan for the forthcoming one. He was glad to be up to his neck in work and, for the first time in a long time, was thriving on it. There was much to do and he knew he would have little time to sleep. That did not bother him too much. The coffee and adrenaline of concurrent murder enquiries would keep him going in the early stages and it was imperative to pull a cohesive plan together or things would go off half-cocked and he would just get confused.

With paper and pen, he started to jot a 'To Do' list under five separate headings.

1. Cold Case
   - search flat again (maybe support unit to do)
   - find ex-house manager
   - annoy Jack Burrows. What is it with her and the Cragg bros?

2. JJ & Carrie
   - see informant again
   - forensics

3. King's Cross
   - liaise with Jane?!

4. Marty/unknown
   - search Marty's house
   - stmt from Ray
   - annoy Burrows
   - forensics from hotel room
   - circulate details of 'unknown'
   - four in a car

5. McDonald's...

That was as far as he got before his eyelids started to droop. He heard movement upstairs and thought someone was going to the toilet, then there were quiet footsteps on the stairs and a sleepy Kate appeared at the living-room door. She rubbed her eyes. She was wrapped in a less than alluring dressing gown. Her short hair as awry and there were tramlines across her face from where she had been lying on pillows. Henry stifled a gasp. She looked damned wonderful.

'Hi,' she croaked with a crooked smile.

'Hello, gorgeous.'

'You busy?'

'Yeah – ish.'

She was wearing big teddy-bear slippers, which she dragged across the floor, stopping in front of Henry. She bent down, picked up his pad and pen and pretended to read his notes. 'Um – very interesting.' She dropped them on to the coffee table before dropping herself into his lap and winding her arms around his neck. She smelled wonderful and musty. Henry had to catch his breath, especially when the dressing gown fell open to reveal one perfectly formed breast and one hard little nipple.

'God, I love you,' she said. 'I don't know why, I just do.'

'And I love you,' he admitted honestly for the first time in a long time.

She gently took hold of his face and kissed him, long, slow, warm, wet. She had amazing lips.

'I know it's late,' she said, snuggling her face into his neck, 'but how do you fancy making love?'

There was no doubt that his body, though exhausted, wanted to oblige.

'Here?' he asked.

'Mm,' she breathed from deep in her throat, 'right here, right now.'

Henry pushed her gown off her shoulders and ran his hands across her soft, white skin. He knew he was where he belonged.

They were waiting for Miller to arrive, sitting in the living room of Ray's house. Crazy was smoking one of his thin roll-ups and sipping a beer. Ray was staring at the porn channel on satellite TV, the sound turned low. He had a bottle of Stella in his hand.

'I just don't see Dix doing that,' Crazy ventured reasonably. 'He doesn't have it in him, doesn't have the bottle.'

'He had the bottle to nick my money.'

'That was just a spur of the moment thing.' Ray shot Crazy a hard look and Crazy raised his hands defensively. 'I'm not defending the cunt. I'm just saying that he probably wouldn't do something like that.'

'He was a good taxman. He put guns to a lot of people's heads. I think he had it in him. I think Marty found him and Dix popped him.'

'So who's the other guy? It doesn't make sense. Dix shooting two people – naah.'

'I don't know who he was, and I don't care,' spat Ray. 'All I know is that silly twat of a half-brother of mine's been whacked and my money is still missing. As I said, I'm not so much fussed about Marty. It's my money I want back.'

'What about your mum?' Crazy asked.

Ray shrugged. 'I'll tell her whenever she lands back. Haven't got a clue where she is and I'm not going out looking for her.'

'Fine,' said Crazy.

There was a knock on the door.

'That'll be Miller.' Crazy stood up. He did not

look out of the window to check. He should have done.

Jack Burrows knelt at the top of the stairs in the darkness, a wet towel pressed to her face, still trying to stem the blood oozing out of her mouth and nose. Her right eye was swollen and closing rapidly. Her whole body ached. There was a pounding noise in her ears, but she was still capable of hearing the conversation between Ray and Crazy in the lounge.

When the knock came at the door, she pushed herself deeper into the darkness, but maintained a position where she could see Crazy opening the door.

'Ray,' Crazy said from the living-room door.

Cragg was engrossed in a screen image of a man being given a blow job by a blonde with huge breasts.

'What?' he said, annoyed.

'It's not Miller.' Crazy's voice sounded strangely strained.

Ray tutted and glanced round, his head fixing into position.

Crazy was at the door, an expression of terror across his face because a man was holding a gun screwed into his side. The beer fell from Ray's hands on to the carpet where it spilt.

On the TV screen, the fortunate man ejaculated over the blonde's face and neck.

Ray and Crazy knelt side by side. Their faces were pressed into the settee. Their hands were bound behind their backs by plastic handcuffs which dug deep into their wrists. They both had the muzzle of a pistol skewered into the base of their skulls, held there in place by two men dressed in dark clothing.

A third man, similarly dressed, came into the room and spoke to a fourth man, who was sitting in Ray's chair.

'All clear,' he said.

'Where is the woman?' the fourth man asked.

Neither Ray nor Crazy answered. To encourage speech, the guns were pressed harder and twisted tighter into their necks.

'She's gone,' Ray said, his voice muffled.

'Why is her car still here?'

'Got a taxi,' Crazy said quickly. 'She'd been drinking. Couldn't drive home.'

'What's going on?' Ray demanded. 'You're gonna fuckin' regret this.'

'Yes, I'm sure I am,' said the fourth man. 'The guns are pointed at your heads, don't forget that, Mr Cragg.'

'What do you want?'

'My name is Mendoza,' the fourth man said. 'Have you heard of me?'

'Should I have?'

'Your brother has been doing business with me for over a year, maybe you should have heard of me.'

'Who, Marty? Doing business? He's a fucking useless businessman, or was.'

'Exactly, and that is why I am here. He kept taking credit from me and never paying me back. You are right, he is not good with money – not like you, I understand.'

'Fuck all to do with me,' Ray insisted. 'I don't know anything about it.'

'Be that as it may,' Mendoza said. 'I called in the debt and decided enough is enough. He had to pay with his life.'

'So the debt's settled,' Ray said quickly.

'No, it has been passed on to his next of kin. That is the way things are in my country.'

'I don't know fuck all about it, so it's nothing to do with me. I'm not his fucking keeper.'

'Sorry. You now own all the debt.'

'How much? Just curious, because whatever it is, you can fuck off. I am not paying.'

'With interest, two hundred thousand pounds, sterling.'

'You gotta be joking!' Ray squirmed. His head was forced back down by the man with the gun.

'No joke,' said Mendoza. 'You now own the debt, Mr Cragg. I know you have the funds to pay it. You have one week to do so, otherwise – you've seen what happened to your brother. The same will happen to you.'

Miller arrived ten minutes later. His senses told him there was something amiss. Something in the air, something about the stillness. Too many tours across the water had sharpened him too much, he thought. I'm always too damned cautious. He drove past Ray's house, noting that the front door was slightly ajar, the lights on throughout. He smelt danger, but did not know why. He drove into the next cul-de-sac and parked his car, walking back slowly through the shadows. He watched Ray's house from a distance and edged closer. His gun was in his hands, in a two-handed combat grip.

It took five minutes to reach the drive, then creep to the front door, flattening himself against the wall, listening, sniffing, breathing shallowly. He moved stealthily to the door and pushed it with his toecap and stepped into the wide hallway.

Voices.

With a shake of the body he relaxed. It was Ray and Crazy talking in the kitchen. Miller kept his gun down by his side and walked to the kitchen door, which he pushed open.

Ray and Crazy turned to stare at him. They were standing back to back, their wrists still cuffed. Crazy had a bread knife in his hand and was attempting to saw through Ray's plastic cuffs without slicing his boss up.

He stopped when he saw Miller.

'Get these fucking things off me,' Ray said to Miller, and twisted to show him the cuffs.

Miller laid his gun on the kitchen table, glad his senses had pre-warned him of something wrong at the house. 'What's gone on?' he asked. He took the knife from Crazy's hand and placed it on a work surface. He opened a drawer, found a pair of kitchen scissors and snipped the cuffs off. 'Some perverted game gone wrong?'

Ray scowled and pushed past him, bounding up the stairs, calling out Burrows' name, angry that she had not come down at his calling. He found her huddled in the cistern cupboard, wedged behind the tank, covered by several bath towels. It was a good hiding place.

Twelve

Professor Baines crossed one of his spindly legs over the other and smiled at Henry and Jane Roscoe. 'As you know I am an expert in many fields where the dead body is concerned, and sometimes even living bodies.' He looked from Henry to Jane and gave a knowing smile and a double raise of the eyebrows. Neither of the two allowed their expressions to change. There was a distinct chill between them that morning.

They were in Jane's office – formerly Henry's – discussing the post-mortem findings with Baines, who had been up much of the night pulling everything together. This, however, did not stop him being bright, bubbly and full of mischief. Even so, when the faces of the two detectives did not alter, he cleared his throat uncomfortably and crossed his legs in the opposite direction.

'It's the dead bodies we're bothered about,' Jane Roscoe said stonily.

'Yes, well – so may I come to the unidentified body of the male?'

'You may,' said Henry.

'Killed in exactly the same way as the unfortunate Mr Cragg. Massive brain damage being the cause of death – in layman's terms,

240

that is.'

Henry glanced down at a set of SOCO glossies of the dead man on the slab, taken before Baines had got to work on him. Henry thought the man had been fairly handsome in a Mediterranean kind of way and it was obvious from his physique that he had been a fairly fit guy in life. No extra fat on him, muscles well developed, even a six-pack gut.

'I was fortunate enough to go to a pathologists' convention in Miami at the tail-end of last year,' Baines said enthusiastically.

'Bet that was a hoot.' Henry grinned.

'It was – actually,' Baines said, slighted slightly. 'Anyway, there was a very interesting session on dental records, fascinating, actually.' He gave Henry a quick smile.

'Something to get your teeth into?' Henry quipped. Even Jane smiled.

'Part of the session,' Baines proceeded, ignoring Henry, 'was dentistry from around the world. It's absolutely fascinating how much difference there is between countries and how stereotypical dental work can be in particular countries. They all have their own way of doing things. I had a very good look inside the mouth of our unknown victim and he'd had some bridgework done. I would say, from my bridgework spotter's guide – yes, it does exist – that the work was done in America. That's not to say he's an American, though his appearance could be classed as Hispanic, but it could assist you in identifying him.'

'Nice one, Prof,' Henry said.

241

* * *

One of the problems in being a nomad investigator, going out to divisions all the time, was that you always had to find office space to make phone calls, or to get some sleep. It really was like being a nomad in some ways. Henry managed to find an empty office and slid in behind the desk into a big, comfy chair. He leafed through his pocket diary, found the number he needed, swung his ankles up on to the edge of the desk and picked up the phone. He punched in the number. And waited for the reply.

'FBI Legal Attaché Karl Donaldson speaking. How may I help you?'

'I wish we could get our bloody employees to answer phones like that,' Henry said.

Donaldson recognized the voice immediately. 'Henry! You wearin' your cloth cap and clogs?'

'I am that, lad,' he replied, dropping into his best broad Lancashire. 'Eeh, look, I can see a red London bus drivin' past and I can 'ear Big Ben chimin' away – an' look over yonder, it's a London copper rockin' up an' dahn on his toes.'

Donaldson chuckled. 'Actually I can see a London bus, but there are no coppers about these days.'

He and Henry had met several years earlier on a case Donaldson was dealing with in the northwest, when he was a field agent, concerning Mafia activities. Since then they had worked together on several occasions and had become very close friends, though they had not spoken to each other for a couple of months now. They exchanged a few pleasantries, gossiped about families and proposed holidays, then the American cut to the chase.

'You only call me when you need me, H. What is it this time?'

Henry explained about the double murder with one unidentified victim with the mouthful of American-style dental work. 'I was wondering...' he said hopefully.

'Fast track? Sure, why not? What have you got?'

'Description, photographs of dead person – not nice – fingerprints, dental observations. We're waiting for a DNA profile.'

'Fax 'em down and I'll put them through our system as soon as I get 'em.'

'Thanks, pal. They're on their way.' From his experience of life, Henry knew it wasn't what you know but who you know that gets results.

It was good to have such a direct and personal connection into American law enforcement. It gave Henry access to FBI computers, albeit unofficially. His relationship with Donaldson, though well known in the higher ranks of Lancashire Constabulary, was not something he boasted about. He kept it to himself, knowledge being power.

He sat back and literally twiddled his thumbs, impatient already for a result from the information he had sent to Donaldson. 'Get a grip,' he told himself. 'Even a fast track will take time.'

He riffled through his pockets and found a folded piece of paper from a jotting pad. He opened it and flattened it out. It was his 'To Do' list written with the splendid assistance of Mr Jack Daniels. One thing that sprang out that he could have done before was the item 'four in a car'. The suspicious motor he had seen near to Ray Cragg's home with four people on board. He dialled the PNC bureau and requested a check on the number he had committed to memory. The reply came back within seconds. Henry closed his eyes in despair. He sighed and kicked himself.

The car had been stolen from London two days earlier. The cop in him was extremely pissed off at having missed the opportunity to make an arrest. But more than that was the question burning in his mind: what was it doing there, within yards of one of the country's biggest drug dealers? With four shady characters on board? What were they up to? Did it have anything to do with Marty Cragg's untimely demise?

As soon as he had finished the call from Henry, the internal phone on Donaldson's desk rang and he was summoned into Philippa Bottram's office to discuss the progress of a case being run jointly with the Metropolitan Police. As the American left his office he heard his fax machine start up and much as he would have liked to wait for it to spew out the stuff from Henry Christie, he did not wish to incur his boss's ire. With a 'Damn' under his breath he closed the door behind him and strode to her office down the corridor for what he knew would be a long meeting.

'Just give me a break,' Jack Burrows pleaded.

Ray had been questioning her incessantly for over an hour, insisting she tell him exactly what Marty had been up to on the side to get himself into so much trouble and debt. 'I don't know, okay?'

'You were fucking him.'

'No, I was not,' she said. 'We were friends, that's all. I'm with you, Ray. You're my partner, not him. He never was, we just talked.'

'Just talked? Just fucked, more like.'

Ray was beginning to steam up now. Burrows could see him starting to bubble and she knew she needed him calm. Otherwise she would be facing another beating and she wasn't strong enough to maintain her lies. If he laid into her again, she would be unable to keep going and she was frightened that if she blabbed the truth about her and Marty she would end up as dead as him.

'We never fucked,' she said. 'Never.'

An hour later and Henry still had not received any reply from London. Not that he expected a result but an acknowledgement that the faxed papers had been received would have been nice. He had spent the hour reviewing paperwork, so it had not been wasted, but he was eager to hear from his American chum because it would mean that something was actually being done to identify the unknown male. Henry knew that unless he could put a name to a face, this murder investigation might stall at the first bend. He needed to know quickly who the guy was. He almost picked up the phone to castigate the

Yank, but thought better of it.

Instead he plumped for a trip to the canteen, although he was slightly reluctant to leave the quiet office he had discovered just in case he lost squatter's rights.

Donaldson shook hands with the Metropolitan Police Commander, who had been a major player in the meeting which concerned Yardie activities linked to a Colombian drug cartel, linked to organized crime in Miami – hence the American involvement – and showed him to the elevator. Once he stepped in and was on his way down, Donaldson returned to Bottram's office.

She was leaning back in her chair, waiting for him, tapping her pen on her desk top. Her breasts were pushed up tight against her blouse.

'Worthwhile?' she asked as he took his seat.

'Certainly promising,' Donaldson concurred. 'We'll all come out of it smelling of roses, I'd guess.'

'Mm.' She eyed him less than professionally. 'Can you stay in the city tonight, Karl?'

His eyes grew wide.

'Business,' she said quickly. Too quickly. 'Need you to meet the new Foreign Secretary. There's a bit of a bash at number 10 Downing Street and I'm invited, plus guest. It would probably be in your interests,' she said with an undercurrent to her voice. She didn't have to add it might be professional suicide to refuse. But Donaldson was not daunted.

'Too short notice – babysitting duties tonight.' He tried to look sad, but there was no way in

246

which he was going to end up alone with her in the big bad city.

'I see,' she said shortly, an icy disappointment on her face. 'I'll have to find someone else, then.'

He did not respond to that, but raised the cheeks of his bottom off his chair in a 'Can I go now?' gesture.

'Heard anything from Zeke yet?'

He sat back heavily. 'Nothing.'

'You'd better do something about it, don't you think?' She was immediately starting to exert her authority over him because of his refusal to socialize.

'I am,' he said curtly. He rose and left the room without a further word, quickly getting back to his office, grabbing the sheets off the fax and slamming them down on his desk. 'Bitch,' he muttered.

He looked down at the sheaves of paper in front of him. There seemed to be reams of the stuff. He was tempted to bin it all then claim technical failure, but when he calmed down, he began to leaf through the received documents carefully. Most were from America, one from Paris. Routine stuff, but important nonetheless. Eventually he made it to the papers Henry Christie had sent him from Lancashire. He almost did not look at these, just considered handing them to an admin clerk to do the business. Curiosity rather than professionalism made him turn over the fax front sheet.

The second page contained a slightly blurred black and white photograph of the deceased.

Donaldson blinked. His lips popped open and a curious taste entered his mouth. The taste of fear.

He stood up slowly, reading the supporting paperwork Henry had sent through, including a description of how the man had met his untimely death. Transfixed, Donaldson walked numbly down the corridor back to Bottram's office. He walked through her secretary's office.

'Sorry, Karl, she's in a meeting already,' the secretary said.

'This is important.' Donaldson's voice was strained.

The secretary nodded and backed down.

He went through and found Bottram talking to another woman he did not recognize. They were sitting on the sofa, very close to each other, curiously intimate. Both looked round guiltily when he came through the door. They were obviously deep in conversation.

'Karl! Can't you see I'm busy,' Bottram said.

Before she could finish, Donaldson thrust Christie's faxes in front of her face. She took them from him and glanced at them.

The other woman looked on quietly, sipping tea, an amused expression on her face.

'Yes – so?' said Bottram. 'Why interrupt?'

'Look at the photo again.'

Even Donaldson had to admit the fax transmission was less than clear, but it was clear enough. Bottram studied it intently, brow lined, then suddenly she realized what she was looking at.

'Oh my God!' she said.

* * *

The three men convened at an innocent-looking car wash which operated on an industrial estate close to Marton Circle on the outskirts of Blackpool. It was one of those businesses apparently operated by several enterprising young men who looked more likely to steal cars than wash them, but they did a good job of washing and polishing.

The business was actually a front for part of Ray Cragg's drug dealing activities, and a profitable one at that. Customers could come and go within seconds and, together with the legitimate monies made from the soap suds, the venture turned over about five thousand each week, all profit. Ray Cragg had ten such businesses spread across Lancashire which sold a range of drugs for the discerning buyer, from cannabis to crack cocaine. They were like little drug supermarkets, but far more profitable than a chemist's shop.

There was an office in a large portacabin on the site at the rear of the car wash where Ray, Miller and Crazy gathered for their conflab. They were joined by two other men, trusted by Ray. Their names were Grice and Raven and both had turned up with flash motors which were being valeted by the lads at the car wash. Grice had been the driver of the van which had ferried Ray, Marty and Crazy from place to place before and after the King's Cross shootings. Raven had arranged disposal of the clothing and equipment they used.

They sat huddled round a small table in the office. There was only one window with horizontal blinds covering it, drawn at such an angle that it was easy to see out but difficult to see in. Outside, the day had turned murky. Business was fairly brisk and most of the customers passing through at that time of day were legit.

'Any sign of anything yet, Crazy?' Ray asked.

'Nothing obvious,' Crazy said. He had just been out to do a recce of the surrounding area and had found nothing untoward.

'They will come for us at some stage, you can bet,' Ray warned everyone. 'Don't think they won't, so be ready. Don't argue, go in peace, tell 'em nothing and you'll be okay – trust me. The brief is on standby, so stay cool, don't panic and there's nothing that can stick to us.'

They all nodded at this reassurance.

'So, the cops are nothing to worry about. We have far more pressing matters to consider than a bunch of dumb jacks trying to get us to talk.'

Henry was still doing his best to avoid bumping into Jane. It was proving to be more and more difficult as the crimes they were investigating became increasingly intertwined. He was only trying to keep away from her because he knew he was weak and he was trying to be strong for once in his life. He had far too much to lose by becoming involved with her and his materialistic streak, thin though it was, was preying on his mind. He was far too old, he thought, to let his heart rule his head. Go for comfort and security, he tried to convince himself. Be Mr Sensible. Don't do it. Don't fall in love again. God, his head hurt.

As he was waiting for the return call from

Donaldson, he decided to sneak out of the station and have a stroll around town.

The day was now dark and dull and chilly. He hunched in his jacket and headed swiftly for the town centre shops.

It was fairly quiet, low season, mid-week. Not much happening from a tourist point of view.

Once out of the wind, he slowed down and window-shopped for a while, before going into Waterstone's to browse the shelves. He began to feel guilty about not being at the station, so decided to head back, then make his way to the MIR which had been set up at Bamber Bridge. Tearing himself away from the bookshelves he left the shop and almost immediately his mobile phone chirped up. He fumbled it out of his pocket and answered it.

'It's me, Karl.'

'Hi – got something for me?'

Before Donaldson could answer, the ring tones on the phone announced he had received a text message. Then it did it again, telling him he had received another.

'Sorry, Karl, messages coming in thick and fast.'

'In reply to your question, the answer is yes, I do have something for you.'

'Brilliant – go on,' said Henry intrigued, but also noticing a strained tone in Donaldson's vocal chords.

'Not over the phone, H. I'm booked on the shuttle this afternoon. I should be in Manchester by three thirty. Can you meet me, or arrange for me to be met?'

Henry blew out his cheeks, taken aback, but not about to question his friend. He did some quick mental calculations. 'I can be there.'

'I'll see you there, then. Terminal 3 of course.'

They concluded the call. Henry looked at the display on his mobile phone and scrolled down to the 'message read' option. The first text was from the DI in Blackburn whom he had liaised with over the murder of Jennifer Walkden and the subsequent arrest and charge of her boy-friend, Joe Sherridan. The message asked for Henry to contact the DI as soon as.

The second text read, 'H, RU avoiding me again? Luv JR.'

Henry stared at it for a long time before deleting it.

Crazy and Miller sat side by side in the portacabin at the car wash. They said nothing to each other, simply stared out through the blinds at the weather, darkening by the minute. Miller sighed. Crazy sighed. Everyone else had gone, leaving them to sort out matters themselves.

Crazy scratched his head. 'Fifty grand,' he said into the air.

'Apiece.'

'Then a bonus on top of that.'

'Yep,' said Miller. 'Fifty grand and a bonus.'

'There's a lot to do.'

'That's an understatement,' said Miller.

'What's an understatement?'

'It's like a vest,' replied Miller.

'Oh.' Crazy's eyebrows knitted together. He shook his head.

A quietness descended between them, each man lost in his thoughts. Rain began to hammer down, smacking on to the portacabin.

'Are you capable of doing it?' Miller questioned him.

Crazy nodded. 'How about you?'

'Oh aye,' he said confidently. 'But is it worth fifty grand and a bonus, I ask myself?'

Their heads turned and they looked at each other. At first their expressions were serious, but then they started to grin.

'You bet it's fuckin' worth it,' said Crazy. 'You in or not?'

Miller held out his right hand and they shook.

'Where do we start?' Crazy asked.

'Simple and local. Then we progress on to the more difficult stuff.'

'I'll have that,' said Crazy.

Henry juggled a number of phone calls when he got back to the police station and fended off Bernie Fleming, who, for some reason, was prowling the building, hustling Henry.

He made it back to the office he had occupied before without bumping into Jane Roscoe, but found that the true occupant had returned. He moved cautiously round the building until he found another office which appeared to be vacant and unused at that moment. He moved into the empty seat and began phoning.

The first call he made was to the DI at Blackburn and Henry loved what he heard the man say, scribbling down notes on a scrap of paper. He thanked the DI profusely, promised to keep in touch with developments, then hung up. Next he called Risley Remand Centre near Warrington and did some smooth talking, after which he called Kate and told her it looked like it would be another late one, but could she put up the spare bed for Karl Donaldson?

The mention of the American's name immediately calmed her down. Henry could tell she was beginning to simmer a little and could hear a trace of suspicion in her voice. He knew she was wondering if he was straying from the straight and narrow again. He was wondering the same.

As he cradled the landline, his mobile rang again. The noise it made hit some nerve inside him and he squirmed.

It was Roscoe. 'Henry, where are you?'

'Blackpool police station,' he said vaguely.

'Whereabouts?'

He stifled an irritated sigh. 'Coming up to the incident room. Be there in a couple of minutes.'

'I'll see you there,' she said, her voice having the quality of best granite.

Henry dropped the mobile on to the desk. There was never any peace with one of them in your pocket, he thought. You are always contactable, never quite able to leave people behind. He was starting to hate the damned thing, yet he had no option but to carry it around with him, switched on and charged up. He swore and stood up. He had no intention of going to the incident room now.

He trotted down the back steps to the lower-ground floor. He crept along the corridor which went past the custody office gate and emerged in

254

brief daylight before going back under the cover of the car park. He drove out, approaching the shutter doors which opened automatically. As he went through, he glanced in his mirror and caught sight of Jane Roscoe hurrying towards him, waving her arms.

He pretended not to notice. In fact, he accelerated away.

There were two doctors walking down the corridor. Green skull caps, long coats, clip boards, stethoscopes, surgical masks covering their faces. They were deep in conversation about some patient or other. Their manner was relaxed, but it was apparent they were in disagreement over the benefits of a particular surgical procedure.

The policeman by the door of the private room did not take much notice of them. Doctors scurried past all day long. He'd seen enough doctors for a lifetime. He was sitting on a chair, browsing with little interest through a magazine for middle-aged women. He was wearing a ballistic vest, had a Glock 9mm strapped to his side and an MP5 slung high across his chest. He was guarding the patient inside the room. Stationed inside was another officer, similarly equipped and bored. They conversed with each other by means of a 'talk group' on their personal radios with earpieces in. They had not spoken to each other for ten minutes and the cop in the corridor half believed that his mate had nodded off. Typical.

The discussing doctors stopped about five feet

away from him. Their talk was quite heated, but still amicable.

'I say he's got to have the lower part of his bowel removed,' the younger-looking doctor said.

'That's a typical stance of the younger surgeon these days. Cut 'em open and chop it out. That's your answer to everything.'

'In this case it is. The patient will die otherwise. His condition is too far gone.'

The older doctor guffawed. 'You're wrong. Give the fucker an aspirin and I'm sure he'll get better.'

The cop on the door had only been half listening, but the remarks made by the older doctor made him lift his head.

'Just kidding,' the doctor said to the policemen. 'Come,' he said to his junior colleague, 'the bowel it is.'

At which point the hand of the younger doctor withdrew from underneath his long coat. Before the cop could react, he had pushed the barrel of the gun into the unwary cop's ear. The older doctor moved quickly. He drew the officer's Glock out of its holster and used a scalpel to cut through the strap of the MP5 and remove it from round his neck.

'Bulletproof vest is no good if you get shot in the head,' Crazy whispered. 'Now get up and go into the room using the same procedure you always do. Nothing outrageous, or you're a very dead cop. Are you with that scenario? Behave and you live, okay?'

The officer nodded.

256

He pressed the button on the side of his radio. 'Bob, coming in in ... Yeah, no probs.' His frightened eyes moved from one false doctor to another. He was annoyed at being caught out.

'Stand up and lead the way,' said Miller. He was armed with the MP5, having pocketed the Glock.

The officer stood on quaking legs. This should not be happening, he thought. Bad guys are not so foolish as to do things like this. His own bowels reacted in a way which made him think he should perhaps have them removed. He opened the door and walked in ahead of Crazy, whose gun was now held at his neck, ready to blow his head off.

The patient was asleep. Drips fed nourishment into his body. A monitor blipped by his side.

The cop in the room was on a chair next to the bed. He was not dozing as suspected, but, like his comrade in arms, he was reading a magazine. He did not look up initially when the door opened, so blasé was he. He only sensed something amiss when his buddy squeaked, 'Bob?'

Bob raised his eyes, then closed them.

'We're not here to harm you,' Miller said from behind his mask, pointing the commandeered MP5 at Bob, 'but if you don't do what we say, you'll both be dead and that's fact.' His voice was cool, controlled and he came across as being very much in charge. His matter of fact tones were steeped in the menace of certain death. 'Drop your weapons, Bob, and don't even think of being a hero. There's too many cops on the roll of honour. Don't join them.'

Bob nodded. He was no fool. He unslung his MP5 and placed it carefully on the floor. Next he unfastened his holster and drew out the Glock. Miller stiffened and prepared to waste him, but Bob put the gun on the floor and sat upright.

'Each of you take out your handcuffs.'

They complied with the order, knowing what was coming. They could see Miller's eyebrows rise as he smiled behind his surgical mask. 'Now, Bob, I think you've guessed. Please hand-cuff your mate here, hands behind his back. You' – Miller turned to the first officer – 'what's your name?'

'Ted.'

'Oh, Bob and Ted. Okay, Ted, kneel down, hands behind your back and let Bob fasten those nasty handcuffs on you.'

'Shite,' said Ted. He dropped to his knees and, his face angry and annoyed at being hoodwinked so easily, put his hands behind himself, wrist to wrist.

'C'mon, Bob, do the business.'

Bob secured his colleague's wrists with rigid handcuffs and without having to be told, sank down to his knees and allowed Crazy to cuff him next to Ted.

'Now then, lads, just shuffle on your knees up to the wall and press your faces right up to the plasterboard,' Miller directed them.

They did as told, Crazy covering them and urging them on with an occasional poke of a gun and a tap of the foot. Crazy was having trouble stopping himself from giggling. When they got to where Crazy wanted them, he ripped out their radio wires.

'Let's see if we can waken sleeping beauty,' said Miller, turning to the patient on the bed. He was propped up at 45 degrees by nice clean white pillows and had not stirred during the confrontation. 'He can talk, can he?' Miller asked the kneeling officers. Neither ventured an answer. 'Bob? Speak to me?'

With a deep, pissed-off sigh, Bob said, 'He can talk all right, he's just a big groggy with sedatives.'

'I'll soon wake him up,' said Miller. He recognized the prisoner as the one Crazy had blasted in the groin. Miller slapped his hand over the man's nose and mouth, constricting all airflow. It took a moment or two before his body reacted. He woke with a panicky start. Miller removed his hand and replaced it with the muzzle of Ted's Glock, which he jammed hard into the guy's mouth.

'Nice man,' Miller cooed. 'Keep very cool, keep calm.' His voice was a whisper. 'Talk to me, tell me what I want to know. Just whisper it to me and things'll be just fine – okay?'

He gave the man enough leeway for him to nod his head.

'Now then, one simple question. Who set up the raid on the counting house? I'm going to remove this gun from your mouth and give you three seconds to answer. If you don't respond within that timescale, I'll shove it back in and kill you.'

Slowly he eased the gun out.

'One,' he breathed, 'two...'

The man uttered a name just loud enough for him to hear.

'Three.' Miller forced the gun back between the man's teeth, breaking several teeth in the process and pulled the trigger. He left the Glock dangling out of his mouth because he had no further use for it but he kept hold of the MP5 because he thought it could be a useful tool.

Henry fully expected his mobile phone to ring, so it was no surprise that it did even before he reached the motorway.

'Yes,' he answered abruptly.

'Den Craven, Scientific Support. Is that DCI Christie?'

'Yes, Den, sorry about the snappy answer, I'm driving,' he said lamely. He wondered what Craven wanted. Henry knew he was an expert in footwear.

'No, it's all right. I just wanted to let you know something about the death of Carrie Dancing.'

Henry perked up. It seemed so long ago. 'Go on.'

'I looked at the marks on the side of her head at the request of the pathologist and I'm a hundred per cent certain that it is an impression from a shoe, a trainer to be exact, and a right foot. Beyond that, I'd estimate a size nine. I am sure, however, that the make is Nike, the model is the Air Max Specter – they have an unusual and easily recognizable pattern on the sole, so it was easy to match it. Made in China. Not very much wear on the sole, so quite new I'd say, but there is a mark across one of the ridges, just a single line, which makes it quite identifiable. If you arrest someone wearing these shoes, we'll go a long way to get a conviction. Oh, and I checked the shoes Johnny Jacques was wearing – they don't match.'

'Brilliant, Den, thanks very, very much,' Henry said. He wanted to ask, 'Do you get out much?' but refrained because this was a major breakthrough and people like Den were worth their weight in jewels. 'Can you fax me those details to the MIR at Blackpool?'

'Will do.'

'Thanks again.'

Henry punched the air. Okay, it wasn't a name, but it was bloody good. He pushed the car up to eighty, smiling, then not smiling any more as his phone announced a text message had landed. The noise set his teeth on edge. He read it as he drove along in the fast lane.

'Shit,' he said and pressed harder on the gas, taking the Vectra up to the ton and trying not to throw the damned phone out of the window.

He arrived too early at Manchester Airport, but was quite happy to kick his heels for half an hour while waiting for the shuttle to arrive. He stowed his very hot car in the short-term multi-storey and sauntered into Terminal 3, which dealt exclusively with domestic arrivals and departures. He went to the café bar and paid an extortionate price for a straight coffee, which he drank while propping up the counter. He would have liked something stronger, lots of something stronger, but that blow-out would have to wait.

Standing there like a seasoned international traveller, he mulled over everything he was presently involved in. Professionally he had just bottomed a domestic murder in Blackburn; had been handed a cold-case review; was involved in the suspicious deaths of JJ and Carrie Dancing, the latter most definitely a murder. Then he found himself running a triple fatal shooting, drugs related, which, somewhere along the line, tied in with a gangland execution and maybe a shooting incident at McDonald's.

Violent Britain, he thought. Why the hell do I live here? It rains a lot, it's always cold, the roads are jam-packed, the infrastructure is crumbling, the health service is a joke, the government is as corrupt as a Third World country's and the police have lost all control. The justice system was weak and ineffective, biased towards the accused and not the victim and he still owed a fortune on his mortgage with the probability that the endowments wouldn't pay out enough to cover it.

He knew why he stayed. He loved catching villains. He loved being pitted against very bad people and beating them, even if the courts were lenient with the bastards. It was his life and death was his trade. He just loved it.

His thoughts moved on to more personal matters. Love. Affairs. Deceptions.

He took a deep breath to stop himself having a panic attack. His personal life was a mess – again – but he knew he had the power to do something about it and end this foolishness with Jane Roscoe before it got on a roll and people really got hurt. He could stay with Kate and make something of his life with her, he knew. It would be a good life, too. Safe, secure, comfortable – yet, some reckless inner demon seemed to push him to self-destruct.

He finished his coffee and checked the arrivals screen to see that the Heathrow shuttle had just touched down. He strolled over to the arrivals hall and waited for Karl Donaldson.

Miller and Crazy could not speak to each other. Miller paced around the small bedsit they had chosen as a base for their operations. Both men had washed and showered since the shooting at the hospital and changed clothes completely, down to underwear and socks, bagging everything up for disposal.

'Not good,' Miller said eventually.

'Understatement,' said Crazy.

'What's one of them?'

'It's like a pair of knickers.'

Miller stopped his pacing. 'We have to tell him.'

'I know.'

'Toss you for the honour. Heads you tell him, tails I don't.'

Crazy sighed. 'I've known him longer, I'll do it.'

'Good luck.'

Thirteen

As the passengers filed out into the arrivals hall, Karl Donaldson stood head and shoulders above everyone else. He always reminded Henry of Superman, but without the underpants. He was big, wide, good looking in a square-jawed sort of way (bastard, Henry thought), still had a college crewcut and piercing blue eyes which had women drooling over him. His muscular shoulders tapered to a slim but proportionate waist and his thighs were tight against the inside of his trousers, muscles rippling. He saw Henry immediately across the heads, smiled and ploughed towards him.

They greeted each other like old buddies. Lots of back-slapping and hugging, but no tears of emotion.

'Good t'see ya, pal.' Donaldson beamed.

'And you. Let me take that.' Henry reached for the shoulder bag the American was carrying. 'The car isn't far away.' Then his mobile rang. 'Hang on,' he said, putting the bag down. Henry had input Jane's mobile number into his phone's memory so that when she rang him from that phone, his display read, 'Roscoe: mob'. Which it did.

'Henry Christie,' he answered formally.

'I think you're purposely avoiding me,' Jane

teased. Henry did not respond. 'Yeah, I'm right, aren't I?' Still nothing from Henry.

Then he said, 'It's not that – it's just...'

'Don't bother. I know when I'm not wanted,' she said crossly. 'Anyway, this is a business call. There's been an incident at BVH. Two of our armed officers who were guarding one of our shooters from McDonald's got jumped by a couple of guys pretending to be doctors and got tied up with their own handcuffs, and the prisoner they were guarding got shot to death.'

'Murdered?' said Henry. 'Holy shite. Are the officers okay?'

'Yeah, more's the pity.'

'And the second prisoner?'

'Untouched. Separate room, separate ward – just as per your instructions.'

'So what happened?'

Roscoe relayed the facts succinctly to him. When she had finished, Henry asked, 'They didn't hear the name?'

'Nope – deaf as well as stupid,' she said.

'Don't be too harsh on them. Whoever did this are very dangerous people and I'd rather our people went home at night than not.'

'Think it could be the two they had a shoot-out with in McDonald's, out to play the Grim Reaper with them?'

'Most likely.'

'What do you want me to do?' she asked.

'Call out an SIO. I'm going to be busy all afternoon.'

'You're not coming?' She sounded disappointed.

265

'No, just crack on with it, Jane. I'll speak soon. Bye.' He ended the call.

'Trouble?' Donaldson asked.

'I think the shit has just hit the paddles. C'mon, mate, let's get moving. You can tell me your story, then I just need to hijack you for something, if you don't mind?'

There was complete silence as the news was digested at the other end of the phone. Crazy did not dare say anything, merely waited and looked at Miller, who mouthed, 'What's going on?' Crazy shrugged. He put a finger on the 'secret' button and said, 'I think he's gone off on one.'

'You are saying to me that Marty set the job up? To rob me?' Ray Cragg eventually said.

'I'm not saying anything, boss,' Crazy corrected him. 'I'm just telling you what the guy said before he got popped.'

'What about the other one?'

'Er, I'm sorry? Are you asking us to kill him too? I don't think so,' said Crazy. 'We don't get to do something like that twice. Miller asked him who set the job up and he said a name – Marty Cragg. And reluctantly I've passed it on to you, Ray. We'll never get to the other one. The cops won't let it happen. We were lucky this once, but we won't be again – and the fact is we got a name for you, however unpalatable it happens to be. Sorry.'

'Yeah, yeah, fuckin' yeah. You sure he heard right?'

'Positive.'

'So the git got himself into debt with some

266

Spanish bastard, doing what I don't know, and he set up this heist to get the dosh to pay him back?'

'Could be one scenario.'

'And I chucked JJ out of a window because Marty told me he was skimming and all the time it was him. No wonder he was so jumpy when we were with JJ, no wonder he wanted him dealt with. JJ was telling me the truth, wasn't he?' Ray's voice was rising in anger.

'Could be,' said Crazy without committing himself.

'JJ skimmed a couple of hundred, tops. Marty skimmed thousands and it still wasn't enough. What the fuck was he up to? You and Miller better find that out for me when you track down that Mendoza bloke. I want the full story.'

'We'll do our best.'

'Anyway,' Ray took a soothing breath, 'you both did really well. Now, get my money back for me, will you? I want Dix topped and then I want that spic hunted down. Are you two up for it?'

'Dix, sure. The Spaniard – he's a different kettle of fish. He'll take some doing, I reckon.'

'Fuck,' Ray said, not really listening to Crazy. 'It's all going wrong for me at the moment. Can anything else possibly go shit-shaped? I'll tell you what it is, Crazy.'

'What?'

'Greed. So don't you get greedy, pal. I'll pay you well, so don't get greedy, you or Miller, understand?'

'Yeah, boss, got that.'

267

'Jeez, I do not deserve this shit, no way,' said Ray.

Henry and Donaldson headed west away from Manchester down the M56, towards the M6. Henry was stunned by what Donaldson had just told him.

The American was still speaking. 'Zeke was one of the best operatives we ever had. Undercover work was his life, particularly after his wife and kid died a few years ago.'

'What happened there?'

'Cancer. Both died within weeks of each other. Tragedy. He threw himself into work and he was good, very good, not reckless as you might have thought under the circumstances.'

'Even the best make mistakes.' Henry had worked undercover during his time on the Regional Crime Squad as it was then named, and occasionally since. He knew how difficult it was to maintain the deception. It ate away at your soul.

'I agree,' said Donaldson, 'but not in this case. I just don't see it.'

'Or do you refuse to see it?'

'No, I just don't see it. Zeke was far too smart to get caught out like that. He lived the life. He was totally immersed in it.'

'Perhaps he was dobbed on, as the Aussies say.'

'Very few people knew of his existence.'

'Maybe you need to start looking at who those people are,' suggested Henry.

Donaldson fell silent. 'The thing of it is,

Henry, he took over where someone else left off, and that "someone else" died doing the same job against the same people in much the same way. Two undercover agents murdered. I don't believe it was a coincidence.'

'What was the job?'

'To infiltrate a gang run by a guy called Mendoza, a Spaniard operating off the Costa Blanca, mainly through the port of Torrevieja, south of Alicante. He's one of Spain's biggest operators, running all the illicit things you can think of: drugs, cigarettes, anything to avoid tax, and of course the biggie of the moment...' He paused.

Henry filled in the gap. 'People.'

'The biggest earner of them all.'

They reached the M6 and Henry went north into four streams of very heavy traffic. He flitted from lane to lane before bearing off on to the M62 and heading back towards Manchester.

'There must be an American link,' Henry said.

'There is,' confirmed Donaldson. 'Organized crime – the Mafia. Joint venture. Zeke was amassing piles of good intelligence against a mob family from Miami who'd been financing a lot of Mendoza's operations concerning illegal immigrants. We were not very far from moving in and closing them down. I guess Zeke's death will put us back twelve to eighteen months. There's no chance of getting someone new in there now without causing suspicion. We'll have to go for them by other means.'

'What a waste.'

At junction 11, Henry came off the motorway and drove south-west into Risley. He pulled into

269

the security gate of the Remand Centre and flashed his ID together with a lovely smile.

In Blackpool, Crazy had finished his conversation with Ray Cragg. Ray had started jabbering on again about his disbelief at Marty's disloyalty and it had developed into a tirade lasting well over ten minutes which only ended when Crazy claimed, falsely, that the battery on his mobile was running low.

'Now I have a migraine,' Crazy complained to Miller, who chuckled.

'Fifty grand plus should ease it,' Miller suggested.

Crazy wiped his eyes. 'Yep. What's next?'

'Besides some sleep? *Cherchez la femme.*'

'Eh?'

'Find the bitch, find the dog,' Miller said enigmatically. 'Flush her out and we've got him, cos a woman is always the weakest link – goodnight!' he snapped and laid himself out on the camp bed. He closed his eyes and began to snore.

'You cool bastard,' Crazy said admiringly, but felt pretty laid back himself. He stretched out on the settee, reached for a pair of earphones and the remote control for the portable CD and pressed play. He lay back as the dulcet tones of Frank Sinatra soothed him into oblivion.

The prisoner was led into the interview room where he was searched again, then allowed to sit across the table (which was screwed firmly to the floor) from Henry Christie. Karl Donaldson

270

leaned nonchalantly against the wall by a reinforced window and watched without comment.

As a 'not guilty' remand prisoner, Joe Sherridan was permitted to wear his own clothing, but it was creased and grubby, as was the man himself. His short period of time on remand was obviously affecting him for the worse. He looked like he had not slept, eaten or relaxed. Good, Henry thought, it's easier to get someone when they're down.

'Afternoon, Joe,' Henry said.

No response, just a glare of contempt.

'Not going well, eh?' Still nothing. 'Well, what can you expect when you stick a knife into your girlfriend's heart? The Ritz? Applause? Sympathy?'

'I'm pleading not guilty.'

Henry shrugged. He did not care.

'All you've got is my confession – and a forced one at that. My brief says I'll walk.'

'Just remember all those little things you told me on tape, Joe. All those little details which only someone who committed the murder could have known about. All those details that no one but you and me knew about. How you wiped the knife on her skirt. How you also wiped it on a kitchen towel. How you tried to lose it down a particular grate in a particular street, the one we found it in. All those sorts of details are the ones known only to the killer and to me. You dug yourself in deep there, Joe my boy, and you didn't know you were doing it, and it's all recorded on tape. Joe, I promise you, you'll get

271

convicted of murder.'

'So why come here? To gloat?' Sherridan ran a trembling hand across his unshaven chin.

'For a conversation that could go one of two ways, Joe. I could either be here to help you or completely bury you. At the moment we are completely off the record, aren't we, boss?' Henry turned to Donaldson for confirmation. He nodded. Henry looked back at Sherridan and winked. 'He's my boss. A good man.'

'Just get on with it,' Sherridan said tiredly.

'Okay,' said Henry. 'I'm thinking of charging you with another murder.'

'What!'

'You heard.'

Sherridan shook his head. 'Off the record – I did stab Jennifer, but she deserved it for playing around and rubbing it in, making me look like a fool, but I haven't killed anyone else, not even in your wildest dreams, pal. Who are you talking about, anyway?'

'I think you beat a girl to death in Blackpool, about a year ago.'

'Yeah, right.' He snorted.

'I'm investigating a murder of a young girl who was a prostitute.' Henry watched Sherridan's reactions as he spoke. 'She worked from a basement flat in North Shore. She was about fourteen years old, thin as a rake, and as yet we haven't identified her.'

Sherridan was doing a lot of swallowing. Henry knew his throat must be the driest place on the planet right now.

'So what?' the prisoner blustered.

'It's very likely that her last client was the one who beat her to death. It was a vicious assault and she died a terrible, traumatic death, poor kid.'

'Goes with the territory,' Sherridan said coldly.

'Murder does not go with any territory,' Henry came back. He did not really believe his words, because he knew murder went with many territories. 'But that's by the by, Joe, because whether you believe it goes with the territory or not, I believe you murdered her.'

'No way, no effin' way.'

'Do you know why I believe that?'

'Astound me.'

'Well, to be blunt, we found your spunk inside her.'

'No you didn't.'

'Yes we did. Shall we have a pantomime here? No you didn't, yes I did?'

'You're talking bollocks.'

'An unfortunate turn of phrase, because I'm talking about what came swimming out of your bollocks, Joe. Your semen, your come, your jizz, whatever pet name you have for it. We found it inside her. Yours, no one else's.' Which wasn't strictly true, but Henry wasn't going to admit that.

'You'll have to do better than that,' Sherridan said.

'Don't need to, Joe. Remember when we took that swab from your mouth after you'd been charged with murder?' Sherridan looked stonily at Henry. 'Do you know what that was for?'

He shrugged. 'Not really.'

'Advances in science. Genetic fingerprinting. DNA, Joe. Your DNA, that stuff which is in every one of your cells, totally exclusive to you, no one else, in every cell in every corner of your body, like a fingerprint, but better, that's what the swab was for. And the result was checked on the national DNA database and was matched up to semen found in a murder victim – another murder victim. My, Joe, you've been a busy lad, a proper killing machine. Almost a serial killer now.'

Sherridan shot to his feet, gripping the edge of the table, towering over Henry aggressively. Donaldson tensed, ready to step in and flatten Sherridan.

Henry stayed seated and calm. He waved Donaldson down and said to Sherridan in a low voice, 'Sit down, Joe, otherwise my boss will take very good care of you. Sit!' Sherridan dropped slowly back into his chair.

'I didn't kill her.'

'But you had sex with her and paid for it?'

'I didn't kill her'

'Answer the question, Joe.'

'Yes, I shagged her and paid for it, okay? But I never killed her.'

'I never thought you did, Joe,' Henry said and Sherridan glowered. 'But I had to put it to you. Your sperm was found inside her, so what am I expected to think?'

'Yeah, suppose so.'

'But I want to know who did kill her.'

'I haven't a clue,' he said, with relief in his voice.

'I'll tell you the deal,' Henry said. 'The deal is this: you tell me everything about your dealings with that prostitute, and I mean everything. How you met her, or were introduced to her, how you screwed her, what condition you left her in, who ran her, who was behind her and, of course, what her name is.'

'Why should I do all that?'

It forced a laugh out of Henry that should have acted as a warning beacon to Sherridan. 'Because if you don't,' the detective said in a measured tone, 'I'll charge you with her murder and I'll go out of my way to make it stick, whether I believe it or not. You might get off, but I doubt it, not with your sperm inside her. It's pretty compelling evidence. But, whatever, I'll make you suffer the indignity of a double trial, because I'm a twat like that. I mean, no one else's sperm was found inside her. Five million little swimmers all with your ugly face on them, all ready to tell their sordid tale. And another reason you'll tell me what I want to know is that I can help you on the original murder charge.'

'How?'

'If you get convicted of Jennifer's murder, which you will, you'll go down for life. I'll make sure the prosecution lay it on thick and you won't even need to think about seeing the light of day for at least fifteen years. How old are you now? Thirty-eight? Let's see, that's...' Henry started to count on his fingers.

'Fifty-three,' Sherridan said glumly.

'Fifty-three, yes. Not too old, I suppose, but fifteen years behind bars – hell! I can help you,

275

but you have to give me everything in return.'

'How can you help me?'

'I can get the murder charge reduced to manslaughter like that!' He clicked his fingers. 'You could be walking in five years, or less if you're a really good lad. I could really lay it on thick for the judge, about how she drove you to pig-sticking her, how she sent you mental, how she deserved what she got – though it is a bit ironic that you stiffed her because of her infidelity when you were being entertained by hookers. That's how I can help you, Joe. Fifteen years down to five. But I want everything in return and if I don't think you've given me everything, I won't help you. I want names, addresses, dates, times, everything about your use of prostitutes. If you don't give, you'll be very old and gnarled when you walk out of prison.'

Sherridan stood up. Donaldson tensed again, but this time the prisoner walked slowly round the interview room, hands deep in trouser pockets, dragging his feet along the tiled floor.

'It's your life you're talking about here,' Henry tossed across to him.

He stopped in one corner of the room and rested his head against the wall, speaking down to his toes. 'There's some bad people involved here.'

'And fifteen years of your life is a long time to spend banged up. Okay, you can start again at fifty-three, but it's a lot easier at forty-three. People have mid-life crises at that age and start all over again, I should know,' he muttered to himself.

Sherridan came back to his seat. Where before his eyes had been dead and lifeless, now they sparkled with hope. Henry knew he had seen the possibilities.

'If you tell me all I want to know, I'll get the charge reduced to manslaughter.'

'When do I need to decide?'

'Now. And the first thing I want to know is the girl's name.'

'Julie, they called her Julie, but she couldn't understand most of what I said to her. Foreign, she was. Albanian, I think he said.'

'Julie from Albania,' Henry mused. He looked at Donaldson and repeated, 'Albania.'

'Sorry it took so long, Karl. I'll come back and speak to him again tomorrow, by myself. I know you're up here for a specific reason and I'm delaying you.' It was almost two hours later and Henry and Donaldson were just leaving Risley Remand Centre.

'It's okay, pal. What he said was very interesting to me.'

'Oh, good,' Henry said dubiously.

'One thing I would like clearing up, though. Is it true that only his sperm was found inside her?'

Henry blanched with discomfort. 'Not necessarily, but he didn't need to know that, did he?'

Donaldson laughed. 'You are a twat, then.'

'Goes with the territory.'

'And it's such a nice, English expression too, so quaint,' said Donaldson who was always intrigued by the vernacular. 'I'd put you down as more of a cunt.'

* * *

Miller and Crazy strolled innocently down the street past the house in Fleetwood they knew belonged to Debbie Goldman, Dix's girlfriend. It was in darkness, as they had fully expected it to be. Crazy had a carrier bag in his hand. They walked to the end of the street and lit a cigarette each, two friends chatting in the early evening, certainly doing nothing remotely suspicious.

Miller drew deeply on the cigarette but exhaled the smoke without breathing it into his lungs. He was not a smoker, never had been, but it seemed appropriate tonight for the sake of cover.

'Looks like no one's home,' Crazy said.

'Didn't expect there to be.'

'You done much burgling in your time?'

'Yeah, course,' said Crazy, affronted. 'Screwed my first house when I was eleven.'

'Ah, late starter then?'

Crazy grinned. 'Made up for it since.'

'Ever broken in and left something behind?'

'No, always taken what was rightly mine. I'm not Robin Hood, just Robbin' Crazy.'

Miller smiled. 'Let's reverse the trend then. Did you see an alarm on the house?'

'Negative, don't think there is one.'

'Me neither.' Miller looked at the sky. Cloudy, overcast, dull – the usual. 'Let's break and enter.'

They ground out their cigarettes in the gutter.

Henry switched the lights on. They flickered and pinged and eventually lit the room brightly.

Down one side were the refrigerators, over a dozen doors, each one with a body behind it.

'Welcome to my home,' Henry said, adopting a creaky, witch-like voice. 'This is my kitchen and those are my freezers.'

Karl Donaldson was not amused.

'Sorry,' said Henry quickly, sensing his friend's serious mood. 'But just at the moment places like this are second homes to me.'

He walked along the fridge doors, reading the name cards as he went, until he found the one he was searching for.

He opened it and pulled the drawer out. It slid easily and noiselessly on its runners.

The body on the tray inside was wrapped like a ghost in a white muslin shroud. Henry hesitated.

'Do it, please,' Donaldson said.

Henry obliged and folded the material away from the face, revealing a grotesque mess, part of the left side of the face blown away.

'Two more bullet wounds in the back of the head,' Henry informed Donaldson.

The big American looked as close to tears as Henry had ever seen him.

'It is Zeke,' he whispered. 'Real name Carlos Hiero, FBI field agent, expert in undercover work – a good man.' Donaldson choked and cleared his throat.

'I'm sorry,' Henry said, knowing the words were inadequate.

'How was he killed – exactly?'

'He was shot in the back of the head. The pathologist believes that the first was to the base

279

of the skull, the gun angled upwards a touch, so it would be a fatal wound. The other two to the back of the head were make-sures, not that they were needed because the first one did the job.'

Donaldson took the information in. 'Calibre of weapon used?'

'Nine mill. Two bullets have been found inside the brain and we can match them to a weapon if we ever find one – your thoughts?' Henry asked. He could see Donaldson was pensive. The American had brought his attaché case with him. He hoisted it on to the edge of the drawer and flicked open the catches. He pulled out some glossy photos of a crime scene and handed them to Henry, who blinked when the images registered fully with his brain.

'That's another undercover agent, codename Barabas. He infiltrated Mendoza's gang and was killed in exactly the same manner as Zeke.'

'And Marty Cragg,' Henry added.

'And at least four other people in Spain and France. Same MO. What particularly worries me is the fact that two undercover agents have been shot dead within the space of a few months, two very experienced guys.'

'Like I said in the car, you need to be asking who knew about them from your side. Maybe there's a leak somewhere. Did you control both of them, Karl?'

Donaldson nodded reluctantly.

'Who else knew – if it wasn't you who leaked?' Henry asked, striking a chord with the American.

'That's what worries me.' Donaldson scratched his head, took back the photos from Henry and slid them into his briefcase.

Henry's mobile rang. He stepped away from the body on the tray and answered it while Donaldson stared sadly down at his shrouded colleague. It was Rik Dean speaking from the Major Incident Room at Blackpool.

'Sir, I've been speaking to Jack Burrows. She wants to talk to you and not only that – she wants to look at Marty Cragg's body. Here's her number.' Dean read it out while Henry, with his phone lodged between ear and shoulder, wrote it down on the back of his hand.

'Is that it, Rik?'

'Er ... yeah, that's it.' He sounded doubtful.

Henry immediately telephoned the number, not being one to miss an opportunity. She answered quickly.

'Thanks, thanks for ringing – I need to see you.' Her voice wavered.

'I'm at the mortuary at Chorley hospital. I think you know where that is, if you want to make your way.'

'I'm about half an hour away. Can you wait?'

'Yes.' Henry thumbed the button to end the call. 'Interesting,' he frowned. 'Mind staying for a little while longer? Call me an old-fashioned detective, Karl, but I think we might have some sort of breakthrough here.'

For two men of their undoubted calibre, the task of breaking into Debbie Goldman's house was very easy. They went in via the back yard, forced the kitchen window causing little visible damage and climbed quickly in. They used fine, penlight torches to find their way around. Crazy went to the front door, while Miller stayed at the back.

What they intended to do was simple and straightforward.

Crazy lifted the doormat out of the slight recess in which it lay and inserted what looked like a wafer thin, black, square metal plate, then replaced the mat on top. He returned to Miller in the kitchen, who was having a slightly more complicated time. He had to ease up the linoleum flooring by the back door before placing a similar black plate underneath it, about eighteen inches away from the door. He pushed the flooring back into place, flattening it with his shoe.

'Need somewhere to put this,' he said. He took a small black box out of the plastic bag they had brought along with them. It was about 6" by 3" by 1" with a small aerial on theside which Miller extended to its full length of six inches. There was an on/off slide switch on it. 'I don't think we need to be too cute about hiding this,' he said. 'She'll be in a rush, won't be hanging about, won't be looking for suspicious things.'

'You certain she'll come back?'

'As eggs is eggs. She's a woman. She'll have to get her totty things. It's just the way they are. You'll understand one day when you start shaving.'

'Doubt it. As long as I can get me knob sucked from time to time, I'm a happy guy.'

'Right. Here'll do,' said Miller. He had walked into the living room. He slid the box behind the video recorder, which was near to the window. 'Should get a good enough signal from here.' He pulled another box out of the carrier bag. This one looked like a hand-held transistor radio, which in some respects, it was. He turned a switch. 'Stand on the mat,' he told Crazy.

'What – just step on it?'

'That's the idea.'

Crazy went into the hall and stood on the mat. Immediately the box in Miller's hand came to life. 'Alarm Code Echo, Alarm Code Echo,' it repeated through its small speaker.

'It's working,' Miller said. He pressed a re-set button and it shut up. 'Let's try the one at the back door.'

Crazy did as bid with the same positive result.

'Hey, that's good,' Crazy said with admiration.

'It's just a radio alarm. Cops use them all the time. Easy to get hold of, easy to install. Now let's get out of here.'

Henry met Burrows in the car park. She turned up in her yellow Mercedes, so it was easy to spot, even in the dark. She parked in a vacant spot next to Henry's Vectra, paused for a while to collect her thoughts, then got out.

'What can I do for you?' Henry asked.

'I'd like to see Marty.' Her voice was flat. 'I didn't get to see him when I was here before.'

The car park was one which was 'secured by design' which meant it had features built into it and around it which tended to make criminals think twice about robbing or stealing cars. One of the things it had was good, bright lighting.

When Jack spoke she lifted her face up to Henry and he got a good look at her. He saw the cuts, the bruising and the swelling.

'Jesus, what happened?'

Her mouth tightened and she winced. Her right eye was purple and puffed-up, her cheek too, her top lip cut. Her eyes fell away. She turned back to her car and reached for the door handle.

'I thought you wanted to see Marty?'

Her fingers hovered by the handle. 'I do,' she said meekly. She kept looking away from Henry as though she was embarrassed.

'But why?' Henry asked. 'Why do want to see the body of someone you claimed not to know initially? Are you just a morbid thrill seeker, or is there a professional interest there, you being an undertaker and all that?'

'You know why I want to see him.'

'Tell me.'

Her face flickered round to him again. This time the car park lights caught the tears streaming down her face. 'Because I love him,' she sobbed.

Henry was hard faced. 'So? You're not a relative and I don't have to let anyone see him but relatives. Even his mum hasn't been to see him yet.'

'She's too distraught, can't get out of bed.'

'Ah well.' Henry shrugged. 'Then you'd better give me a good reason why I should let you see him. I could get into trouble for allowing you to.'

'I said I love him. Isn't that enough?'

'No, not in my book, Jack.' Henry was actually

284

on the verge of cracking and letting her have her way. Her tears and emotion were getting to him, despite his rock-like expression. He could never stay hard for long. He was too nice.

She stood in front of him, a vicious debate going on inside her.

'Come on, Jack, I haven't got all night.'

'Okay.' She swallowed nervously. 'Let me see him and I'll give you Ray Cragg on a plate.'

Fourteen

Crazy returned with a take-away, handing Miller his chips and pie covered in a curry sauce. He had a doner kebab for himself, everything thrown on, and a portion of chips. They were in a pub car park about quarter of a mile away from Debbie's house with the alarm receiver on the dashboard of Miller's second car, a rather battered Ford Granada. Crazy pulled off his crash helmet and sat in the car next to Miller. They had decided it might be wise to have two vehicles at their disposal and when Crazy told Miller he owned a 750cc Honda which travelled faster than light, it seemed to be the right thing to use.

Earlier in the afternoon, Miller had taken Crazy to visit one of his contacts in Blackpool, a guy who was a radio technician, once actually having worked for the police, but who now made his money from house alarms, person-to-person radios and other such useful items.

He had provided Miller with the footpad alarm for £100 and had also fitted a radio into Miller's car for free and one on Crazy's bike plus an earpiece in his helmet for an extra £150.

Crazy had been impressed. He folded open the paper surrounding his kebab. Miller folded a curry-coated chip into his mouth.

Donaldson, again, observed what was going on without interrupting. Henry stood back while Burrows looked at the body of Marty Cragg on the tray sticking out of the fridge.

'Marty, oh Marty,' she said sadly.

His face was a terrible mess, blown apart, skull splintered, brains oozing out, left eye completely missing. She sighed and touched his cheek tenderly. 'I don't know why I love you,' she said. 'I just do, I just do.' She looked over her shoulder at Henry. 'All Ray's bothered about is his money. He didn't care about Marty getting hurt, it didn't bother him at all. I hate him for that. His own flesh and blood – and I hate him for what he did to me.' Her shoulders shook as a sob made her convulse.

Henry did not reach out and touch her. He wanted to know what the hell she was talking about. What money? What was all this about? He clamped his teeth together, not wanting to say anything, trying to judge how best to take this forward, because he knew that if he said anything out of place, he could jeopardize the possibility of catching Ray Cragg.

'Yeah,' he agreed, 'flesh and blood.'

She ran her fingers down Marty's face and ice-cold neck, then touched his distorted lips with her fingertips. 'I loved him kissing me,' she said.

Henry held back the urge to shove two fingers down his throat. The idea of Marty, dead or alive, kissing anyone repulsed him. Burrows faced him again and Henry only just about managed to get his face back into sympathetic mode. Not that easy a thing to do quickly and he thought that Burrows may actually have seen him ready to hurl.

'You probably won't believe this,' she said, 'but Marty was good to me. We had a great time, had fantastic plans for the future.' She could not tear her eyes away from her dead lover and she looked longingly at him again. Then she did something that almost made Henry spew for real. She kissed Marty's lips, a soft, tender brushing of mouth to mouth. She hovered over his face and said, 'I can make you beautiful again. I'll put you back together so that no one will know how bad you've been. I'll make you look like Marty again. Handsome ... gorgeous...'

And a woman beater and maybe, Henry thought, a woman killer too. Why did women like bastards like him? he wondered.

Burrows stood upright. She inhaled deeply, pulled herself together. 'When the body is released, I want to do the work on him,' she stipulated. 'That is a condition of me telling you everything.'

'Fine by me,' Henry said.

287

'Right, I think I want to become a protected witness now, if you don't mind.'

As far as Henry was concerned, there was no time to waste.

'Sorry about this,' he whispered hurriedly to Donaldson, 'but I need to get things moving here. A bit of a twist I didn't anticipate.'

'That's okay. I'll go along for the ride at the moment.'

'Cheers.' He punched Donaldson on the shoulder then cowered away when the big man made to return the gesture. 'Can you take her car to police headquarters at Hutton? Do you know the way from here?'

'I'll find it, I've visited it often enough.'

'Good. Park it somewhere well out of sight of the road and I'll arrange to have you picked up at the sports and social club, if that's okay?'

'Sure.'

They were standing in the car park outside the mortuary. Burrows was leaning on her car, sobbing. Henry's mind was working fast. He strode over to her, followed by Donaldson.

'Give him your car keys,' he told her.

'Why?'

'Because we're going to look after it for you. For a start it's a very obvious car, turns heads, and if you get seen in it, it might turn the wrong heads.'

She delved into her shoulder bag and came out with her keys which she gave to Donaldson. He peeled the car key off the fob and gave her the remainder back. Henry pulled her away from the

288

door to allow Donaldson space to get in. His big frame squeezed uncomfortably into the sports car and he fired it up and opened the window.

'Got your mobile phone?'

'Yep.'

'Keep it on ... I'll be in touch soon.'

Donaldson nodded, reversed and was gone. Henry quickly dialled headquarters control room from his phone and told them that Donaldson was on his way to HQ and for them to tell the security people at the gatehouse to let him in. He noticed that the battery on his phone was running low and he did not have a car charger.

'Right, Jack, first things first. Where does Ray think you are now?'

'At home, I suppose.'

'Will he be trying to contact you?'

She fished her own mobile phone out of her bag and said, 'He hasn't done yet.'

'He doesn't know you were planning to come here?'

'No.'

'Right.' His mind whirred. 'I'm going to drive you to your house now. Because of what you are going to tell me, I think there's a pretty substantial threat against you, so I want to get you to a place of safety as soon as possible tonight. I don't know just where, yet, but it probably won't be very comfortable tonight, okay?'

She nodded understandingly. Henry thought how unlike she was now from when he had first met her a few days ago, when she had been cocky and confident. Now she was low and pliant. Love, he thought. And a beating. Amazing.

'You are going to tell me everything, aren't you?' he asked. 'That includes about Marty, too.'

Again she nodded.

'Okay, let's get going.'

He led her round to the passenger door of his car and seated her firmly before getting in himself. A minute later he was driving towards the motorway, trying to keep to speed limits, but finding it hard because his fast-beating heart made him want to step on the gas.

He looked at the battery meter on his phone which told him how low it was. He needed to phone someone and hoped it would not pack up, though he could have used Burrows' phone, he supposed. He dialled a number.

'Henry? Where the hell have you been? It's bloody chaos up here,' came the panicky voice of Jane Roscoe.

'Just listen, Jane,' he said urgently. 'In one hour I want you to meet me at ... er ... let's think ... Kirkham police station.'

'Henry, I can't just drop everything. There's been one of our prisoners murdered at the hospital, or had you forgotten?'

'Listen. Just meet me, okay? This is very important and I don't want to say any more over an open line.' His tone quietened her down. 'It's very, very important.'

'I'll be there.'

'And bring someone along to help.'

Henry's phone bleeped a warning that the battery was now almost lifeless. 'Bloody things,' he mumbled and slotted the phone down between

290

his thighs. He glanced at Burrows. She was staring blankly out of the window. 'You okay?'
'No.'
'We'll look after you,' he said and tried not to guffaw. 'Now, you need to listen to me and do some thinking.' She turned to him. 'I don't need to tell you the danger you're in, do I? We are now going to your house and what I want you to do is this: think about all the things that are valuable to you and the things you're going to need of a practical nature. When we get there, go straight in and start to pack a suitcase. Do it quickly. Take whatever things you feel you need which are emotionally valuable to you. Make sure you've also got all your bank cards, credit cards, birth certificate, passport, driver's licence, stuff like that. You can't afford to dawdle. Just get in and do it, okay?' He wanted to know that she understood his every word. 'Things'll be fine, I promise, but we need to move fast. Don't be tempted to make any phone calls or anything.'

They hit the motorway and he upped the speed. He breathed out long and hard, feeling very excited.

They reached her house in less than half an hour. He drew on to the drive and went into the house with her.

'Go and pack quickly and please don't make a phone call from the house.'

'Okay.'

'Where is your stop tap?'

'What?'

'You know, where's your stop tap? The pipe

where your water comes into the house?'

'I have absolutely no idea, why?'

'You go and pack. I'll find it myself.' He watched her trot upstairs, averting his eyes and thoughts away from her bottom, and went into the kitchen. The stop tap was where he expected to find it, under the sink. He reached under and turned the water supply off. Next he found the central heating control panel and slid the buttons to the 'off' position. His next job was to read the meters. He found a small torch in a cupboard and found the triangular key for the meter cupboard on the wall outside. He took a note of the readings, just in case Burrows never came back to the house again, which he doubted she would. She would have to pay the bills up to date. Back inside, he shouted up the stairs, 'How are you doing?'

'Okay,' came a fairly weak response.

'Mm, right,' he murmured.

She came downstairs a few minutes later, hauling a suitcase. She dropped it on to the hall carpet and went into the lounge where she opened the sideboard and scooped out a bundle of official-looking papers, placing them into a small flight bag. She then worked her way round the room, picking up photos and ornaments, putting some of them into the bag too.

'Finished,' she declared. She was on the verge of breaking down. Henry knew this would be a critical point and that he had to get her out of the house before severe doubts made her change her mind.

He picked up her suitcase, which was so heavy

it almost tore his arm off at the shoulder socket. 'We'll go now,' he said, wishing to keep on top of the moment.

Her house phone rang, making both of them jump. She stared at Henry, wanting a steer.

'Don't answer it.'

It rang and rang, then finally stopped. Almost immediately her mobile started to ring. She got it out and both looked at the display, but it was anonymous.

'It'll be him. If I don't answer, he'll get suspicious.'

Henry relented. 'Short and sweet.'

'Hello ... Hi, Ray,' Burrows said. 'Yeah, I'm coming round ... Ooh, that sounds great ... Can't wait ... See you. Bye.' She sneered at the phone. 'He said he wants to suck my tits,' she said with disgust. 'The bastard.'

The words were music to his ears because it meant her resolve to drop shit all over Ray from a very great height was still there. 'Come on,' Henry said, 'let's make a move.'

She went out ahead of him. He carried out the bags and made sure the door was closed and locked, unable to stop thinking that he himself would not mind doing what Ray had said, though he might have found a way to say it in a more diplomatic fashion. He would probably have used the word 'breasts' rather than 'tits.'

At the last moment, Henry had a deliberate change of plan. He stopped at a telephone kiosk outside the town of Kirkham and called Jane Roscoe's mobile. He fed a pound coin into the

293

phone as she answered and saw it reduce immediately to 80p, then 70p. This urged him to get a message across as succinctly as possible.

'Sorry – total change,' he said. 'You'll see the reason why, so bear with me.'

'I am waiting at Kirkham police station.'

'Well done. Now I want you to go to Ormskirk police station. There's a police hostel above the nick and we're going to need two rooms for the night. Can you arrange that via a land line? Make sure we can get into the station, too, because I think it shuts to the general public at midnight. And make sure there are rooms to be had. Okay?'

'Right, will do.'

With one penny to spare, Henry hung up and returned to the car. He explained what was happening and Burrows accepted things without a qualm, apparently.

'You can't be too careful,' he said.

He headed back towards Preston and picked up the A59 southbound, which ran directly past police headquarters at Hutton, south of Preston. He turned in through the main gate, now properly guarded and controlled since a baddie had been bold enough to walk on to the site and toss a grenade at the force helicopter parked up on the rugby pitch. Henry was recognized immediately by the security guard and the barrier was raised for him. He turned right and pulled up near the single-storey social club situated behind the main HQ building. It was 11.30 p.m. and business was over for the evening, but he

294

found Donaldson clutching the remains of a pint of lager at the bar, chatting to a starry-eyed barmaid who was definitely under his spell.

Jack Burrows saw her chance as Henry disappeared around the corner of the club. She got her phone out and called Ray Cragg.

'And just where the hell have you got to?' he demanded instantly.

'Can't tell you that, Ray, other than to say it's all over between you and me. I hate you and don't want to see you. I've had enough. It's true, Marty and me were lovers. He treated me right, didn't hit me like you've done.'

'You were one of the lucky ones, then, you bitch.'

'Yeah, I am, and there's more, much more. I'm going to tell the cops everything I know about you. I'm in protective custody now and I'm going to destroy you for the way you treated me and Marty.'

'I don't think so,' Ray said confidently. 'You'll be dead before you know it.'

'Naah, Henry Christie will look after me. He fancies me and I fancy him. He can suck my tits, you bastard. You are going down, you complete and utter evil bastard! DOWN!'

Henry knew the barmaid. He said, 'This man is happily married.' He saw her face crease. 'Sorry.'

'Just my luck.' She shrugged philosophically, pulling herself together. 'It was nice talking to you, though.'

'You too,' said Donaldson. He drank the last of his lager and stood upright.

'Maybe another time when you're passing through,' she said hopefully.

'Maybe, ma'am.' Donaldson tipped his head and winked. Henry thought she looked as though she had orgasmed on the spot.

'Come on, you big lug,' he intervened before full sex across the bar became a very real possibility. He herded Donaldson away from her.

'She was cute.'

'Sure – and so is your wife.'

'And I cannot believe how cheap the beer is up here.'

'Lancashire prices.' He pushed Donaldson out of the bar to the car. 'You still okay?' he asked Burrows as he got back in.

'Fine,' she said and smiled wickedly. 'Do you know what "Fine" means? Fucked up, insecure, neurotic and emotional, so yeah, I'm fine.'

Henry sensed a change in her. He started the engine and looked questioningly at her, a horrible feeling in his guts.

They were at Ormskirk police station fifteen minutes later, the traffic being light at that time of day, making the journey fast. Henry parked in the rear yard and pulled up at the back entrance.

Already he was beginning to feel jittery about things and it all emanated from the smile that Burrows had given him. There was something behind it and he thought he knew what it was. He decided he would broach the subject later.

He rang the intercom by the door and asked the

voice which answered to send the inspector to the door to let them in. The voice obviously belonged to a public enquiry assistant working on the front desk. She chuckled when Henry mentioned an inspector.

'There isn't one here at this time of day,' she told him. 'Nearest one is at Chorley, I think.'

'How about a sergeant?'

'Nope – covering from Skelmersdale.'

'A PC?'

'The two who are on duty are out. I suppose I'll have to do.'

'Guess so,' said Henry wryly

The lady appeared at the door a minute later and demanded to see Henry's ID, which he gladly showed.

She led them into the station, then up to the hostel used mainly as accommodation for single police officers, though other waifs, strays and divorcees were often found to be lodged there. The rooms consisted of a bed, wash basin, wardrobe, dressing table and desk, all quite nice and modern. Showers and toilets were separate. There was a kitchen/dining area and a TV lounge.

The PEA showed them an empty room. 'This one should be okay. Next door is free, too.'

'I'll have the keys for both, if you can put your hands on them,' Henry said. He smiled and she softened.

'See what I can do.' She scurried away back down to the front desk. It was not far off midnight and she would be locking up soon.

A bloody PEA in charge of a police station,

297

Henry thought and wished briefly for the good old days when every job was taken by a policeman. 'You'll be staying here for the night,' he said to Burrows, 'but I guess you've already sussed that. If you need a take-away or something to drink – which I do – we'll arrange it, okay?'

She went into the room and sat on the edge of the bed. 'Home from home,' she said, bouncing up and down on what looked to be a hard mattress.

'Can I have your mobile phone?' he asked, holding out his hand.

'Yeah, sure, why?' She handed it over.

Henry checked the last number rang. 'Is this Ray's number?' Burrows nodded and closed her eyes. 'You must never contact him again,' he told her firmly. 'It's too dangerous.'

'I know, I know. It's just ... I had to.'

'Fine, but no more, Jack. You can't do it, okay? You must trust us with your welfare and safety, but you have to play the game with us.' He pocketed the phone. 'Right. Food and drink. Karl, sorry about this, but can you bear with us?'

Donaldson was fine about things. After all, this was the girlfriend of the man who had been killed alongside Zeke. He had much to learn from her, he was sure.

Henry heard footsteps on the stairs. Jane Roscoe emerged, trailed by Rik Dean. He went to meet them down the hallway.

'This better be very good,' she warned Henry.

'Better than good,' he whispered. 'Someone who is going to give us Ray Cragg on a plate. I

298

want you in on it, because it's your job, but I also think there's much more than just a shooting.'

'Who is it?'

'Jack Burrows, Ray's girlfriend. She's come to us.'

He looked at Dean, who looked, for all the world, like he'd seen a ghost.

Crazy had fallen asleep, his chin on his chest. Miller was wide awake and alert, knowing he could remain so for very long periods when he had to. Not that he needed to stay awake. The volume was up high on the alarm receiver on the dash, loud enough to wake the dead. Yet he stayed awake. His mobile rang. It was Ray Cragg.

'How's it going? Any sign yet?' Cragg wanted to know.

'Nothing.'

'Think she'll come tonight?'

'I don't presume anything,' said Miller. He stifled a yawn. Not one of tiredness, but one of boredom. This was the sixth call from Cragg that evening and Miller was getting pissed off with him.

'Something else has come up. I need to see you both now.'

'You want us to leave here?'

'For the time being I do. This is more important and it'll mean a lot more for you if you pull it off.'

Miller shook his head. 'Whatever. You want to see us now?'

'Yes, right now.'

Fifteen

It was a Chinese take-away and they sat and ate it in the dining room at the hostel. It was one of the best Henry had eaten and he devoured it with relish. He was ravenously hungry too, and that helped. One or two curious officers who lived in the hostel passed through with frowns on their foreheads, wondering who this strange quintet of people was who were invading their space. Mostly it was quiet and also very hushed between the people who were sharing the immense banquet. Small talk was minimal.

Henry did not mind. He noticed how uncomfortable Rik Dean was. Very bloody uncomfortable. Dean and Burrows made occasional eye contact, but on the whole Dean kept his eyes on his Won Ton soup and crackers. Henry also noticed that Jane was watching him. He smiled pleasantly at her, but she puckered her brow and shook her head.

Donaldson partook in the food and enjoyed watching the unspoken interactions between the participants, happy not to be involved in any personal way.

At the end of the meal, Dean tidied away the boxes and foil containers. Henry drew Jane into a corner.

'What's the plan, Henry?'

'Is there any way you could stay with her tonight?' he asked hopefully.

Jane blew out her cheeks. 'Other than the fact I have no night things, no wash bag, no change of clothes. That I have been wearing this lot since seven this morning, I probably smell like a fish, my knickers feel like they're ready to walk in protest. My husband will go spare – yeah, no problem.'

'If you can stay, I'll get Rik to collect a change of clothing for you from home. D'you think your better half would be okay about that?'

'He'd have to be. I'll ring him.' She stared at Henry. 'Are you staying?'

'I have Karl to sort out.'

'And what about us?'

Henry went zip-lipped.

Jane's mouth twisted. 'Thought as much.'

Miller and Crazy met Ray at one of the bedsits in South Shore. Miller arrived in the car, Crazy on the motorbike. Ray was already there, holding a bottle of Stella. Two empty bottles were by his side, suggesting he had been busy consuming.

'It's all just gone to fucking rat shit,' Ray said, beerfully. 'Marty ripping me off – and what's the full story behind that, I do not know. Him shagging Jackie, my bird. The fucking foreigners. Dix pissing off with my money.' He hurled the half-empty bottle across the room. It thudded into the plasterboard, leaving a hole, and fell to the floor, its contents spraying everywhere. 'Shit,' said Ray unhappily. He folded his arms.

301

Miller watched the display with bemusement, wondering why they had been summoned. 'We'll get your money back,' Miller promised.

'With interest,' Crazy added.

Ray scratched his forehead, then sighed. 'Yeah, I know you will. I trust you two, can't trust any other git, though, can I?'

The two henchmen knew when to speak and when not to. They clammed up.

'And now this,' Ray said, shaking his hands angrily. 'The bitch. I cannot believe it!'

'Believe what?' Miller asked, wishing to be put out of his misery.

'She's gone to the cops. She's going to grass on me.'

'What are your plans?' Donaldson asked Henry. They had retired to the games room downstairs, knocking balls around the snooker table in a desultory manner. Henry aimed a cue and belted the white ball into a cluster of reds, sending them spinning round the table.

'Keep her here tonight, tucked away. Then in the morning move to another police station, maybe, so we don't stay still. Then start debriefing her and if she gives us the goods, a written statement, that is, which condemns Ray Cragg to a life of crushing rocks, we'll look seriously at putting her into a witness protection programme.'

'Do you think she'll need that?' Donaldson potted a black.

'Yes, I think she'll be in big danger and I don't think she's done herself any favours by making that call to Ray. Sheer stupidity. That means we have less time to play with because he now knows she's defected, if you'll excuse the Bond-like terminology. He'll be out to get her, probably even as we speak, so we have to keep on the move for a little while before things are arranged. If she gives us a statement, I can have her out of the county by tea time tomorrow, holed up in a half-decent house.'

Henry lined the cue up on the white and slammed it into the pink so hard that the ball bounced and flew off the table. Donaldson caught it in his left hand.

'What I would like to do is get her used to talking now, even though it's late. That's what I'd like Jane to sort out. Chat her up, put her at ease. I'd like to leave her with a voice-activated tape recorder, but I can't just put my hands on one.'

'I always carry one in my case,' said Donaldson, placing the pink ball back on the table. 'I prefer pool,' he said.

The games room door opened. Rik Dean stood shamefacedly at the door.

'Boss,' he said to Henry. 'Need a word.'

Henry racked his cue. He knew this had been coming.

'It would be better to get her before she makes a written statement,' Miller said, thinking hard. 'Then no matter what, there's nothing they can use in court.'

'Good speech,' said Ray.

'They won't have started formally interviewing her yet. They'll be softening her up, offering her inducements, but they'll get into her ribs tomorrow, I'd guess.'

'So we don't have much time?'

Miller shook his head.

'I want her taken out before she makes a statement.'

'Easier said than done.' Crazy sniffed.

'Think I don't know that?' Ray snapped.

'Is there any way your informer in the intelligence unit could find out where they're keeping her?' Miller asked.

'Doubt it. She's just a bloody admin clerk.'

Miller scratched his head, then had an idea. 'Got it! What is the name of the cop involved in it?'

'Henry Christie.'

'That twat!' Crazy spat.

'He's the key to this,' Miller said thoughtfully. 'He can lead us to her. We follow him, he takes us there. Just follow him from home.'

'We don't know where he lives.'

'Couldn't your admin clerk find out?' Miller asked.

'She doesn't have access to personal records. I've asked before.'

'Doesn't matter,' Miller said. 'I know how to find his address.' He turned to Crazy, winked, then said to Ray, 'This will cost you big bucks, Ray. This will not be easy.'

'Tell you what – afterwards, when you find Dix, because I still want that to happen – you two split the money. Hundred and forty grand each, give or take a bob or two. How's about

304

that? Worth it to me.'

Miller and Crazy nodded. It sounded very good.

Henry lounged against the wall on one side of the corridor, Dean stood opposite. Henry regarded him coldly. He knew Rik was an excellent detective, but Henry also knew he had done something very stupid. Dean's face was mainly floorward, his eyes occasionally rising to meet Henry's, but only fleetingly.

Dean sighed heavily. He shook his head with disgust. 'I've been a fool,' he admitted, and said no more.

'Tell me.' Henry's voice was tough.

Dean's head continued to shake. 'You know I took that statement from Jack Burrows regarding the young girl who was murdered in one of her flats?'

'I do.'

'Shit.' He screwed his eyes up, finding it hard to continue. 'I slept with her. There! Said it. I slept with her.'

'I thought as much,' Henry said in a clipped tone. 'What did you tell her?'

'Nothing, nothing much.'

'Pillow talk,' said Henry. 'Did you keep her up to date with the investigation?' Dean nodded. 'Did you know she was involved with the Cragg brothers?'

'Er ... no.' It was an unsure answer.

'Tell me the truth, Rik.'

'I had an idea.' He winced.

'Was the fuck worth it?' Henry asked.

'It wasn't like that.'

'Oh, what was it like? Was it love?' he asked harshly. 'So during your post-coital chats you told her how things were going on with the investigation? Yeah?'

'Suppose so,' Dean said miserably.

'And the fact that her boyfriend could have been a prime suspect didn't enter your idiotic bonce?'

'I didn't actually know he was her boyfriend, did I?'

'It doesn't matter, Rik, because what you did was jeopardize a whole murder enquiry. Why the hell do you think she let you sleep with her? Because you're a good shag? It was the woman who owned the flat where the girl was murdered, for God's sake. Why? Ahh! Even she's a fuckin' suspect, Rik.' Henry could have screamed. He threw his hands up. 'Once this is sorted, I'll deal with you,' he said, bringing the conversation to a close. 'And don't think for a moment you're going to get off lightly – you're not!'

Miller had left the flat, gone to his own place and returned about half an hour later with a laptop computer. He flashed a CD-ROM. 'Let's have a look at this.'

Miller opened the laptop, plugged it in and booted it up. He perched it on his knees and the other two men got into a position where they could see the screen. They were intrigued. He opened the CD drive and inserted the disc.

'What's the cop's name again?'

'Henry Christie.'

'And where do you think he lives?'

'Somewhere in Blackpool, I guess. Definitely Lancashire,' said Ray. 'What the hell is this?'

'It's a CD-ROM which contains the names and addresses of every person in the UK who is on a voters' list.'

'Bloody hell!'

'Very useful for tracking people down. Got it free with a computer magazine.' He tapped a few keys and the disk set off on its memory search, whirring as it spun. Moments later all the people with the surname of Christie who lived in Lancashire were displayed. There was only one Henry James Christie. He tabbed down to it and pressed enter. Henry's address appeared on the screen.

'How about that, then? Not bad for a free gift, eh?'

Another corridor, another conversation. This time Henry and Jane Roscoe.

'Chat to her and use this.' He handed her Donaldson's tape recorder. 'Rik will go and get you a change of clothing and I'll be back first thing. You okay with that?'

She nodded. She was exhausted.

'Good lass.'

'Henry! Oh, it doesn't matter.' She turned away and walked down the corridor. Henry watched, strangely drawn to her, but knowing that ultimately he was doing the right thing for himself and his family, although it was damned hard. Jane went into the TV lounge where Burrows was sitting. Donaldson appeared by

307

Henry's elbow.

'She really has the hots for you, that one. I knew that when I met her last year. Plain as the day is long.'

'I'm a new man now, though. In my formative years I would have done something very silly, but now, at my tender age, I know better.' Henry smiled. 'I just fuck 'em and leave 'em now.'

'Hey, you're growing up at last, Henry.' Donaldson patted his back.

'Yeah, Mister Mature, that's me.' Henry scowled and checked his watch. It was very late, or very early depending on viewpoint. 'We can be at my house in under an hour if you like?'

'I need to be back at the airport by seven thirty, but I would like to see Kate and the girls, however fleetingly.'

'Good.'

'And I have a confession to make to you.'

'I'm a cop, so you can tell me anything.'

'I overheard your conversation with DS Dean.'

'Silly, silly man. Him, not you.'

'People make mistakes. They often don't realize they're doing it at the time, but it has made me think of something.'

'You've slept with someone you shouldn't have?'

'Not recently ... but I have a feeling I know someone who has.'

They left Crazy's bike near the flat in South Shore and Miller drove them both to a housing estate on the outskirts of Blackpool, not too far from the motorway junction at Marton Circle.

308

They drove past Henry Christie's house just once, and returned to South Shore to pick up the motorbike. Ten minutes later they were parked up separately near the detective's house, keeping in touch with each other by radio. Miller settled himself at the top of the avenue on which Henry's house was situated, with a clear view of the house and driveway. He settled down low in his seat, reclined it and relaxed.

At 4 a.m. he was roused from a sort of sleep by a car driving past him. He sank further into the seat and watched it park on the Christies' driveway. Two men got out.

'He's landed back,' Miller said to Crazy over the radio.

'In that Vectra?'

'That's the one.'

Miller watched the two men enter the house. He assumed the driver was Christie, not having seen or met him before. Both men were big and handy-looking and for the first time in a long time, Miller had an uneasy feeling inside him.

Sixteen

It was Kate who roused them. Henry in the same bed as her and Donaldson in the spare bedroom. They threw coffee and juice down their throats and said a quick goodbye to Kate, but not the girls, because they were still in the Land of Nod.

It was 6.15 a.m. when they reached the motorway and Henry knew that barring accidents or other travel delays, he would have his friend at the airport well in time for the shuttle.

'Have I slept?' said the bleary-eyed American.

'Not really.' Henry yawned once, then could not stop from yawning.

At least the day was fine and pleasant as the night gave way to dawn. The sky was lightly clouded with hints of blue beyond.

Miller and Crazy were following, Miller in his Granada and Crazy on the motorbike, each hanging back, occasionally one passing the other. The following was easy because Christie was driving fast and it is far easier to follow a quickly moving vehicle, not least because the driver is usually more concerned about what is going on in front of him rather than behind. At 90 mph, this was very much the case with Henry.

* * *

Henry made it to the airport for 7 a.m., dropping Donaldson off at Terminal 3. Traffic was busy around the airport roads and Henry knew he could not stop long. Donaldson leaned back through the nearside door.

'Thanks, Henry. At least I know what's happened to Zeke. I'll inform his family as soon as I get back to London and start making arrangements to get his body back to the States. How soon do you think we'll be able to have him?'

'As soon as I can arrange it,' Henry promised. 'It might be that we'll have to arrange an independent post-mortem to be carried out before the coroner will release him, but I'll get on to it today.'

Henry leaned across and they shook hands.

'Much appreciated,' said Donaldson.

'Take care,' called Henry as Donaldson slammed the door and stood back to watch Henry drive off. His eyes narrowed when he saw a black-suited motorcyclist pull away and slot in behind Henry's Vectra. He did not know why it made him feel uncomfortable. It just did. Fed instinct. He shook it off and strode into the terminal.

The traffic had built up considerably by the time Henry got to the M6, but even so he was driving into the back yard at Ormskirk police station about forty minutes later. He called Rik Dean on the radio and he came down to let Henry into the police station, which had not opened for public business yet. Dean looked as tired as Henry felt.

'Any problems?'

311

'No,' said Dean.

Henry held his tongue, wanting to make a quip about Dean and Burrows because he was still very annoyed about it. Instead he said, 'Is the witness okay?'

'Yes.'

They went up to the first floor and found Jane and Jack Burrows eating toast and drinking coffee in the dining room. Jane had obviously showered and was in her change of clothing. She looked fresh and beautiful and Henry's insides did a quick whirl, making him think, 'If she does this to me every time I see her, should I really be dumping her?' He was getting confused again. He shelved his feelings and turned his attention to Jack Burrows. She needed a shower and a change of clothing, but that could not detract from the fact that she looked as stunning as ever. On one level Henry could not blame Dean for his indiscretion, but on another, a professional one, he condemned the guy totally.

'Morning, ladies,' Henry said.

He got a grunt from both of them.

'A word, Jane.' He tipped his head to indicate she should follow him out on to the landing. 'How has it gone?' he asked quietly.

'Good. We talked until about five thirty, then decided to get some shut-eye.'

'Did you record your conversation?'

'Yeah, if the tape recorder's working.'

'Interesting?'

'Very, very, very interesting.'

'Gimme a flavour,' Henry said enthusiastically.

'Let me make you a brew first. You look like you need some sustenance. It's a long story.'

Ormskirk police station is situated on a main road leading into the town on a corner plot just outside the shopping centre by a set of traffic lights. It is a relatively new building, constructed in the 1980s. It has a cell complex, a few offices and a first-floor hostel. Apart from the hostel, the police station is very underused. Spiralling policing costs mean that the station is open to the public for a restricted number of hours only and that all but very short-term prisoners are taken to the cells down the road in Skelmersdale. It has a large enclosed car park at the rear, with only one way in and one way out.

This meant that, whatever happened, Henry Christie could only drive out in one direction and if he had his protected witness with him, they would be an easy target.

Miller smirked. Trapped like rats, he thought, as he surveyed the red-brick police station and its environs.

If she is in there, that is.

Henry and Jane sat in the lounge area while he ate some toast and drank the tea she had made for him. It was too busy to talk confidentially because of the number of sleepy hostel residents wandering in and out in various stages of undress. Henry wondered if he had missed something by never living in a police hostel in his younger, single days. The lifestyle had some appeal to it.

'Let's go to the room I slept in,' Jane suggested when Henry had finished his toast. 'Better to talk,' she added. Each with a drink in hand they went into her room. The bed was made, there was no mess; her clothes from yesterday were hung up neatly on a hanger. Henry could smell that she had been there. Her aroma made him slightly dizzy as he sat on the edge of the bed.

Jane sat at the desk, keeping some distance between them, and placed Donaldson's hand-held tape recorder on it.

'Summary,' Henry said. 'Detail later.'

'Okay ... Jack Burrows is the only daughter of the well known transport boss and haulier, Bill Burrows, who has depots all over England and the continent. She had an undertaker's business which she sold and went into property. I think you know some of this?'

Henry nodded. 'But go on, it's worth hearing again.'

'By her account, she was always a bit of a wild child and when she met Ray Cragg, his lifestyle appealed to her for some unknown reason. Money. Excitement. All that sort of stuff, I suppose,' said Jane dismissively. 'Anyway, she got in with him and they became an item, but all he was doing was using her as an accessory, she says. Bit of posh totty. He didn't really care about her, treated her like shit. Anyway, because of this she falls for the delectable Marty, Ray's younger, stupider, half-brother, who, totally out of character, treats her like a lady.'

'First time for everything,' Henry commented.

'Unless he was using her as well,' said Roscoe.

314

'It seems Marty was always trying to emulate and better Ray, but never quite succeeded. He was never quite as tough, never quite as hard, never quite as successful. He got bitter and twisted and decided to screw Ray as much as possible, including screwing his girlfriend, which is why he treated her well, I think, because Ray didn't. There may be another reason why Marty treated her so well, too.'

'Let me guess,' interjected Henry. 'The transport business.'

'How did you know?'

'Just brilliant, I suppose.' He licked a finger and marked the air.

'Apparently Ray does a lot of pimping, controls a lot of prostitutes. He saw the potential for bringing asylum-seeking girls in from Eastern Europe. He made contacts with some gangs on the Continent, but never quite pulled anything substantial off, though he had plans to expand in that direction. During this time, Marty met a guy called Mendoza who headed a Spanish gang which specializes in providing girls for prostitution to UK criminals. Marty decided to go into business with them without telling Ray. At the same time he proposed to bring in loads of paying asylum seekers by using Burrows Transport.'

'How?'

'Jack is well in with a number of bent drivers.'

'Thought as much. So he's been importing people in general and prostitutes in particular? The people get dumped and the hookers end up working in grotty flats – am I on the right track?'

'More or less, except that Marty being Marty, nothing was quite so easy. He needed a lot of start-up money, apparently, which he didn't have, so he took out loans from the Spaniards. Trouble was, Marty was terrible with money. He couldn't add up, but he managed to subtract a lot into his own wallet and lost a lot through gambling: horses, casinos, the lot. The loan repayments kept being extended until such time as they were called in and Marty found himself repaying to a deadline, which he could not meet. In a panic, Marty skimmed from Ray, but could not accumulate enough and blamed others—'

'Such as JJ?'

'Yes. Then he had the big idea to get all the money together in one fell swoop.'

Henry was puzzled.

'Apparently Ray counts his weekly takings in a little terraced house in Rawtenstall. Marty simply arranged to rob him. Hired four dimbos from Manchester to do the business, but Marty being Marty, it all went wrong. Two of them got whacked, two got away and one of Ray's trusted men got greedy and did a runner with all the takings in the confusion. About two-fifty, two-eighty grand, supposedly.'

Henry whistled. 'Marty gets left with nothing other than debt and gets executed by a very pissed-off bullfighter. Things are slotting into place now. So Ray doesn't show any feelings about Marty's death, he accuses Jack of sleeping with him and beats her up, so Jack is really pissed off with him and decides to drop him in it.'

'The money is still on the run and Ray wants it back because it's his and because – and get this for a kind of rough justice – the Spaniard has threatened Ray and told him he now carries the debt incurred by his brother.'

Henry laughed. 'What goes around comes around.'

'Ray's got two goons trailing the man who stole Ray's money as we speak. A guy called Miller and that one who was at Ray's when we went round.'

'Crazy.'

'And those two are very dangerous guys. They're the one's who took out the guys who tried to rob Ray, then dumped their bodies over the county line. They're also the ones who came off best in McDonald's. They've also been contracted to murder the Spaniard.'

'What about the King's Cross shooting?'

'Ray and Marty did that. Crazy drove them.'

'Wow,' said Henry, taking it all in. 'So how's Jack? Will she put pen to paper, do you think?'

Jane nodded confidently. 'She's up for it.'

'We'd better get it done as soon as possible. These people need to be taken off the streets – Oh,' Henry had a thought, 'did she say anything about the dead prostitute?'

'No, didn't ask. Sorry.'

'Okay, you've done bloody well so far. What I want to do now is keep her on the move. I'd like to get her to the rape interview suite at Morecambe, just for today. It'll give us some breathing space and while you're sorting her out statement-wise, I'll get a move on with the witness-protection stuff. She needs to be moved soon for her own safety, I reckon. From now on I think we should all watch our backs until we get Ray, Crazy and this other guy Miller into custody. I'd say they'll be out to get her and anyone daft enough to get in their way – i.e., us.'

The entrance to the car park at the back of the police station was by way of a rough road through a small area of derelict land and some grassed-over humps. It was easy enough for Miller to position his car to have a view of all the comings and goings at the rear of the station without arousing too much suspicion.

Henry came off the phone, which seemed to have been pressed to his ear for over an hour. He had been making arrangements, letting the right people know what was happening, but not letting any names slip. By 9 a.m. he had done the necessary to get the ball rolling, but could not help but feel nervous. He knew he was up against a ruthless gang who had their backs to the wall. They would stop at nothing to protect themselves and destroy others. Henry knew he had to assume there was a very substantial threat against Jack Burrows, even though one had not yet been made. The phone call she had sneakily made last night worried him. It meant that Ray had been alerted. But what could he have achieved overnight in terms of pulling some-thing in place to get at Jack Burrows this morning? Henry pondered. Nothing, he assured himself. Ray did not have a clue where she was and once Burrows committed herself to paper later today, there would be no way in which Ray could ever find her, unless she was foolish enough to compromise herself.

But Henry was on pins and needles.

She was safe and secure in the police station. Once outside on the road she became vulnerable.

He went upstairs and found Jane Roscoe, Rik Dean and Jack Burrows in the TV lounge. He beckoned Jane out to the landing.

'The rape suite isn't being used at the moment and though I know we shouldn't really use it for this, I'm going to. We can spend some time debriefing her and getting it all recorded.' He clenched his jaw. 'I want to move as soon as possible, cos I'm starting to get a bit jumpy. We'll travel to Skem and pick up the M6 from there. Probably take an hour to get to the suite.'

Jane nodded. 'I'm beginning to feel jittery, too.'

'I'd like an armed escort, but the only trouble with that is the bureaucracy. It would waste time and I want to get her moving as soon as. What do you think?'

'I know what you're saying, but it isn't likely that Ray knows where she is at the moment, is it?'

'No, but she's still under threat. I don't want to put her in any unnecessary danger. I'll speak to Bernie Fleming about it.'

He went back downstairs to the CID office and called Fleming on the land line and put the conundrum to him.

'Well,' said Fleming, 'under the circumstances, just get her moved, then we can have a proper look at having pre-planned firearms escorts for any future movements, once she's made her statement.'

I'm not a happy chappie, Henry said to himself as he hung up.

Henry emerged from the front door of Ormskirk police station and walked across the small concourse to the traffic lights at the junction. On the opposite corner was the library and opposite that was the traffic-free road leading down to the main shopping centre. He breathed in the fresh air and watched the traffic flowing for a while, before strolling down the slight incline away from the town centre, then cutting across the grassed area and walking back into the car park behind the station.

His eyes were roving constantly, seeking potential problems, searching for signs of danger.

There was nothing. People were coming and going all the time. Many cars were parked on the waste ground outside the police station walls. A guy in motorcycle leathers, helmet on, was standing astride his bike, chatting to another man in a car, both smoking. They didn't even look at Henry. He did not give them a second glance.

Yet he was still feeling pretty unhappy.

He reversed his car to the rear door of the police station. As soon as he got there, Rik Dean came out and did the same with his car, parking it in front of Henry's so they were in convoy.

Henry waited for him and they both went back into the station. Jane and Jack were waiting behind the door.

'We're ready,' Jane said.

'I'm not,' said Henry. He left the three of them standing there and went into the CID office where a lone detective was beavering diligently away at paperwork. Henry picked up the phone and dialled the divisional communications room. He asked where the Armed Response Vehicle was at that moment. Chorley, he was told. At least twenty minutes away.

'Tell them to make their way to Ormskirk police station immediately and to liaise with me, DCI Christie.'

Back with the three waiting people, Henry told them the good news. They were not going anywhere yet.

'Looks like they're preparing to go,' Miller said to Crazy as he watched Henry Christie walk back into the police station car park and manoeuvre his car to the back door.

'What's he up to?' Crazy said.

'Checking,' said Miller. 'He's a bit worried, and so he should be.' Miller smiled. 'He's on the ball. I wonder if he clocked us? If he did, he didn't show it.'

The ARV rolled into the police station fifteen minutes later, the engine reeking of heat and smoke. They were in a fully liveried Ford Galaxy with smoked-glass windows and they had pushed it all the way.

'Armed cops,' Miller said.

'He must have clocked us then,' said Crazy.

'I don't think so. He's just being careful. Shit,' breathed Miller.

'What do we do?'

'I've just added up fifty grand and one hundred and forty grand, plus what other stuff I have put away for a rainy day,' said Miller. 'To me that adds up to a nice lifestyle in a hot, cheap country. I don't know about you, but I'm up for this.'

'The money's not in our hands yet.'

'It will be. We'll easily find that idiot Dix and then we'll be laughing all the way to wherever.'

'It might mean killing a cop.'

'Yeah, true. So be it. Needs must.'

Henry watched the ARV come into the back yard and manoeuvre backwards to become lead vehicle of the three-car convoy. He trotted down to meet the two officers at the door as they were buzzed in.

He introduced himself and said, pleased, 'You made good time,' then quickly briefed them and asked if they had any problems.

'No,' one said, 'but can we covert arm?'

'Yes,' Henry said, making a big decision. It meant they could arm themselves, but that their weapons would have to stay out of sight, but be accessible.

'Go and sort yourselves out and we'll be out soon.'

Henry collected everyone from upstairs and led them down to the back door of the station.

Jane dropped into the front passenger seat of Henry's car, while Henry opened the back door of Dean's car, ushering Jack Burrows out of the station and into the back seat where she laid herself out full length. 'Keep down until we reach the motorway, then you can sit up, okay?'

Rik Dean got into the driver's seat and Henry got into his Vectra. He gave the word, 'Go,' on his radio.

The ARV began to roll slowly towards the exit. Dean released his handbrake and crawled behind, with Henry bringing up the rear.

Henry was feeling the strain, particularly in his throat, which felt dry and sore. He took a deep breath to help him settle down. Maybe he was just letting his police senses get in the way of his common sense. 'But why do I have a very bad feeling about this?' he thought and only realized he had said it out loud when Jane shot him a query-filled look. 'Sorry.'

As the ARV reached the exit, Henry's mobile rang out.

'Hi – Henry Christie,' he said, happy to answer it: he knew it could not be Jane because she was sitting next to him.

'Henry, it's Karl ... Just something preying on my mind, might just be a load of bollocks, as you might say, but just be careful when you move that witness, will you? I saw a motorbike behind you when you left the airport and while there was nothing wrong about it, it just seemed out of place, somehow, like it could have been following you.'

Motorbike! Shit! Henry's mind spun like a

323

vortex. That could be how Ray Cragg might be able to get to a witness quickly. He could have followed Henry from his home and Henry would have led him right to the witness. His mind processed these thoughts as the convoy turned out of the car park and approached the junction with the main road. Henry did not even thank Karl. He threw his phone down and grabbed his radio, about to cancel the trip north until he could put together a full armed escort.

He was too late.

The Ford Granada came out of nowhere, from the side. It was the car Henry had seen earlier, the one with the motorcyclist standing next to it.

It wheels spun on the gravel, churning up stones and dust. Henry saw a flash of the hooded driver. He also saw the leather-clad, helmeted motorcyclist at the side of the road, sitting astride his powerful-looking machine.

The Granada smashed into the driver's side of the ARV, crushing the PC who was driving and making the vehicle undriveable.

Henry slammed his brakes on and was already half out of his car, his brain only just registering what was happening.

The driver of the Granada was out of his car faster, spraying the side of the ARV with a broadside of slugs from the H&K MP5 in his hand – the one he had stolen from an armed officer at Blackpool Victoria Hospital. This done, he ran to the back of Dean's car, stood by the back door, rose on his toes, and pumped every last remaining bullet into the back half of the car where Jack Burrows was lying.

Henry could do nothing but cower behind his door. Roscoe, hands to her face, screamed uncontrollably. Rik Dean had thrown himself underneath his steering wheel for protection.

Then it was over. The gunman threw the H&K down and ran to the waiting motorcycle and jumped on to the pillion. He waved and with a skid and a swerve of the rear wheels, the bike shot away and headed towards Preston.

'Pull yourself together,' Henry screamed at Jane. He ran to Dean's car and peered in through the shattered windows. 'Fuck,' he said when he saw the state of Jack Burrows. Rik Dean, shell-shocked and shaking, literally rolled out of the car and fell to the ground.

'You okay?'

'I think so.'

'Get sorted and call an ambulance.' Henry ran to the crash damaged and bullet-splattered ARV. The driver was trapped by the steering wheel and looked like he'd taken a bullet in the shoulder. His colleague on the other side of the vehicle was unhurt, just a little shaken, but still cool. He was already out of the car, reaching in for his weapons.

Henry ran back to his car. Jane was still in shock.

'Get out, get looking after the wounded and protect this scene,' he ordered her sharply. She got out numbly, seemed to pull herself together as she stood up and ran to Dean's car, opening the rear door. Jack Burrows slumped out, covered in blood, but apparently still alive.

Henry jumped into the driving seat of his car,

reversed in a cloud of smoke, slammed it into first and drove around the chaos. He stopped at the road and shouted, 'Get in,' to the unhurt ARV officer. 'These other people will look after the wounded.'

The PC, carrying two H&K MP5s and his own Glock at his waist, got in beside Henry and dropped the assorted weaponry into the footwell. Henry jammed the gas pedal down and screeched out through a gap in the now stationary traffic in the direction the motorbike had gone. He knew he had little chance of catching it, but he steered with one hand, recklessly, while he held his radio in the other and relayed details of the incident to the control room and circulated details of the escaping bike, which, he said, would be easy to spot because the passenger was not wearing a helmet.

He gunned his Vectra towards Preston once he reached the A59, though he did not know for sure if he was even going the right way. The bike could easily have gone towards Liverpool. Or could now be abandoned in a side street and they could be tootling along in a nice car. All Henry knew was that it was more than likely they would be making their way, by some route or other, back to Blackpool. Or maybe not. Shit, he thought.

One of Lancashire Constabulary's objectives for the year was to make roads safer. This meant that there were often traffic patrols operating radar speed traps on roads where speeding had been the cause of accidents, or where it caused a

326

danger to the public. Parts of the A59 north of Ormskirk are such a problem, particularly on the north side of a small town called Burscough. Here the A59 is often subject to traffic-officer attention, especially in the 30 mph limit as the road winds out of the north end of town. On that day, two traffic cops had set up a speed trap, one on the radar, one stopping the offenders, and were keeping themselves very busy with cars coming into Buscough from the direction of Preston. Easy pickings and great fun.

Travelling south down the A59 that morning was a PC from Ormskirk who had been to head-quarters clothing stores for some new uniform. He had been on duty since seven and was return-ing to Ormskirk, ready for a very big, fat-boy's breakfast. He knew that the traffic cops had set up a radar north of Burscough and he slowed right down as he sailed into the 30 mph zone, fully aware that the gutter rats would have no qualms in booking him, even though he was on duty and driving a police van. No love lost there.

This combination of police on the A59 at that time of day was not particularly unusual. As the officer drove past the tripod-mounted radar at 29 mph, he waved at the traffic cop, then hid his one-fingered salute. Up ahead he could see the motorcycle cop standing next to his machine, wearing his hi-viz jacket, ready to pull in wrong-doers. He accelerated a little.

All these officers received Henry Christie's

coolly transmitted circulation at exactly the same time, and their reactions were similar because they realized that this motorbike could well be en route to them and, as motorcycles tend to go like the proverbial shit off a shovel, it might be there within seconds.

Miller clung to Crazy as he took the machine underneath them up to speeds which were, like his nickname, crazy. The road surface was generally smooth and excellent. If no other traffic had been about, it would have been a fantastic ride as the bike swept round long corners and flew down straights. Unfortunately, other traffic did impede progress a little, but not too much. Crazy was good. He looked well ahead, made sound decisions, veered round and in between vehicles and made superb time.

They were on the southern outskirts of Burscough within minutes. Crazy throttled back a little and disregarded the red of the traffic lights just outside the town, weaving dangerously between crossing traffic and hitting the humpback bridge just before the small town centre at 90 mph.

The bike left the road at the crest of the hill, thumped down on its rear wheel, swerved madly, but Crazy held it upright and braked down to about 50 mph for the town centre, then, once he had negotiated the pelican crossing and the mini-roundabout without knocking anyone over, he opened the throttle again up the hill over the railway line.

Miller could not help but laugh. The wind in

his face and hair, the roller-coaster ride he was having was fantastic. The feeling was unbelievable, that combination of speed, danger and blood-letting.

Then he heard Crazy scream an obscenity.

The A59 is not a wide road as it snakes out of Burscough, so it was very easy to place the police van and the traffic cop's plain car at an angle and effectively block the road completely. There were no footpaths on either side, with nowhere for vehicles to go, unless they chose to go off-road into the recently ploughed fields on either side.

The motorcycle cop stood astride his powerful BMW. The other two officers stood in the road, stopping traffic and working their way on foot down the short line of stationary cars and puzzled drivers, towards Burscough, anticipating the arrival of the pursued bike.

It came speeding into view.

Henry was speaking calmly into the radio, telling the three cops up ahead to take extreme care and not to put their lives or others' lives in jeopardy. The men on the bike were dangerous in the extreme.

They acknowledged his warning.

Crazy braked hard and almost launched himself and Miller over the handlebars as the speed of the bike reduced from eighty to zero within a fraction of a second. He stopped about fifty metres away from the two cops on foot, who started to approach hesitantly.

Miller had his pistol in his waistband. He produced it and rested it on Crazy's shoulder to take aim at the officers. They dived for cover behind a car and the police motorcyclist cowered down, hoping his machine would offer protection. Miller did not fire. He patted Crazy on the back and indicated for him to about-face.

Crazy revved the engine, released the clutch, spun the bike on the spot and headed back towards Burscough.

Behind him the two officers on foot raised their heads slowly from their cover and spoke on their radios. The one on the motorcycle set off in pursuit.

'Coming this way,' the ARV constable said to Henry. He racked his MP5 so it was ready. He was a happy man. He had been trained for this sort of thing and was looking forward to putting it into practice.

Henry reached the set of lights that Crazy had ignored. Three cars had been involved in a minor bump, blocking part of the road. Henry could not see any injuries, so he sneaked past and speeded up towards the town, wondering if he was actually going to come face to face with the motorcycle.

He hoped so. He had already decided that, given half a chance, he was going to ram the bastard off the road and fuck the consequences.

'Which way?' Crazy shouted over his shoulder, the wind taking his voice away with it.

330

'Back into town,' Miller screamed into his ear. 'Left at the roundabout towards the motorway down the back roads.'

Crazy acknowledged these directions with a thumbs up.

He was approaching the railway bridge at 70 mph.

Henry reached the mini-roundabout as the motorbike came into view on the crest of the railway bridge just ahead of him. He screeched to a halt. The bike kept coming.

'You might want to close your eyes, cos I'm going to ram him and I don't want any witnesses,' Henry said to the armed constable.

'You have my permission to go for it, sir.'

Henry pressed the accelerator, brought up the clutch with a dithering foot, and held on to the handbrake as he built up the revs. He thought how much he had actually come to like the Vectra. It had been a good workhorse. Now it was going to go to the knacker's yard.

Crazy saw the Vectra. So did Miller. They recognized it as the one Henry Christie was driving. Both knew he would go for them because he had to. Otherwise he was going to lose them.

Crazy powered the bike down the short hill, went wide across to the wrong side of the road to get into the best position to cut left at the roundabout. He leaned over at such a sharp angle that his knee was almost touching the road surface, and only the edges of his tyres were in contact with the tarmac. The bike twitched.

Crazy corrected it expertly, then its back end twitched again; he corrected it instantaneously.

He saw the Vectra leap forwards.

In his mind Henry had prepared himself for the ram. He was going to go for it. He brought the clutch up, dropped the handbrake, virtually stood on the accelerator.

And probably for the first time since he was seventeen, he stalled a car.

The Vectra lurched as though it was going to be sick, then died.

Crazy was ready for the impact, but it did not come. He laughed out loud when he saw what had happened, then screwed back the throttle to take him out of the corner, across the edge of the roundabout. His rear end twitched, but this time he could not control it. As his rear tyre touched a minute patch of diesel spilt on the road, the wheel whipped away. Crazy fought for control. He could not pull it back and the bike went down in a shower of sparks and slid at a speed of about 60 mph across the road and under the front end of the Vectra.

Henry saw the bike go. He gripped his steering wheel, ducked his head uselessly, lifted his knees up and braced himself for the impact. It all happened within a millisecond, yet he saw it all in wonderful, coloured, sharp detail. The sparks were spectacular, like a Roman candle burning. The rear passenger took off in flight from the pillion and zoomed like a missile out of Henry's view. The rider held on tight to his machine, fighting desperately with it all the way until the moment of impact when it collided with the front of the Vectra with a crash so loud and distorted that Henry would never forget it.

The bonnet crumpled up like a blanket and the front of the car lifted as though on a jack.

Then it was over.

'You okay?' he asked the ARV officer.

'Never better.'

Henry got out on shaky legs and looked at the motorbike and rider, both trapped tightly underneath his car. The rider was still moving, but Henry saw that his left leg was sticking out at a hideous angle below the knee and shards of bone had pierced his leather trousers. Then the rider was still.

'Boss!' the armed officer called to Henry.

Henry looked across the twisted bonnet of his car. The pillion passenger had rolled across the pavement and slammed up against a wall. He was now, miraculously, on his feet, staggering, gun in his right hand, towards the ARV officer who had his MP5 in a firing position. The passenger was covered in blood. His left arm hung loosely at his side and his face seemed horribly deformed. He was trying to raise the pistol and fire it.

The armed officer was getting very tense, very close to shooting this man down. Henry could see the tension in the constable's shoulders.

'Armed police,' he shouted. 'Drop your weapon, drop it now!'

The man still came towards him.

'Armed police,' he said again. 'Drop your weapon or I will fire.'

With what looked to be an amazing feat of strength, the injured man raised his gun, but as he did so he lost his balance, toppled over backwards and discharged the gun once into the air.

Seventeen

It was a very tired, harassed and angry Henry Christie who, at 6 a.m. two days later, took part in the briefing of a full firearms team and a full squad of hefty support unit officers at Fleetwood police station.

Prior to this Henry had faced many hours of relentless scrutiny following his, allegedly, very ill-judged decision to move a witness who was under a substantial threat without putting in place a pre-planned firearms operation. It had been a harrowing time for him as his decision-making was continually criticized as being poor and also because he received no support whatever from Bernie Fleming. Henry would not have minded so much, but he was, misguidedly it transpired, trying to protect Fleming from the fall-out. But Fleming seemed to have developed a case of memory loss and, oddly, could not recall receiving any phone call from Henry prior to the incident taking place.

All anyone could see was the result. The so-called protected witness was currently still in intensive care and unlikely to pull through; an injured ARV officer who would be okay was already talking about suing the force; and there were two dead offenders. Added to that DS Rik Dean off sick with stress, also planning to sue the county.

Only one good thing had happened to Henry over the preceding forty-eight hours. He had received the results of the DNA test taken from Marty Cragg's dead body which matched the DNA from one of the semen traces found inside the body of the dead prostitute. Henry pulled together a few disparate pieces of information such as Marty's involvement with bringing asylum-seekers into the country, some for the purposes of prostitution; Marty's association with Jack Burrows, which gave him access to the dead girl's grubby flat; his penchant for beating up women, his sperm inside her, of course, and the fact that Marty had a scald mark on his arm, which Henry had noticed while inspecting his body before sliding it into the mortuary fridge. At the time Henry had not thought anything about the scald, but it tied in with the scald mark on the girl's body nicely. Henry believed he probably had enough there to get a conviction if Marty had still been alive. When he got the chance, he would put pen to paper and write off the murder.

It still troubled him deeply that the girl, Julie from Albania, remained unidentified.

He felt a journey to Albania coming on. He

knew the police out there were keen to work alongside other European forces, and maybe he could use them to help find her family. If, indeed, she did come from Albania.

So that was the only good thing.

And now he was going for Ray Cragg, although he did not know how much good would come from sweating him in interview. Ray was a seasoned criminal and would say nothing and probably get away with everything, particularly if Jack Burrows died, which was a distinct possibility. An interview was about all Henry had. Ray was so forensically aware it was frightening. If only he had made a mistake somewhere along the line.

Henry looked at the assembled faces of the firearms and support-unit teams. He thought they looked pretty mean and would not like them coming through his door at any time of day.

Next to him was Jane Roscoe who was co-running the operation. She had taken the bulk of the briefing with Henry chipping in where appropriate. He had watched her talk and had been impressed.

The briefing was over at 6.30 a.m. Everyone was then given the chance to have a quick brew before turning out to be ready and in position to hit Ray Cragg's house at seven on the dot. Henry knew Ray was in because he'd had a surveillance team tracking his movements for the last thirty-six hours.

Henry and Roscoe had a cup of tea each, but said little to each other. He finished first and with relief said, 'Time to go.'

They left the back door of the station together and were approached by a man bearing a large bouquet of flowers. Henry held back the urge to say, 'For me?'

The man went up to Jane.

'Tom!' she said, taken aback. 'What are you doing here?'

'I needed to see you, needed to sort things out with you.'

'Can't you see I'm busy?'

Tom glanced at Henry and the corners of his mouth turned down, as though he knew something. Henry's breathing constricted for a moment. Tom looked back at his wife. 'Please.'

Jane shook her head in disbelief and looked pleadingly at Henry.

'You talk,' Henry said. 'I'll sort this job out and you catch up later. Not a problem.' He jumped into his pool car, a rather tatty Astra which had temporarily replaced his Vectra, and set off behind a support-unit carrier. He saw Tom hand the flowers over to Jane. He wished them well.

Henry, wearing a ballistic vest, with two armed and dangerous officers standing behind him, was towering over Ray Cragg at five minutes past seven. Ray was in such a deep sleep he had not heard the front door being battered down, nor the thud of heavily booted coppers wading into his house, clearing each room with a shout as they went. Neither did he hear his mother's screams, or the grunt of her latest lover, as the firearms team entered her bedroom and pointed their machine pistols at them.

Henry shook Ray by the shoulder, thinking, The sleep of a man with no conscience.

He took a lot of rousing. Henry wanted to slap him – hard – but knew it would only backfire.

'Come on, Ray. Come on, sleepy head.'

Eventually his eyes flickered open. Henry thrust his warrant card and badge in front of them and introduced himself, although introductions were probably unnecessary. He immediately cautioned Ray and told him he was under arrest on suspicion of murder, conspiracy to murder and supplying controlled drugs. 'And whatever else I can think of in due course, but that'll do for now,' Henry finished.

Ray smiled mockingly. 'Whatever. I'll be back here in an hour.' He sat up, rubbing his eyes.

'This is a nice bed you've got,' Henry commented. 'Very comfy.'

'Had it since I was ten – it's brill.'

'Unfortunately I don't think you'll be sleeping in it again – ever.'

Ray glared sharply up, a touch of concern on his weasel-thin face. It quickly disappeared to be replaced by an expression of contempt. 'Don't think so.'

'Get dressed.'

Ray stumbled to the wardrobe, eyeing the two armed officers. He removed his ragged underpants and began to clothe himself. He sat back on the bed as he pulled his socks on and glanced round for his footwear.

Henry bent down and picked up a pair of trainers tucked under the bed.

'These?'

338

'Yeah, give 'em here.'

Henry smiled and handed them over.

'Nice ones. Had them long?'

'Few months, why?'

'Nothing,' Henry said innocently. 'Let's go, pal.'

They conveyed him to Blackpool central police station where the pre-warned custody sergeant and gaoler were waiting to receive Ray with open arms.

'Bag up his clothing and shoes,' Henry told the sergeant.

'You let me get dressed, you twat,' Ray said to Henry. 'Now you want me to strip again!'

'I know. I'm like that.'

'Why do you want my clothes?' Ray demanded, a sneer on his lips.

'Forensics.'

'As if,' Ray said cockily. He undressed and was given a paper suit in replacement. He then called his solicitor, who said he would be there in half an hour. Ray was led to the cells by the gaoler. Henry instructed the sergeant to ring when the solicitor landed. He then made his way up to the MIR to prepare for a tough interviewing session. It was 8.30 a.m.

He was surprised to see Bernie Fleming in the MIR. Henry's mouth twisted. Fleming was not his bestest friend at this moment. In fact, Henry had struck him off his Christmas card list.

Jane was also there, sitting on a chair at the allocator's desk. She looked pretty uncomfortable. Henry wondered if she and her husband had made up and were now united against the world together.

'I need to talk to you,' Fleming said ominously.

'What about?'

'Not here, eh? DI Roscoe's office.'

As there was no one else in the room at that moment, Henry said, 'Here'll do fine.'

'As you wish.' Fleming shrugged.

He cleared his throat and Henry thought, Oh, fuck! He experienced a tightness across his chest and found he could hardly breathe. Somehow he knew what was coming.

'I'm sorry about this,' Fleming went on, 'but a decision has been made at the highest level that you should be suspended from duty.' Henry shivered as the words sank in. Fleming went on, 'You'll be on full pay pending the outcome of the inquiry into the incident at Ormskirk. Your professional judgement has been called into question and it is not felt appropriate to allow you to remain on duty under the circumstances.' It was as though Fleming was reading it off a card. 'I'm sorry, Henry.'

Henry held his tongue. What he would have said, he would have regretted. Instead, he said absolutely nothing.

'I'm afraid you are now barred from entering police premises, other than the public areas. I want your warrant card and badge. I have been told that I should escort you from the station. Please give me your car keys, too, as well as your swipe card. You can arrange to come into headquarters later today to clear your desk.'

'Thanks for nothing.' Henry handed over the

required items. 'I take it DI Roscoe is running with Ray Cragg now?'

'She is.'

'Just one minute before I leave.' He shouldered past Fleming and stood in front of Jane. 'Ray Cragg is in custody. His clothing and footwear have been seized. Just cross-check his trainers with the footwear mark found on Carrie Dancing's head, will you? It could be a match. I think he's slipped up there, so if nothing else you'll get him for her murder.'

'Thanks,' she said, not raising her eyes. 'Henry, I swear I didn't know about this.'

'It's okay, Jane. I'll be fine. Good luck with it, and with your life. And just for the record, I'm sorry I treated you so badly. Guess I'm just one screwed-up individual.'

Her face crumpled, but he turned away and without a backward glance walked out of the police station. It was four miles to his home. He walked there without stopping.

In the end, after much argument, Dix relented and allowed Debbie to go to her house to collect her things. Her reasoning that it was safe to do so was fairly sound now: Marty was dead and Ray had been remanded in custody charged with murder; their two henchmen, Miller and Crazy, were no longer in the land of the living. Debbie argued that Ray wouldn't be bothered keeping tabs on her house now as his organization was in total disarray. She said that it would be better to go there sooner rather than later, because if they left it too long Ray could well get his act together from prison. Dix was pretty impressed by her thought process. She was starting to think like a crim and he felt flushed with pride. Even so, he was still nervous about it.

They had been lying low in hotels in the Lake District, staying in nice places, one night here, a couple of nights there, but not flashing the money around. But both knew they could not maintain such an unnatural lifestyle for ever. They decided they had to get out of the country and settle somewhere cheap and cheerful, so Debbie wanted to get some stuff before they left, including her passport. This had caused further friction, because Dix said he knew someone who could get her a passport, but she said she wanted her own, real one. And she wanted to know why he wouldn't go back to his flat and retrieve his own passport, but he declined to tell her. That, he had said, was too damned risky. He would get a passport done for him by a man he knew who lived in Crewe. It would only entail a short stop off on their way south.

On the morning in question, he drove them down to Fleetwood. They were still using her car. He parked within a quarter of a mile of her house, near enough for her to walk the distance. He was feeling very tense.

She went in by the back door, not noticing the slightly damaged window frame, nor the slightly raised square underneath the lino on the kitchen floor.

She was quick and efficient. She knew what she wanted, where it was, and within five minutes everything was in a small suitcase and holdall. Then she was out, never to know she had activated a radio alarm which was not received anywhere as the box in Miller's car had been damaged beyond repair when he had driven into the side of the ARV.

Debbie hurried back to Dix, flopped into the passenger seat and breathed a sigh of relief. She smiled victoriously at him, threw her arms around him and gave him a big smackeroo. She was getting very used to being with him night and day and it was a great feeling.

'Let's get out of this hell hole,' she said. 'Never bloody liked Fleetwood anyway. Too many bloody fishwives.'

He spun the car round and headed for the motorway. His intention was to keep driving south, stop in Crewe for his passport, then go, go, go. Eventually they would catch the ferry to Santander and drive south to one of the less developed Costas and see if they could settle down in the sun.

The roads were busy, but he made good progress in her slow car. He joined the M55 at junction 3 and accelerated down the slip road. He kind of knew there was a heavy goods vehicle in the slow lane travelling alongside him as he began to filter on to the motorway. He expected it to move out to the middle lane to allow him on, but it stayed resolutely on his shoulder.

'Fuck,' he said, pushing Debbie's car a little harder, hoping to nip in front of the HGV, but its engine was not designed to outrun anything. It responded sluggishly.

Then the HGV veered towards him, the driver, unbeknownst to Dix, having dropped asleep at the wheel. Dix braked and tried to avoid the beast. He drove on to the hard shoulder. The HGV slewed right across and collided with the little car.

Dix remembered nothing more until he found himself regaining consciousness upside down in the car in a field next to the motorway. The HGV was on its side, its load of hardcore having burst out everywhere. Dix shouted for Debbie. He could not see her. She was not there. He got his seat belt open and crawled out of the wreckage, a severe pain in his head and left leg.

'Debbie,' he yelled.

Then he saw her. She had been thrown clear of the car and had landed about twenty metres away in a ditch. Her body looked twisted and badly hurt.

'Debbie!' he screamed, his eyes trying to focus properly, his head hurting badly. 'Jesus! Oh no!' he cried at something else he had seen.

The holdall containing all their cash, which had been in the back seat, had also been ejected from the car. It had ruptured when it walloped against a tree and now the contents of the bag were being blown across the field, towards the motorway. All thoughts of Debbie evaporated from his head as he ran to the holdall and desperately began collecting the money which was scattered everywhere.

When the police arrived at the scene, they found Debbie still alive in the ditch, no thanks to Dix. The offending driver of the HGV was also alive but trapped in his mangled cab, both legs and pelvis broken. Dix was in the middle of the motorway, chasing his banknotes at the same time as trying to avoid oncoming traffic. He was clutching a few thousand pounds to his chest, but the bulk of almost three hundred thousand pounds had disappeared in the wind.

Karl Donaldson spent every night for two weeks in London, much to his wife's annoyance. She was reassured, though, when he promised he would make it up to her in more ways than one.

It took him that long to get what he needed. It was a complicated process, carried out furtively, and he hated doing it, but he knew he had no choice in the matter.

On the morning of the fifteenth day he presented himself unannounced in Philippa Bottram's office.

She was deep in her work and looked up, startled. 'Hello, Karl.' She was always pleased to see him. 'Do we have a scheduled meeting? I'm sorry, I forgot.'

'No. I just need to chat. Important and urgent.'

'Very well, take a seat.'

He drew up a chair to her desk, sat down and placed a large buff envelope on the desk.

'Not sure where to begin,' he admitted. Bottram thought he looked very tired and troubled. 'Is is about Zeke?' He nodded. 'Still preying on your mind. Don't feel guilty, Karl.'

'It's not that, but he is still preying on my mind.' He had a flash of the memory of informing Zeke's parents of his death and their

345

reaction. It had been very hard to deal with. He had also made it his job to accompany the body back to the States to hand it over to them personally. Their grief had rubbed off on him deeply.

'What can I do for my favourite legal attaché this morning, then? Begin at the beginning,' Bottram said benignly.

Donaldson opened the envelope and extracted a large number of photographs which he did not immediately show to Bottram. 'I've spent a lot of time researching Mendoza, his associates, relatives, friends, etc. I've pulled together everything we know about him and managed to get photos of many of these people.' He paused uncertainly. 'As we know, Mendoza arranges for a lot of people to enter the UK illegally and I've spent time analysing what we know about the people connected to him and how they help him – all those sorts of things.'

'Very creditable,' said Bottram.

'Okay, that's one prong of my fork, shall we say? The other is that I believe Zeke must have been compromised somehow because, to this day, I do not believe he would have been so unprofessional as to let his guard down.'

'Maybe, maybe not. Where is this going?'

Donaldson showed her a photograph. 'Do you know this woman?'

Bottram looked and gulped. Donaldson could tell she had suddenly gone ice-cold.

'She is married to a Spanish diplomat based in their embassy here,' she said. 'I met her once briefly at a function there. Just fleetingly.'

346

Bottram, who was tanned by means of a sunbed, had lost much of her colour and had gone slightly green.

'Didn't I see her here?' Donaldson asked. 'On the day I learned what had happened to Zeke. Remember, when I showed you those faxes?'

'Ahh, possibly,' Bottram said vaguely.

'It was her. I checked the visitors' book, Philippa,' he said and ploughed on. 'It turns out that she is related to Mendoza, some distant cousin or other, and that both she and her husband are suspected to be on Mendoza's payroll. In fact the Spanish police are very close to arresting the husband on corruption charges. She, incidentally, is known to be bisexual.'

'What are you getting at, Karl?'

'You really want me to go on, Philippa?'

She stared hard at him, so he showed her more photographs. 'I've had a metropolitan police surveillance team working for me for the past two weeks. Remember that nice commander who was here a while back, the one dealing with the Yardies? He arranged it for me. I've had them watching and following you, Philippa. I've also had your phone calls from here monitored?'

'You bastard – on what authority?' She picked up the photographs and for a moment looked like she was going to hurl them across the office.

'On my own, as an FBI agent investigating the murder of a fellow agent. The photos show you consorting with this woman on several occasions over the last two weeks, because you are bisexual too, aren't you? You've been screwing her and she's been using you, Philippa. Pillow

347

talk. She seduced you and you went along for the ride because you were lonely. Philippa, you've been very stupid and it cost two agents their lives.' He paused for effect. 'And now I've come to get you.'

One month later, Henry Christie, Kate and their two girls were on holiday in Lanzarote. As he was suspended on full pay, he was determined to take advantage of his free time. The garden at home was now wonderful. The house was in the process of being redecorated. His music collection had expanded and he was spending quality time with his wife and children.

He was strolling alone, out to buy rolls for their breakfast in their self-catering apartment. He was on the seafront at Playa de los Pocillos, breathing in the fresh air and feeling the hot sun on his face and head. He had the beginnings of a good tan.

He had heard nothing from the inquiry into his terrible judgement. No one had contacted him, even from a welfare point of view, which did not surprise him. That was the way the organization worked. It purported to be caring, but in reality it wasn't.

Yet he felt strangely serene. He should have been stressed, going out of his tiny mind, but he wasn't. He believed that the inquiry would vindicate him and that he would be reinstated, but would probably return to his original rank of inspector, as opposed to temporary chief inspector and then be transferred – or sidelined – into some nondescript, out-of-harm's-way job where he could do no damage. But it did not bother him too much. It was fairly obvious that the powers that be did not want him to catch villains any more because they didn't trust him. He had thought that would have destroyed him, but it didn't.

What had happened was that this enforced break had allowed him to re-assess his priorities in life. Now he knew that his family came first – being a good husband and father – and way back in a poor second place came the job of being a policeman. Beyond that, nothing else really mattered.